The Frozen Waterfall

The Frozen Waterfall

GAYE HIÇYILMAZ

faber and faber
LONDON · BOSTON

First published in Great Britain in 1993
by Faber and Faber Limited
3 Queen Square London WC1N 3AU

Photoset by Parker Typesetting Service Ltd, Leicester
Printed in Great Britain by Clays Ltd, St Ives plc

Gaye Hiçyılmaz is hereby identified as author of
this work in accordance with Section 77 of the
Copyright, Designs and Patents Act 1988

A CIP record for this book is available
from the British Library

ISBN 0–571–16794–2

2 4 6 8 10 9 7 5 3 1

To Jale and Ilhan,
Onur and Özgur

One

In the very early morning when it was still cool, Selda sat on the garden wall and watched for the taxi. Up near the old house her grandmother was sweeping together the rubbish which the cats had scattered during the night. They were a wild lot and roamed the neglected garden in a shabby and defiant band led by a huge, one-eyed ginger tomcat. A couple of lemon-eyed blacks, as darting and treacherous as snakes, stalked behind him followed by a tattered tangle of kittens as sharp and thin as winter twigs. They mewed shrilly, all except one, which was clearly ill. It watched the others with clouded eyes from behind the jasmine root, and it shivered. Selda's grandmother swung her brush threateningly at the cats so that they stayed clear of the kitchen door.

Then the old woman looked over at the sick one and tossed it a fish head from last night's supper.

'Dirty things,' she grumbled, 'carrying diseases and fleas. When you've all gone and I can have a moment to myself, I'll be able to look after this garden properly. I'll clean it up and scare off these cats. You can't be too careful with animals. And don't you forget that over there in Switzerland, where you're going.'

'Forget what, Grandmother?'

'Don't forget that animals are dirty. I've heard that over there they keep animals in the houses. They even let them sleep on the beds! Your father told me that his Swiss neighbours washed their dog in the bath! Can you imagine it?' Her grandmother scowled in disgust and Selda pulled a face in sympathy. It did sound quite revolting.

1

'It's not only that,' grumbled the old woman, 'foreigners are not as clean as we are. People say that they walk straight from the street and into their nice rooms with all the street filth still on their shoes!' Her grandmother shook her head in disbelief and banged the rest of the household rubbish out of the tin and on to the heap in the corner of the garden. Then she kicked at the tom which had crept forward again. It leapt just out of reach but managed to snatch some of the tumbled fish gut and make off with it, jerking and trailing behind him. The other cats sprang yowling after him.

'Nasty, greedy brute,' muttered the old woman. Yet Selda knew that her grandmother had been feeding that ginger tomcat for years. She had even put titbits aside for him when he lost the eye in a fight. Selda swung her legs and watched her grandmother. Although she was so old, she was still a complicated and contradictory sort of person and in the two years that Selda had been living in her grandmother's house, she had tried to learn some of the caution of those cats. Now she hoped that these uneasy and difficult years were over. The endless half hour that had stretched before her when she first climbed up on the wall had wasted away to a hurrying, scurrying rush of minutes. Any moment now the taxi would stop in front of the house. Then she and her two sisters and her mother would get in, and wave goodbye and be off.

It was quiet along the street. Nobody else seemed to be up and the early morning noises from the flats opposite had hardly begun. Selda had half hoped that her friend, Demet, would come over from the flats to say goodbye. They had said their goodbyes once already, of course, and had exchanged addresses and promised to write and remain friends for ever, but Selda still secretly hoped that Demet would get up and come over for another dramatic, last-minute parting. Now it did not look as though she would. The curtain at Demet's window opposite had not moved. She had probably overslept or been forbidden to come out by her aunt. Poor old Demet:

that would be just her luck. That dreadful aunt of hers watched over her as closely as if she were a dangerous prisoner. Selda and Demet had been friends for two years, best friends, too, although recently Selda had been annoyed and irritated by her. 'Poor old Demet', that was what everybody called her. She was the sort of girl for whom nothing ever went right. Demet's parents were workers in Germany but Demet had been sent back to Turkey in disgrace. Somehow, she had never settled down in Germany and had twice failed her class in school there. The German school authorities said that she must go to a special school for children who found learning extra difficult. Demet's parents had not agreed. They had been furious and had sent her back to this aunt in Izmir. There Demet had been for the last two years, waiting and hoping to return to Germany.

Selda thought about her friend a great deal: and Demet's fate filled her with dread. Selda feared above all things that she too would fail in school in that distant, foreign country. She was afraid of failure and her fear scared her although she knew that she and Demet were very different. Demet had not even settled back into school in Turkey. It wasn't that she was lazy. She worked ten times harder than Selda. She slaved at her lessons and rarely came out to play. Late at night Demet's light would be burning and she still 'studying'. Actually, Selda knew that her friend would be going over and over her exercises, changing things again and again, and making it all worse than it was before. Demet panicked in school orals: her mind went blank and she dissolved into tears and couldn't say a thing. The gossip along the street was that Demet only passed into the next class because her parents had sent the teacher expensive presents from Germany. Selda's grandmother strongly disapproved of such gossip, but it was a bad business, and Selda knew it. Although it spoilt her excitement at getting away finally from her grandmother's house and finally, finally, joining her father and brothers in Switzerland,

3

Selda was determined not to be sent back, like poor old Demet.

She shifted her position on the crumbling brick wall and craned forward to look for the taxi.

'So! I see that you just can't wait to get away from me!' Her grandmother called out suddenly.

'I was only looking for the taxi. Mother told me to.'

'Well, you can look for it just as well from inside the house. Whatever will people think? A great big girl like you, sitting out on the street at daybreak! You can't be too careful.'

'They'll only think . . .'

'Be quiet! I've heard quite enough from you these last two years. You and your smart answers! Just you wait, my girl, you won't be making any smart answers over there in Switzerland. So you had better start getting used to it now.'

'Yes Grandmother.'

Selda got off the wall and went back to the house. She was horribly afraid that her grandmother might be right. She would not be able to say anything at all in German, let alone anything clever. And it wasn't only that which worried her. She was very afraid of flying. She would not have said so, ever. Nothing in the world would have made her admit it, for she was the brave, clever one of the girls. When she opened the house door she saw her elder sisters, Pembe and Fatma, lolling sleepily amongst the dangerously swollen suitcases. They were talking, of all things, about plane crashes.

'Anyway, if it does crash, you wouldn't know anything about it,' said Fatma determinedly.

'How can you be sure?' Pembe was still worried.

'It happens too quickly. There's an enormous bang and there you are, in bits in the clouds. In very little bits . . .'

Pembe, who had kept out her best dress specially for this, her first flight, was upset. She licked a tear from the corner of her mouth. Fatma regretted her impulsive words.

'What I mean is,' she said quickly,' it wouldn't hurt, because

4

it would happen too fast. There's an enormous bang and there you are, in little bits, like I said. You wouldn't feel it,' she added helpfully.

'Really?'

'Oh yes. And lots of people escape.'

'Escape? With parachutes?'

'Yes. And with those floating things for the sea. Father told us about them. They have these jacket things under the seats and when the plane lands in the sea, you put one on . . .'

'But I can't swim!'

'Oh, Pembe! That's why you put the jacket thing on. It holds you up out of the water so that you don't have to swim. There's even a whistle, so that rescuers can find you in the dark.'

'In the dark? Oh, Fatma, I should die of fear in the dark.'

'Don't worry,' said Fatma,' we're not flying at night.'

Pembe smiled, but Selda wished that they would talk about something else. She was beginning to feel odd: hot and sick and giddy. Her sisters, resting in the hallway, with their bare feet on the tiled floor, let their fears and worries simmer and bubble away, like water left on the stove. Selda was different. She forced her fear back and felt the sweat begin to trickle down her spine.

'Are there any sharks in the sea?' Pembe returned to her anxiety as one returns to pick at a torn nail. Last summer they had all seen a horror film about a monster grey shark. Since then Pembe had been afraid of the sea and sharks.

'There isn't any sea, not between Istanbul and Switzerland. Haven't you ever looked at a map?' Selda spoke more sharply than she had intended to. Pembe, who had been almost resigned to a daylight rescue with her white dress wet but not ruined, changed her sniffing to sobbing.

'Anyway, most accidents happen when the plane takes off or lands,' snapped Selda. 'And most people suffocate.'

'They don't.'

5

'They do.'

'Not if they get out quickly,' said Fatma, who was an optimist.

'They don't get out. They get poisoned by the smoke.' Selda wanted to stop but couldn't. 'Don't you know anything? It was in the newspapers and on television: all the plastic on the plane burns and you're suffocated within seconds.'

'Planes aren't made of plastic!' cried Fatma, red faced but triumphant.

'You're thinking of toy planes! You think you know everything but you don't!'

'I know more than you!'

'So what? You just wait. In Switzerland you won't know anything!'

Pembe, encouraged by Fatma's victory, jumped up and inspected herself in the old, cloudy mirror in the coat stand.

'I expect we'll *all* be bottom of the class,' she murmured evenly, smiling at her reflection. She suspected that being pretty would make up for a lot of things.

'We might be bottom at the beginning,' said Fatma, seeking a middle way.

'Not me,' said Selda. 'I'm not going to be bottom of any class. Not ever.'

'Well, you won't have much choice, will you? Since you don't know any German.'

'I do.'

'What? Counting to ten with poor Demet? That will be a great help!'

'I know more than that. And I'll learn.'

'We *all* will. But . . . '

'Yes, but I shall learn better . . . '

'Oh, you would,' cried Fatma crossly. 'You just have to be better than us!'

'No! Not better than you, that's not what I meant. I want to be better than them, than the Swiss. That's what I care about.'

'Them? Who cares about them?' asked Fatma.

'I do. That's what matters to me,' said Selda and shivered as though the hallway were really cold.

Her sisters were not impressed. They turned their backs on her and went through the patterned glass doors and into the salon. She lingered on and heard the sound of their voices, but not their words and she saw their pale shapes, but all their details were blurred and changed by the intricate, old-fashioned patterns in the glass.

Was it really what mattered most, this beating the Swiss? She shivered again. Her fear of the school and of failure in that distant land, where, overnight she must become a silent stranger, towered above her now like a mountain of ice. She could imagine its peak: brilliant with dazzling snow, when you reached it, but the way up would be treacherous. It would be as slippery as the blocks of steaming ice upon which the fishermen laid their catch in the bazaar. She was secretly afraid that she would find no grip on its smooth surface and that her nails would break against the unbearable cold. She was afraid that, despite all her efforts, she might slip down like poor Demet and be sent back to Turkey, as a failure.

'It's come! It's come!' The others had been watching for the taxi from the balcony and now had seen it first.

Suddenly everybody was in tears. They searched for their shoes and their bags, their tickets and their jackets. Fatma had run halfway to the gate before she remembered that she had not even said goodbye to their grandmother. Now the old woman, who had grumbled bitterly about the burden of looking after them all every day for the last two years, hugged them fiercely to her. She held them all so tightly and wept so that the taxi driver had to come in and remind them that the plane would not wait.

And then, everything happened too fast. Selda, because she was the youngest, had to sit in the front, beside the driver holding the bulging bag of food that was to feed them on the

7

journey to Switzerland. She could feel the soft warmth of the cheese pie pressing against her knees. She knew that her grandmother had got up in the dark to bake if for them. Her mother and sisters climbed into the back of the taxi and settled down on the sagging seat. For a moment they smoothed their skirts and smiled at each other, like ladies setting out on a visit. But when the taxi started they remembered, and twisted round in panic, craning out of the windows and pushing each other aside. They called and waved to the old woman who was left behind on the street, watching. Fatma was quite desperate.

'I won't go!' she cried. 'Mother, tell him to stop and let me out. I won't go! I've changed my mind.'

'Grandmother,' moaned Pembe,' please don't forget me.'

Only Selda, still clutching that great bag, did not turn round and wave. She couldn't. If she let go of it, she could imagine how the peaches and apples, the black olives and hard-boiled eggs, the marrow seeds and the roast chick-peas and all the other odds and ends, would fall tumbling down her legs and over the floor of the taxi. Somewhere, hidden in the middle of the bag, was a large ring of *suçuk*, which she knew that her grandmother had put in secretly, despite advice from the neighbours that, over there in Switzerland, people would not like foreigners who munched slices of garlic sausage. Her grandmother never took her neighbours' advice. Selda could smell the sausage even now. How obstinate her grandmother was: they didn't really need any food at all, and the wretched bag had stopped her from waving. She was sure that her grandmother would notice and remember that she was the only one who had not turned back and waved goodbye. And now it was too late: the parting was over and they were already gone.

The old taxi swung round the block, lurching a bit, to avoid the potholes. Then, her grandmother's house and garden, the last reminders of the old sea-side villas in a street of new flats,

8

were left quite behind. Selda's school, with its empty yard and flash of red flag, was gone too. They passed the bazaar, where the lorries stood waiting to be unloaded and the bazaar men still slept, wrapped in their blankets on top of their stalls. They left behind the little park, empty at this early hour. Only a three-legged dog turned his head and blinked and then went back to lazily licking up some drops of dried ice-cream. They turned into the main street which was lined with little shops. Most of them were still shuttered. Just the bakery door stood open and as they passed they could smell the soft dough rising under its golden crusts.

'You'll be surprised,' said Sevgi Hanım,' there are hundreds of different types of bread in Switzerland.' Their mother, Sevgi Hanım, had been on a two-week trip to visit her husband in Switzerland last year. Now she felt that she knew all about the country.

'I expect you father and brothers will have been out and got some bread in for us,' she said. She smiled fondly at her memories of the visit. It was such a quiet, well-run country. 'They always go shopping on Saturday afternoons, when the factory is closed. They love shopping,' she added.

Selda found it very difficult to imagine this other life that her father and brothers had been leading over there in Switzerland. At home, in her grandmother's house, when her father and Ali and Ahmet came back on holiday, they never did any 'shopping'. They never did a thing. They would hardly walk down the street to buy a lettuce from the bazaar. If they wanted a drink of cold water they called one of the girls to bring it to them. When they were hungry their mother and grandmother asked them what they would like to eat and then hurried off to the kitchen to prepare it for them. Selda could not think how they had survived in Switzerland without a woman in the house. She certainly could not picture the three of them 'shopping' on Saturday afternoons!

Her father, Turgut Bey, had first gone to Switzerland years

9

ago. The family had expected to follow him soon afterwards. Selda had been very little then and had not really understood it all. She became used to the fact that her father was never at home. There were several families in the village whose fathers had gone abroad to work. She missed him but accepted it. Her mother stayed on in the village, running the grocer's shop in her husband's place and working his small-holding too. How busy she had been in those days. They had all been quite comfortable, especially as Turgut Bey was sending back some of his wages. Her elder brothers, Ali and Ahmet, had started up a milk round. They had all helped and for Selda those had been happy times. One of her earliest memories was of going along the rows of potatoes covering up the first, dark green shoots. She had enjoyed the work and liked being praised for doing it so well, unlike Pembe, who was slow and dreamy and got slapped for being careless and breaking off the stems. They had been full, cheerful days and Selda, as the youngest of five, had been everybody's 'little sister'. She had been Ahmet's favourite and she had loved him best because he had been endlessly kind and patient. Now, when she saw them on their summer visits, these brothers had become distant. They were more like relatives from another town. She hated it most when they talked to each other in German, which she could not understand. She felt that they were shutting her out of their world and she did not like being silent. For she was the talker in their family, she was the one who had ideas about everything. She was the reader and scribbler, who, in the opinion of the grown-ups, knew more words than was good for her. Oh, how she had hated her brothers when they sat in the balcony and chatted in German and she could not understand. She liked to understand.

Selda could still remember the actual moment when she had learnt to read, silently, and understood the words all by herself. She had been walking home from the village school and reading all the street signs aloud to herself: *banka, sokak, polis*. Later, that same afternoon, she had been minding the shop. An old woman had come in asking for rice-flour; she wanted to make baby food for her little grandson. Selda had glanced up at the shelves and read along the hand-written notices that were pinned there: wheat-flour, cornflour, salt, flour, rice-flour, sugar, baking-powder. She had understood them all in her mind, without having to say them out aloud. It had seemed like magic. She had climbed on a box, stretched on tiptoe and proudly reached down the packet of rice-flour.

'Are you sure that's it, not soap or something?' The old woman had looked at her doubtfully.

'Yes. I'm sure. It really is rice-flour.' Selda had turned the packet over and quickly read the instructions on the back. 'Look,' she had said, holding it out,' it says so here.'

'If you're sure, dear.' The old woman had smiled at her then. 'I never learnt to read, but I dare say you're right. Reading must be very useful.'

It was more than useful to Selda. It had been like stepping into a new place, this other world of printed words. She had read everything and had been so happy in school. Her teacher had helped her and loved her and she had loved him. She had admired him more than anyone she knew. She had sometimes wondered if she loved him more than she loved her father and she felt very guilty about it. She vowed that when she got to Switzerland, she would make up for it. When she was with her father again, she would be a proper daughter at last and admire him.

It was just that she had waited so long. She had secretly begun to think that perhaps he would never send for them. She had begun to suspect that he did not really want them. Then, at the end of one summer visit, he had taken Ali and Ahmet back with him and she had been so jealous.

'Take me! Take me too!' She still remembered clinging to his jacket, trying to hold him back and the family all laughing at her. It made her all hot and uncomfortable just to think about

11

it now. He had not taken her, of course. 'Couldn't' was what he said, but she was obstinate even then and had not quite believed him. Soon after the men had gone, she and her mother and sisters left the village and moved into their grand-mother's big, old house in Izmir. It was only to be for a very short time, just until her father found a big enough flat for them in Switzerland. Then he would send the plane tickets.

In the beginning Selda had watched for the postman every day. She had confidently expected him to hand her a fat airmail envelope with the familiar Swiss mountain stamps in the corner. But he didn't. Ahmet often wrote, but no tickets arrived. Selda started the fourth year of primary school in Izmir, and in those early weeks she had run all the way home as soon as school was over. As she turned the corner she was already yelling up to her mother and grandmother who usually drank tea on the balcony at that time: 'Have the tickets come yet? Have they?'

Then one afternoon her grandmother had met her at the garden gate and pinched her arm and told her to stop her shameless shouting.

'You thoughtless girl! Can't you ever keep your mouth shut? Don't you think I have enough to worry about, with the burden of looking after you four, without you telling the whole neighbourhood that your father can't afford to send you the tickets?'

Selda had pulled away, shocked but furious too.

'That's not true! We're not a burden! Father is looking after us. He sends you money every month. I know he does. And Mother gives you money too! Mother says you must be get-ting quite rich on both . . .' Selda had not meant to say the last bit.

'So your mother says that, does she?' Her grandmother had turned and made for the balcony like a cat after a sparrow.

There had been a terrible argument and it had not even been about the air tickets. They had quarrelled about every-

12

thing, from the way Sevgi Hanım wasted precious water when she washed up, to the fact that Fatma wore shoes with holes in them because Grandmother was too mean to get her new ones. Her mother said that Grandmother loved the Swiss francs more than she loved her grandchildren. Grandmother said that they were ruining her house and garden and that the worry would give her a heart attack. It had been quite horrible and the three girls had crept out and sat unhappily on the steps and listened, as had half the neighbourhood. Like all quarrels, it had solved nothing.

The plane tickets still did not come. Autumn gave way to winter and then to spring. Suddenly they were in the midst of another scorching Izmir summer and still no one planned the journey. Her father and brothers came and went. The hot summer nights were unending. Selda used to wrap herself in a sheet to keep off the gnats, then stay up late reading by the light of the single, bare bulb. She would listen to the grown-ups and to the street and to the noises of the cats who fought and scratched and yowled in the dusty shadows.

She began to spend more and more time on her school work. She sought out the quietest corners of the house and sat there with her books. She also tried hard to think before she spoke. She was learning to be wary of this grandmother who was proud and clever though she had never been to school and seemed to feel the injustice of it as sharply at seventy as she had felt it at seven, when she had had to stay at home and watch her brothers going off with their books and pencils. Now, the sight of Selda and her books seemed to make the old woman particularly angry. She often said that she had forgotten more than Selda was ever likely to know. Despite her age, her grandmother was a sharp, tough sort of person. She was independent and rather feared in the neighbourhood and was not one to lean out of her window and gossip. She would work in her kitchen, complaining about her granddaughters, and bringing her knife down upon the parsley stalks with the ruthless strokes of a machine. People said that Selda looked like her grandmother and Selda hated them for it.

If Selda had been unhappy during the long two years in her grandmother's house, her elder sister, Pembe, had not. Idle, clumsy Pembe had blossomed there, under her grand-mother's care. Pembe did not mind people telling her what to do. Everybody said that in a few years she could have married very well indeed. She was such a pretty girl and had such a gentle nature. Her grandmother was proud of Pembe and when the plane tickets finally arrived she had been bitter at the loss of her favourite granddaughter.

'Why don't you leave her with me?' she had said. 'I'll look after her like the pupil of my own eye.'

Pembe had blushed and giggled and looked very closely at her newly varnished nails.

'I'll stay, Grandmother,' she had whispered, 'if *she'll* let me . . .' and she had looked wistfully at Sevgi Hanım

'Pembe, you know you can't stay. Your ticket has come.' Their mother was trying to be reasonable.

'Why can't she? You can always return the ticket. That's no good reason!' Their grandmother, who was not trying to be reasonable, had spoken sharply. 'I'll tell you why you won't leave her: it's because you don't trust me!' The old woman's words had points as fine as needles.

'If I left her with you,' said their mother, sounding weary,' I know what would happen! In five days' time you would be telephoning us in Switzerland and begging us to come and get Pembe, because the burden of looking after her was giving you a heart attack.'

Pembe had cried, but then, Pembe often cried. Oh, those quarrels and those tears. Oh, those hot summer nights in the old house, where somewhere a mosquito droned and some-where somebody tossed and turned and sniffed back tears. Selda had hated it. She never cried. She had fallen down the rotten steps at the side of the house, tumbled from top to bottom, during an evening game of hide and seek and had skinned her leg like a grated carrot, and she hadn't cried. She had been unfairly passed over at school when she should have been in the general knowledge team, and she had not cried. Her own teacher had pleaded for her; her class had sent a petition to the Head Teacher, but Emine, whose father was a local politician and soon expected to be a Member of Parliament, had been chosen, and Selda had not shed one tear, well, not in public, at least. Selda was tough and proud of it. People said that she should have been a boy with her bravery and her dark complexion. Look at those scowling black brows, they said, look at those big hands and feet. Perhaps they were right. She had so enjoyed the company of her brothers when she was little and she seemed to miss them more now that she was older. She was sure that if they had been seated around her grandmother's house, like dark, watchful statues, there would not have been so many furious, tearful arguments.

Well, it would be all right soon. She settled the bag more comfortably on her knees and dared to stretch her legs a little. The taxi rattled through the dusty streets, leaving them to the glare of the strengthening sun which had begun to flash and flicker through the gaps in the buildings. It would all now be left behind, like poor Demet, like her school and her teacher, like the old house and its neglected garden and like her grandmother herself.

She thought again of her grandmother. She imagined the old woman who was thickset and awkward now, going back up the steps into the empty house. Her rough, red hands with their swollen knuckles would grip the rail with fierce determination as she pulled herself up from step to step. She would never, ever have admitted that she found the climb difficult now. No, not her. She would leave her garden shoes at the door and step into her slippers and walk through the cool, tiled hall. Then she would push open the glass doors and the

15

whole house would be hers again. And would she really be pleased to be alone?

Last night, something strange had happened. Her grandmother had come into the room where Selda was pretending to be asleep. She had rummaged around in a chest of drawers, noisily opening and shutting it, as though unable to find something which she wanted. Then she had spoken sharply in the dark, as if she knew that Selda was awake all the time.

'You'll write, won't you Selda?' she had asked, slamming a drawer shut as though she were punishing it. And then she had added, sourly: 'If it's not too much trouble for you to write to your only grandmother.'

'Of course I'll write. I'll write every week. I'll send you lots of postcards.'

'Don't make promises that you won't keep, Miss.'

'But I will.'

'Oh no you won't. I know you. And I don't want postcards, thank you very much. With postcards everybody in the street will know my news before I do. I want letters.'

'Letters?'

'That's what I said, wasn't it? Or have you gone deaf?'

'No, but . . . '

'Oh well, I expect you'll be too busy.' Her grandmother sighed loudly. 'You'll be so busy with your new life and all that German that you won't want to find time to write to your old grandmother. I know what will happen.' She sighed again.

'I will write, I promise. We'll all write!' Why did her grandmother have to be so annoying?

'I haven't asked *all* of you to write, have I?' She had reopened the door and stood there, a heavy, black shape against the shaft of light. 'I've only asked you and I expect I've wasted my breath as usual!'

'But . . . '

'See? There you go! "But" this and "but" that. Why can't

16

you just say "yes Grandmother" for once in your life? Do you have to be so clever?'

Then she had stamped away and Selda had lain awake listening to the clatter and crash in the kitchen as the old woman worked on there in the middle of the night, getting things ready for them.

She had only been going to ask her grandmother how she would read the letters, but perhaps it was a good thing that she had not mentioned it. It would only have infuriated the old woman more. Anyway, it was too late now. The taxi was taking them further and further away from one life and nearer and nearer to the new one. In Zurich, her father would be waiting. In Izmir her grandmother would perhaps be sitting on the balcony, drinking her tea quite alone. Selda wished that she had risked dropping the bag. She wished that she had turned round and let all the food tumble down and that she had yelled, shamelessly from the car window: 'I'll write, Grandmother, I'll write!' even if her grandmother could never read the letters.

Two

The taxi stopped at the checkpoint in the wire fence surrounding the airport outside Izmir. The driver exchanged a few words with the soldier on guard who waved them through.

'Are you flying direct to Switzerland?' the driver asked Selda.

'No. We're flying to Istanbul first. My uncle will meet us in Istanbul and then we fly on to Switzerland tomorrow.'

'Then I need to take you to the Internal Flights. There we are. Aren't you lucky?' He smiled at her. 'I'd give anything to get to Europe. You can't make a living here these days.' He shrugged and added: 'Got your chewing gum I hope!'

'No! I forgot all about it.' She smiled back at him. He was Husein, the fisherman's son and he was a friend of Ali and Ahmet. Sometimes in the summer they took the boat out together, though the catches were no longer very good. That was why he also worked as a taxi driver, she knew. He was the only person her grandmother had trusted to take them to the airport.

'Shame, you'll need your chewing gum. It's more important than your passports.' He grinned at her so that his deeply sunburnt face broke up into hundreds of fine lines.

'Passports? Husein, stop my son, stop!' Sevgi Hanım suddenly called from the back seat in a panic. 'Stop the car, Husein, and let me make sure I have the passports. How you've frightened me.' She began frantically to stir up the contents of her handbag until Selda reminded her that she had the passports, there on her lap, with the food. Husein grinned more widely.

'All safe?'

'Yes, yes, Selda has them. Oh dear, how you scared me, talking about forgetting things! My heart stopped for a moment! I swear it.'

The car accelerated.

'Why do we need chewing gum, Husein Abi?' Pembe's voice was like warm, slow water, flowing over sunlit stone. 'Is it for when the plane crashes?'

Selda squirmed. Husein started to laugh. Then, glancing into his mirror, he saw the reflection of the girl in the back of his taxi and he stifled his laughter. She looked very grown-up, in the white dress.

'No, don't worry. It was a joke. It's for your ears.'

'For my ears? What's wrong with my ears?' Pembe put up her little hand and touched the gold loops in her ears and met his glance in the mirror.

'Nothing,' he said, 'there's nothing wrong with your ears. It's . . . it's . . .' Husein looked uncomfortable and Pembe was wrinkling up her forehead.

'Your ears won't go pop . . .' he said, lamely.

'Go "pop"?'

'He means that it alters the pressure in your ears,' said Selda fiercely. She had had enough. 'You swallow your spit when you chew gum and that equalizes pressure so your ears don't hurt any more.'

They all looked at her as though she had said something quite rude. Then Husein rammed a tape into the cassette player and turned the volume up loud.

They had a very long, hot wait in Izmir airport, which slowly grew more and more crowded. Although they had been rather dreading the moment, when the flight was finally announced, they rushed forward with an unexpected sense of relief. Selda even pushed and wriggled her way in front of people, so eager was she to get on the plane. The jet engines made a terrible screaming noise and a hot, gritty wind stung their eyes and blew up their skirts. It was confusing and chaotic and not at all like what she had seen on the television. In films, people always settled themselves coolly and elegantly into half-empty planes; they leant back in wide seats and sipped clear drinks as they watched magnificent views from the plane windows. Here, people pushed and shouted and banged their bags and parcels into the backs of her legs. There were disputes about seats. Solid Turkish ladies sat themselves firmly down in the places they fancied and then would not be moved, not by anyone. Family men fussed and fretted and jumped up and down and made their wives and daughters change places so that they did not have to sit beside other family men. Children discovered the ashtrays and tables and made them click in and out like crazy grasshoppers, stretching their legs. A girl in front of Selda was trying to ram two huge water-melons under her seat and other people were trying to squeeze past her. The tourists, who all seemed to be very tall, stood in the aisles and leant over the backs of the seats, helplessly checking the numbers against the numbers on their tickets. They shrugged their shoulders and rolled their eyes in humorous bewilderment and Selda could not help staring at all their undressed, sunburnt skin. Some of them were still dressed for the beach. Beside Selda an old lady who was as white haired as her grandmother, was wearing bright pink trousers and a T-shirt. When she sat back in her seat, Selda saw that the T-shirt was printed with a mouse sunbathing under a palm tree. Those were children's clothes, surely?

A tall, slim, short-haired tourist, who was wearing blue jeans and a checked shirt with the sleeves rolled up to the elbow, said 'pardon' and eased past Selda's hastily drawn-in knees. The tourist sat down beside her and it was only when they reached for the safety belt and Selda heard the jangle of silver bracelets falling down to the wrist, that she realized that her neighbour was a woman. Selda smiled to herself: nothing was as she had expected it to be. Nobody was sipping cool drinks, the plane windows gave no view at all and the seats were so narrow that you had to take care not to touch the person beside you. Then, to her astonishment, a hostess came round and told her that she could not sit there with the bag on her lap. Selda just stared back at her in tired confusion.

'You must put the bag in a locker,' said the hostess in an exasperated voice.

'A locker?'

'Yes. Up there!' The hostess now pointed irritably to the rows of little doors above the seats. Selda struggled to get up and couldn't. She had forgotten that she had already fastened her safety belt. She fumbled with the buckle and was aware of the hostess standing watching her and not offering to help. She finally got free only to hear her mother call out: 'Miss, Madam, we need that bag, we need it near us, it has our food and . . .'

The smart hostess eyed Sevgi Hanım; she knew exactly how to deal with inexperienced fliers like this: 'Food, did you say? Madam, it is not *I* who make the regulations. All bags must be safely put away during take off and landing.'

'I didn't know . . .' Sevgi Hanım looked around her for sympathy, but nobody else was interested, so she hung her head while Selda struggled with the impossible bag. She was sure that by now the whole plane could smell the garlic sausage. She heaved the bag up but could not quite reach. Her mother, still shrinking before the hostess's stare, did not come to her aid.

It was the neighbour in blue jeans who rescued her. She touched Selda's shoulder, took the bag from her and reached easily up and put the bag in the locker and closed the door. Selda felt tears, not in her eyes, for she was the one who never cried, but they threatened her, for a second. She hated her mother who had not helped her and the hostess who despised them and she hated everyone who had watched her

21

embarrassment. Then, as they sat down again she impulsively turned in gratitude to the stranger. *'Danke, danke sehr,'* she said, using some of the few words poor Demet had taught her.

'Bitte, bitte.' The woman smiled back, delighted, and then, perhaps because neither of them could say anything else, she offered Selda some sweets. Selda smiled back and, breaking one of those laws of childhood, which said that you must never accept sweets from strangers, she took a piece of the chocolate. She sucked it and so celebrated her first step into the new land: she had spoken German and been understood. And anyway, she wasn't really a child at all, not now.

The plane took off like a person suddenly deciding to run and jump over a wall. After rolling gently along, it accelerated and lurched upwards and Selda had just begun to think 'oh no', when it seemed to be over the worst and straightened out. And there was the Bay of Izmir, sparkling below her. Her companion leant back and held aside the little curtain so that Selda could see out better. By the time they had had their snack of cake and cherry juice, Selda had managed to understand that the woman had spent two of something in Kuşadası, which she knew to be a holiday place outside Izmir. The woman flipped busily through a small book, then put her nail against a line and showed it to Selda. It said: *'Woche = hafta'*. *'Zwei Wochen,'* said the woman, then read out more slowly: *'i-ki- haf-ta?'* *'Evet, iki hafta.'* Selda laughed with surprise. She had never thought that anyone would want to learn her language. Soon she was so busy looking for more words in the tourist's dictionary, that she forgot to be scared about the landing. She looked out of the little oval window to see Istanbul sprinkled around the edges of the sea, like blown blossom on a blue pool. She thought she might have glimpsed the palaces of Topkapı amongst the crowding roofs by the water's edge, but she was not sure. This was her first sight of Istanbul. She had not thought that it would look so huge or that the sea would be so very, very blue, or that the pale sands would go down under the sea and then gleam through whitely to the clouds above. She wanted to see it all, to notice every single fishing boat that rose and fell amongst the glistening waves.

It was wonderful and beautiful and she was so glad that they had left Izmir behind. She was excited now. She hardly held her breath as the plane touched down. In the airport she was the one who found out where the luggage trolleys were kept; she tugged their suitcases off the carousel and it was she who ran over to look for the moustached face of Kemal Amca who was to meet them.

There he was, waiting by the barrier at the very front of the crowd. He opened his arms wide when he saw them. It had been at least a year since he had visited them in Izmir, and he swung Selda up in the air, and kissed her on both cheeks and said that she was prettier than ever. It wasn't true, but it was very nice to hear. He complimented Pembe on her dress and Fatma on her beautiful long hair, and Sevgi Hanım, who was his sister, on her skill in getting them all to Istanbul safely. He praised the new airport and then said goodbye to a policeman, clapping him on the shoulder as though they were old friends. He put his arm around Selda again and said: 'Well, Black Eyes, take a good look around you. You're looking at the most beautiful city in the world.' He took control of the luggage trolley and steered them all out into the brilliant midday sun, where the sound of the call to prayer drifted on the white light.

Kemal Amca had a small haulage business and it was to one of his own red lorries that he now led them in the car park. Sevgi Hanım eyed the mud-splashed vehicle with some apprehension. Pembe said straight out that she hoped the inside was cleaner than the outside. Her uncle, who was a man of endless good nature, only laughed. He teased them all for being too smart for the likes of him. Then he swung the

23

cases and then the girls into the open back of the lorry. There they found that somebody had thoughtfully spread out a thick, clean rug, and laid on it several cushions, so that they should be comfortable. It was a long, busy drive from the airport to Kemal Amca's flat. The last few minutes, along a mud track, were so bumpy that they had to cling on to the sides of the lorry to stop themselves tumbling in a heap. They had come some distance from the main road and when they jumped down the soil was sandy. An old woman sat on a bank near by watching a sheep graze the last of the summer's grass. It seemed like a patch of real country although Selda could still hear the roar of the main road in the distance.

'That's the "E5",' said her uncle, following her gaze. 'That road goes straight on to Ankara and then on to the East and then on to India, or even the Far East, they say. Or, if you turn south, you can go right down to the border with Iraq, even round to the Red Sea, if you wanted to.' He looked away and shaded his eyes and Selda would have liked to ask him more questions, but just then her aunt and two cousins came running out of the flats to greet them.

During lunch Kemal Amca offered to take them on a sightseeing trip that afternoon. He had to drive back on to the European side of the city and he said that if they liked, they could come too. Afterwards he would show them around. Selda hoped that her mother would accept but Sevgi Hanım declined, pleading a dreadful headache. Pembe, who had not enjoyed the bumpy ride, said that she did not want to go either, so their aunt said that she too would stay, to keep them company. In the end it seemed to have turned out for the best. Although Selda and Fatma hardly knew their cousins, five minutes of bouncing about in the lorry made them feel like old friends. It was much easier to chat, clinging on to the ropes and with one's eyes screwed up against the dust and glare, than it had been to talk face to face across the lunch table.

They soon learnt that Alev, who was about Fatma's age, was planning to become a teacher. Atilla, who was nine or eight, said that he wanted to be a pilot, a fighter pilot, naturally. As the lorry crawled slowly over the Bosphorous Bridge, Selda leapt from side to side, trying to see up to the Black Sea in the north and down to the Aegean in the south. It was so busy a waterway and Atilla, leaning beside her, nodded at the big Russian tanker making its way down the centre of the water and said: 'Yes, I'd like to be a pilot, and if not, then I'll be a captain and sail all over the world.'

She understood what he meant. It was all so wonderful and, if Istanbul was like this, what then was Switzerland like? For everybody said that Europe was much, much better than Turkey.

'Well?' said Kemal Amca. He had made the delivery and they were now strolling across the square in front of the New Mosque. 'Well, Black Eyes, what do you think of our Istanbul?'

'It's . . . it's . . .' she pulled a helpless face and smiled up at him, and Kemal Amca nodded as though she had said exactly the right thing. Behind them was the quayside where three or four old ferries swung and clanked against the rotting timbers like great, chained beasts, come in to feed. Beyond them the sea splashed and twinkled as pretty as the bright ribbons on a bride. A hundred street sellers were dotted all over the pavements, half hidden by the waves of people going in and out of the bazaar behind the Mosque.

'Isn't it . . .' agreed Kemal Amca, and stretched wide arms behind them, and Selda did not know if he were safely shepherding them through the crowds, or drawing the city and all its millions towards himself.

'Or,' said Atilla, who was a determined boy, 'I could be a soldier, couldn't I? A general, actually.' His father smiled down at him and nodded.

'What about you, Selda?' he asked.

'Me?'

'Yes, you. A doctor maybe, or a lawyer? That's the fashionable thing in Istanbul: all the girls want to be lawyers. And I'm all for it. Nobody wants to be just a wife and mother any more. You ask my Alev.'

'I do,' said Fatma. 'I'm not going to work.'

'Then I suppose you'll want a rich husband.'

'Yes.'

'How about a Swiss one?' her uncle teased.

'No! Never!' They were all surprised by the strength of her answer.

'Why not?' asked Kemal Amca. 'I hear that they're very rich.'

'I don't care! I'd rather die!' She shook her head in real horror and when Kemal Amca tried to get her to explain what she meant, she wouldn't.

There was a silence and to fill the awkward gap Selda tried to joke: 'Grandmother says that foreigners are dirty. They wear their shoes in the house and they let animals sleep on their beds. Just think of that. So maybe Fatma's right.'

'You're the Devil's hind legs, Selda,' joked Kemal Amca. 'You'll be all right over there, if you can remember to laugh, and not just at other people, either.'

'Do you think I will be all right, Uncle?' She wasn't laughing now.

'Yes. Yes, I really do.'

'That's not what other people say.'

'Then don't listen to "other people", my girl. Listen to yourself, or even better, listen to me. I've been about. I've seen the world, believe me.' He had his arm around her as though she were his own daughter and as though he really cared about her. She thought again of her father and of how much she had missed him in that household of women. It would be so good to be with him again.

'I tell you what,' said Kemal Amca, turning aside, 'there's

someone over here who knows about the future even better than I do.'

'Who?' Had he seen a friend in all this thronging, swarming crowd of people?

He pointed to an elderly man in a black coat who sat on an old fashioned wooden chair at the base of the grey stone steps which led up to the Mosque. In front of him were a couple of boxes covered with a black cloth, but he seemed to have nothing to sell.

'Who's that? What does he do?' asked Selda.

'He tells fortunes!' cried Atilla, who had been there before. 'Father, can I have mine told, please?' He jumped about and shook his father's arm.

'Why not? Today is a special day, after all. You can all have your fortunes told.'

As they drew close, Selda saw that there was nothing on the cloth except four, chipped old coffee cups, whose patterns had almost worn away. Each held some tiny, tightly rolled scrolls of coloured paper, some yellow, some green, some a bright, purplish pink and some black. The old man was worn and tired like some bent but still standing tree and Selda saw now that what had appeared to be a black coat was really a very long jacket, patched and repatched, layer upon layer, so that you could not tell where the original garment was. It looked as though the fortune teller never ever took it off, but just stood there while someone sewed on another patch. His eyes were a very pale grey, as faint as sea mist, with the pupils just a pencil dot in the centre. Selda was reminded of the wet, unclear gaze of a baby. He spoke to them with such indifference that she wondered if he wanted any customers or not. She found herself looking at the black grime under his yellowed nails and she remembered her grandmother complaining that these people of the streets were no better than thieves and robbers. They were cheating beggars, and lazy scoundrels, according to her.

The fortune teller seemed to be looking beyond the funnels of the ferries and across the waters of the Bosphorous to the far shore, where some of the hills still kept their groves of old cypress and pink-barked cedar. He spoke to them, but Selda, who had been looking at the far shore too, did not understand what he had said.

'He's asking you if you want the rabbit or the chicken,' said Alev, helpfully.

'Rabbit or chicken?' giggled Fatma, who had also not understood.' I'm not very fond of either, but chicken, if I have to.'

'Not to *eat*,' cried Atilla, doubling up with laughter. He was glad that he, a proper city boy, had not made such a mistake. Fatma blushed.

The fortune teller bent down and lifted a plump, white chicken from under the curtain. He held it closely to him, talking to it and telling it to do its work well. It nestled against him and clucked and crooned in reply and then stretched out its beak and gently tweaked his ear. He looked towards them with his old, veined hands sunk into her soft, white feathers and he said: 'That's all right then, children, she says that she is ready to tell your fortunes.'

He placed the white hen on the black cloth and stroked the little, red comb which fell to one side of her delicate, curious head. 'She said to me, that, if you are in agreement, she could pick out a green fortune for you.' His voice was unusual but how, exactly, Selda could not tell. It might have been sick, or foreign or just very old. It might almost have been somebody else's voice and Selda found herself looking round to where an old woman squatted on the pavement, selling tins of corn for people to toss to the pigeons who fluttered all around.

'Is it, then, to be green?' he repeated. They nodded, all except Selda.

He picked up a white stick which rested against his chair and he banged on the ground with it three times. The suddenness and sharpness of sound made them all start. The chicken turned its head from side to side, then went along the black cloth on its slender, neatly stepping legs that were the colour of fresh lemon skins. It came to the cup with the green papers. It paused, turning its head from side to side as though considering. The red comb danced anew at each turn. Then, it pecked into the cup three times and brought out three rolls of green paper: one for Atilla, another for Alev and the third for Fatma.

When the old man opened his hands, the little hen scuttled back into his arms and he stroked her and congratulated her on work well done. Then, he reached down with her and Selda, peering over the edge of the boxes, saw that he set her carefully into a straw-lined basket behind the cloth. They heard her claws amongst the canes as she scratched a bit and settled down.

'So you, little lady, would like a fortune of another colour,' said the fortune teller, and Selda knew that he was speaking to her although he had not once looked at her.

'Yes, please. I should like black.'

'I thought you would. As soon as you came near I knew that you would seek a fortune that was black. But I must tell you,' and he spoke more loudly now so that passers-by stopped to listen, 'I must tell you that it is not so easy to read what is written in the night.'

'Unless there's a moon . . .' said Selda quickly. He looked at her then. She had not meant to be difficult or to show off, she'd only meant to agree with him, in a way. He stared at her, or perhaps he didn't. Perhaps he had only gazed at the wave of pigeons that rose up, fluttering and flapping against the grey stone of the Mosque. It seemed that they would rise higher and higher, sweeping up above the minarets themselves, but they didn't. They fluttered and fluttered and fell back to the ground and pecked greedily at the grain that was scattered for them.

'So,' he said, 'a black fortune for this girl.'

'And with the rabbit, please. If it doesn't cost any more.' Selda did not want to make any extra expense for her uncle, but she did so want to see the rabbit.

'Fortunes of all colours have their price,' said the old man.

'In that case . . .' Selda wanted to say that it did not matter after all and that she did not mind if the chicken chose her fortune too, but the old man interrupted her sharply: 'It could cost nothing at all,' he continued. 'It all depends on how good or bad your fortune is. Some fortunes are worthless and some, my daughter, are so precious that we can never pay their price.'

Selda looked up to her uncle for guidance and saw that he only smiled as patiently and easily as he ever did, so she smiled too and said: 'The rabbit, then, please.'

The others had started to unroll their papers and were reading out the verses and laughing. She moved away from them and her heart beat faster as the fortune teller reached under the cloth again and brought out the rabbit.

It was a little brown rabbit, with quivering ears laid back along its sleek, crouched shoulders. One paw and its chest were white. As it made its way over the cloth to the cup which held the black papers, every hair and whisker of its fragile body seemed to shake and tremble. When it stopped, a murmur of surprise ran through the gathering crowd. It paused, wrinkling and twitching its nose. Its tail stood out like a tiny bunch of new-plucked cotton. The old man banged his stick. The rabbit leapt in the air and turned right round. Selda thought that she had never seen anything so pretty in all her life. If only she could have had a little animal like this. Instantly she felt that she too understood those Swiss people who let their pets into the house. If she had had a rabbit like this she would have let it sleep on her bed. She held out her hand for the paper, but the little rabbit came forward without it and, instead, rocked its nose from side to side, then, very gently, began to lick her hand. She felt its tongue, like damp silk on her skin, and she gasped. The old man banged his stick again. The rabbit jumped back. It darted to the cup, plucked out a black paper and gave it to her.

The crowd clapped, for it had been a very good show. Her uncle paid generously and they stepped aside to make way for a smart young officer and his girlfriend, who wanted their fortunes told.

'Open it, Selda. Quick, what does it say?'

She fiddled with the thread that bound it up and was unwilling to untie it. She did not want to read it out aloud. She was afraid that the verse might be foolish and spoil the magic. She shivered: she could still feel the touch of the rabbit's tongue on her skin.

'It's only a game, anyway,' said Kemal Amca kindly, leading the way into the fruit market behind the New Mosque. She followed him gratefully and they looked at the stalls piled high with the beautiful ripe fruits of late summer. There were grapes as long as your little finger and the air smelt of warm skinned apples. Selda felt that she was being secretive and ungrateful when her uncle was being so generous, so she pulled off the thread and smoothed out the paper and read:

> 'Plant pretty roses in your garden,
> Plant sweet herbs by your door,
> But bury secrets in your heart
> To keep them safe for evermore.'

'Is that all?' asked Fatma.

'Yes.'

'Well, that's not bad advice,' said Kemal Amca, peaceably. 'What's yours Fatma?

'Mine's stupid too. Listen:

> 'Dogs are fast,
> And men may be faster,

31

But watch where you run
Or you'll run to disaster.'

'I mean, what a stupid rhyme! Do you think he writes them himself?'

'Well, I don't know, since he's blind.'

'Blind?' cried Selda and Fatma together.

'Oh yes,' said Alev, 'didn't you realize?'

'No,' said Selda, feeling that if anyone were stupid, it was herself. It was obvious, now she thought about it. She had seen his white stick and his distant unfocused gaze, and never thought.

'Actually,' said Fatma, loyally, 'I didn't realize either.'

'Oh yes,' said Kemal Amca. 'He must be very old. People say that he's been blind since he fought in the battle of the Dardanelles when he was hardly more than a boy. He's been here as long as I've been in Istanbul. Summer and winter, he's sitting there. He was even there in that snowy weather. It must have been bitterly cold for an old man like him.'

'And for the rabbit,' said Selda.

'I dare say you're right. I suppose that somewhere there is a home that he goes to and I'd guess that somewhere is somebody who writes out those riddles for him.'

'Do you think that they are all different?'

'He says that they are.'

'That's a lot of riddles,' said Selda, impressed.

'There are a lot of fortunes in the world,' laughed Kemal Amca, but she did not mind because she knew that he was not mocking her.

'Come along,' he added, 'I'll buy you all some ice-cream.'

'Sakız ice-cream?' asked Atilla.

'Why not, if they have any left.' They walked through the narrow streets of the bazaar and found the ice-cream seller, who held out the gleaming cones above the brass-lidded tubs.

They walked back to the lorry, climbed aboard and leant

against the cushions licking their ice-cream slowly, letting the delicious taste of the pine resin trickle over their tongues and icily down their throats. Kemal Amca drove the lorry around some of the other great sights of Istanbul. They saw the floating domes of the Blue Mosque rising like clouds on the breeze above the fountain which played before them. They got down and peered around the leather curtain across the entrance to the Mosque and they saw the thousand different blues of the tiles inside that Selda was reminded of the vast blueness of the sea. They crossed the street and looked up at the impossible ceiling of Santa Sophia and at the mild, staring faces of the frescoes on the walls. Selda would have liked to climb up into the galleries to look more closely at those painted eyes which gazed down and yet did not see, but her uncle said that they must get back and that she must wait for another time.

Once in the lorry they were very quiet. Atilla had fallen asleep instantly. The evening light was fading and Selda felt drowsy too. She heard Alev asking Fatma if she really wanted to go to Switzerland.

'No!' Fatma replied unexpectedly. 'Not at all. I even thought of running away.'

'Did you really?' asked Selda in surprise. She had not realized that her sister felt like that.

'Yes, I did. Really. But you won't tell anyone, will you?'

'No, of course I won't. But why? I thought you wanted to go?'

'Well, I don't. But nobody asked us what we wanted, did they? So it wasn't any good saying anything. But I don't want to go.'

The day passed finally into night and there was only the darkened sky above. It seemed even easier to talk with the stars beginning to come out.

'I don't know why I feel like this,' continued Fatma. 'I just don't want to go. Do I have to have a reason? I was happy in Izmir. I don't want to leave Turkey. But I'm going, just like you. Do you know,' she turned to Selda, 'we're no different from that chicken: somebody bangs the stick and tap, tap, tap, we do as we're told.'

'I didn't know that you felt like that,' said Selda quietly.

'Oh, forget it,' said Fatma, more cheerfully. 'I don't feel like that all the time. Just sometimes, like now. Anyway, I can always come back, can't I? Nobody is going to make me do what I don't want to do! Not when I'm older, anyway. I'll come back, whatever anybody says!' Fatma sounded very determined.

They fell quiet. The warm wind blew the evening sounds of a great city into their faces. They heard the lap of the waves against the shore and the click, click of the halyards against the masts of the moored yachts. They heard music and voices from the still-open windows and they heard the roar of thousands and thousands of other vehicles, moving and stopping and turning, all over the city. Selda realized that her uncle was driving near the sea again but then she must have dropped off to sleep too.

Suddenly she was almost awake but dreaming of the rabbit, caught by one paw, and there was her uncle pulling at her arm to make her sit up.

'What did *you* think of it, Black Eyes?' he was asking.

'I think,' she began, rubbing her eyes and trying to clear her head,' I think it frightened me a bit.'

'Frightened you?' He looked at her in a puzzled way.

'Yes. The thought of somebody knowing all those thousands and thousands of fortunes . . .'

'Not *that*, sleepy head! You've been dreaming about the fortune teller. Wake up. I mean, what did you think of the Bosphorous Bridge at night? I sometimes think it looks even better by night.'

'What bridge, Uncle?'

'The Bosphorous Bridge!' He swung Atilla down to the ground.

34

'Oh, Uncle, I'm sorry, I didn't see it. I must have fallen asleep.'

'Don't worry.' Alev laughed. 'That's the best thing you can do when Father starts talking about roads and that bridge. I think I've been shown that bridge more than any girl in Turkey.'

'Ah, you young people! And to think that this girl, my daughter, wants to become a teacher.' He put his arm proudly around Alev and Selda could see how alike they were, with the same plump, pale face and the same wavy, brown hair. 'Young people.' He laughed. 'I drove all that way so that you could see it by night and it just sent you to sleep! I was going to say that the view from the top is one of the wonders of the modern world. You can laugh at me, but I reckon that that bridge is as good as the Hanging Gardens of Babylon, or the Pyramids. Why, if you look at it carefully from underneath, then you can see how wonderfully it's made. But I don't suppose you noticed that either.'

'No, I'm afraid I didn't.'

'Never mind. But do you know why I took you there?'

'No, Uncle.'

'So that over there, in Switzerland, where you're going, you can be proud of your country and tell them that we too have fine things. You can tell them, but with a smile, that we are not just some poor, forgotten people, knocking like beggars at the doors of their country, but that we too have made great things. After all that is the only bridge in the whole world which joins two continents, Europe and Asia.'

'I can still tell them, can't I, Uncle? Even if I didn't see it by night?'

'Why not? That's the idea! You tell them. You'll do fine over there, so don't worry. Now come along. Your aunt will have the supper waiting.'

And to think that this was the uncle of whom the family was a bit ashamed! 'Kemal?' people would say when they talked about him. 'Oh, he hasn't done much with his life. He's just a lorry driver in Istanbul.'

When he swung her down from the lorry he gave her an extra swirl in the air, and she remembered that years ago, before he went off to Switzerland, that was what her brother Ahmet had always done.

That night, before she curled up on the sofa and tried to go to sleep, Selda hid the riddle away inside her pencil case. She decided that as soon as she got to Switzerland, she would write and tell her grandmother all about this day in Istanbul. The old woman would particularly enjoy hearing about the fortune teller even though she always said that she did not approve of such things. In Izmir there had been a rough man who brought a dancing bear in to the town on public holidays. Last year he had suggested to the onlookers that the pretty, ragged girl of about Pembe's age, whom he had brought with him, should wrestle with the bear, for extra money. People had watched impassively from their windows and balconies, nudging each other and grinning. Selda's grandmother, grumbling and complaining, had shouted out that he should be ashamed of endangering his daughter so. Other women had murmured their agreement. Her grandmother had threatened to call the police. The man had laughed up in her face and told her to run and call them. Then he had blown the first, wailing notes on the pipe. The bear had lumbered across the road and the girl had got up from the pavement where she had been squatting. She had smiled, showing a mouthful of gold teeth and Sevgi Hanım had hissed in horror that that was what these gypsies did for a dowry: they knocked a girl's teeth out and replaced them with gold ones, when she married!

Then the girl had called up that, instead of money, clothes would do . . . and she had started to pull her şalvar up her slim, brown leg, as if to show them how threadbare the material was. Selda's grandmother had actually laughed and shaken her head and sent Selda running down the steps with a pink jumper and a pair of quite good shoes which she said pinched her feet. The man inspected them swiftly, nodded up at them, accepting the bargain and then had struck up his tune. After the bear had danced the traditional dance, the man goaded it into wrestling with the girl. All the neighbours in the flats had leant down, watching. They had cried out and cheered and Selda had heard her grandmother cheering too.

She had stayed down, watching from the garden wall and she had been quite frightened. She had been near enough to see the bear's teeth and to smell the strong, strange smell from his matted fur. Then her grandmother had tossed down more coins and the gypsy had called out a blessing on her for her generosity. But when Selda came back into the house, her grandmother had been protesting: 'Why, he's nothing but a cheap thief, that man! He's had a perfectly good pair of shoes and money, and given nothing in return. He didn't even make that bear wrestle properly. In my young days they used to get the girls right down on the pavement.' She had stamped off to make more tea and had talked endlessly of the gypsies and bears who had roamed the streets in her youth. Then, the bears had been as agile and clever as actors and the men who beat the drums had made a sound so strong that you thought that armies were marching by. And the girls, in those days, had been as beautiful and enchanting as the Devil himself.

'But I thought you said it was wrong . . .' Selda had protested, puzzled.

Her grandmother had turned on her and told her to mind her own business and Selda wished that she had not spoken, for her grandmother had not said another word. But all the same, Selda was quite sure that she would love to hear about the fortune teller and the rabbit. As soon as Selda got to Switzerland, she would settle down and write to her grandmother and tell her all about it.

Three

It was pouring with rain when they arrived in Switzerland. They could see the rain teeming down outside the airport building, but they could not hear a single splash. It was so very quiet. The floors of the terminus were covered with thick, soft black plastic, so that their very footsteps were unheard as they walked along the endless corridors to Passport Control. Selda wanted to shout and cry out: 'Look, it's me! I'm here, I've come, at last!' But instead she became as quiet as all the other passengers who marched along those hushed tunnels. It was almost as though speaking were forbidden here. Even the group of young Turkish men, who had been noisy and a little drunk on the plane, fell silent as they approached the glass boxes where you showed your passport.

They waited in quiet, orderly lines. The man in front of Selda handed in his little navy book and then leant very close to the glass. His feet shifted and shuffled uneasily as though he feared that his shoes might stick to the yielding, bubbled patterns on the floor if he stood there too long. The woman in the box turned and smartly re-turned the pages in the book. The man leant closer but still did not speak. Perhaps he couldn't. Perhaps he was like Selda and could not speak a word of German. Whatever would she do if this woman said something to her? Selda had the feeling that this time it would not be enough to know the numbers up to ten, or how to say '*danke*'. Perhaps she could smile at the woman. That was what Kemal Amca would do.

The woman looked up. She handed the passport back to the man in front of Selda without a word or a sign. He fled like a cat getting away from a dog in the street. Then it was Selda's turn. The pages were flapped over briskly and then it was handed back. And that was it, except that the woman had smiled at her, briefly.

She was in Switzerland, at last. She flew down the remaining steps and into a huge, half-empty hall. The other passengers were just melting away. Selda recognized their suitcases tumbling down on to another carousel and she hurried towards them. A crowd of people was standing beyond a huge glass wall. They were waving and pointing to the arriving passengers. Some held newspapers, others notices and a few clutched bunches of flowers as though they were expecting some film star to arrive. Amongst them she thought she saw her father, but was uncertain. This was a bearded man. But he was also not pressed up against the glass, eager to recognize them, as her father would be, who had not seen them for a year. Perhaps she had been mistaken, and anyway, her brothers were not there, and they, surely, would have come. The man was like her father, though.

She could not force herself to walk over to make sure. She could not bear to walk in front of all those curious eyes behind the glass. What if she was mistaken and smiled at some man who was not her father? She had made that mistake once, as a very little girl. In the crowded bazaar, fearing that she had lost her father, she had reached out in panic amongst the shifting, pressing crowd and caught hold of a man's hand. He had turned and looked down at her and it was a strange man. She still remembered the sense of shame that she had felt as she jerked her hand free and saw that her own father had only paused for a moment to buy fruit.

Now she pretended that she had not seen anyone but must be busy with the luggage. She saw the line of luggage trolleys and was returning with one when she noticed her sister, Pembe, drifting across to the glass wall. Pembe was smiling and she seemed to greet everyone as she searched calmly for

39

the faces of her father and brothers. She acknowledged the way the wall of people admired her in her beautiful white dress. If the glass had not been between her and them, it seemed to Selda that her sister would have reached out and accepted the bouquets as a just tribute to her beauty. Selda looked away and grabbed the handle of the biggest case and pulled at it.

The loaded trolley would have been difficult to steer for one person. It was impossible when the four of them tried. They all four seized it and then banged and barged through Customs. Then one of them accidentally grabbed the brake and the thing stopped suddenly and one of the cases fell off the top and on to somebody's foot. Selda was sure that they were going to be stopped, that a Customs' Officer was going to call them over. She glimpsed somebody else's striped pyjamas and socks being piled up on the counter beside packets of pistachio nuts and tea. Please, please let them pass through. She thought that she would die of shame if the Customs people searched through her underclothes or found the hidden garlic sausage.

'Didn't you see Father?' Pembe asked, breathless with excitement.

'No . . . I was looking for the cases.'

'Oh! He looked so distinguished!'

'Who?'

'Father, of course. That beard makes him look just like a film star.'

And there he was. He certainly did look very different in a dark suit and a buttoned-up shirt with no tie. So it was him, this solemn man, with his sombre, greying beard who nodded at them. He did not swing her up in his arms but, of course, the airport was very crowded. He greeted them and kissed the girls on both cheeks and asked them how their journey had gone. Then he introduced them to another man with a beard who was standing beside them, watching. This man, he explained, was his good friend, Adnan Hoca. Adnan Hoca nodded to them all but did not offer his hand. Then her father smiled, and rubbed the tips of his fingers together and said that if they would like to follow him, he would lead the way out of the car park. He did not offer to help them with the luggage.

'Adnan Hoca,' he said, smiling deferentially at the stranger, 'is a true friend to us Turks in our town. He has kindly offered to drive us all home from the airport.'

'How very kind of you, and what a trouble on a weekend afternoon,' said Sevgi Hanım, pleasantly. She stepped forward happily to take her husband's arm, but in the confusion Turgut Bey did not seem to notice her and linked his arm through Adnan Hoca's instead. Then the two black-suited, bearded men walked off together, talking earnestly, as though eager to finish some interrupted conversation. Sevgi Hanım stood for a moment with her arm still outstretched, then she grabbed hold of Pembe and Fatma, as though they might all lose each other in this strange land. Selda, left in sole charge of the luggage trolley, released the brake and gave it a vicious push. She wondered if she dared to let it run 'accidently' into the back of Adnan Hoca's rather baggy black trousers.

They drove for half an hour in utter silence along fast, clear roads that shone with rain. It was a world of green and grey and sometimes, in the downpour, those tones swirled together like the spoiled colours in a paintbox. Selda, squashed in the middle, half on and half off Pembe's lap, felt very car sick, but did not dare to say so. At last the car turned off the main road and went nosing down several steep, narrow streets. It stopped in front of a block of flats and there, at last, when they got out and looked up, was Ahmet. He was leaning over the top balcony and waving. They heard him come running down, flight by flight. They heard his leaping, eager step echoing in the concrete stair-well. Then he towered over them. He folded his mother in his arms and took the girls in too, hugging them and kissing them.

Then he raised his head and yelled: 'Ali! Ali, they've come!' He must have disturbed the quiet street and Selda loved him for it. She noticed that he barely nodded to his father and that he totally ignored Adnan Hoca. When he kissed her she felt his shirt wet against her cheek and she realized that he must have been standing out in all that rain, watching for them. She also saw to her astonishment that he was wearing a gold earing! It was a single, gold ring and he, a man, was wearing it. She wondered if the others had noticed.

Adnan Hoca refused Sevgi Hanım's invitation to stay and take tea. He let it be known that there were several really important things that he had to do that afternoon.

'Is he a taxi driver?' asked Pembe, innocently, when the big car had slid away.

'Oh no,' said Ali, who had come down too, 'he's just an Imam.'

'He's *our* Imam,' said Turgut Bey stiffly, 'and he's a very important man.'

The flat seemed very small. There were three bedrooms and a living room, but Selda could not help comparing it to her grandmother's old house, with its many high, half-empty rooms and its rambling, chaotic garden, so securely enclosed behind the old stone wall.

'Well, girls, what do you think?' Their father stood smiling at the doorway of the bedroom which his three daughters were to share.

'It's beautiful,' cried Pembe and she jumped off the bed which she had chosen and ran up to him and kissed him. 'I've never seen anything so beautiful, except in films.'

'Do you really like it?' He stepped back and looked around the room. They could all see that nearly everything in it was new. There were three white beds, each with a new, pink cover and beside each bed was a little white dressing table, with a mirror. A big white wardrobe stood along one wall. The room had been newly decorated and, indeed, smelt strongly of paint.

'We had quite a rush to finish it last night,' said their father proudly.

'It's like a room in a magazine,' said Fatma.

'However did you do it all?' asked Sevgi Hanım, coming in and inspecting the new pink curtains.

'Oh, you can do anything here, if you've got money,' he said casually. There was even a bowl of pink plastic flowers on the window ledge.

'This,' he promised, 'is only a beginning. I'll turn our girls into princesses. Just you wait.'

Selda, who had begun to unpack her things, realized guiltily that there was no table where she could work. She wished that she had not noticed, and she kept quiet, reminding herself that, of course, things would be different here.

She did not even see the mountains until early on Monday morning. Pembe and Fatma still slept deeply under their pink covers. Selda slipped from the room. The kitchen was empty although the remains of breakfast were still there. She found her mother out on the balcony, shaking the bed sheets over the rail. Selda went to help her and then stopped in amazement. Beyond the steeply sloping roofs of the houses opposite, beyond the green hills and above the low, white clouds, there were the mountains: two white peaks reared up out of the mass of clouds, one larger and one smaller, but both covered with snow. And it was still summer. A strong wind blew and the sheet flapped wildly and nearly got away as Selda, staring in fascination at the mountains, let her end slip. A dark cloud billowed out and cast its shadow over them, while in the distance the sun still shone upon the glittering mountain tops. It was breathtaking and it was what she had been waiting to see. This was Switzerland. She would go straight out and look for a postcard of this view and send it off

43

to her grandmother in Izmir. If the old woman had known about sights like this, she would not have been so rude about postcards.

Then Selda saw the lake. It extended further than she could see in both directions. It must have been as large as the bay of Izmir, but under the black cloud it was as dark and still as a well. Mist drifted along the far shores. It hung in the air like smoke that has been cooled by a winter's sky. When she turned back, the great cloud and the mountain were gone. Rain began to fall and they hastily took in the bed clothes but Selda stole out again, oblivious to the drops spattering down on her pyjamas. She spied on the little town. It was to be her town now, and she wanted to watch it coming to life. She hoped that if she watched it all with sufficient concentration, she could perhaps understand it. The rain fell more heavily so that finally she too stepped inside, shivering. Her mother handed her a glass of tea, but she could not sit down at the table. She had to stay, pressed close to the window, watching. It was the children who fascinated her. They all seemed to be carrying umbrellas! From the height of their fifth floor flat she could not see their faces, she could only look down upon these brilliant circles, twirling and bobbing along the wet, black pavements. Sometimes she glimpsed their coloured plastic boots, in red and yellow and blue and green. Many of the children actually seemed to be dressed from head to foot in coloured plastic. They were all moving in the same direction, past the flats and on, down the hill. The school, then, must be there, yet to Selda, they did not seem like school children at all. They were more like the bright new plastic figures that were sold in toy shops. You could have collected them up and put them in packets and then decided on a price.

Only when her mother called her again, did Selda reluctantly sit down at the table. She wanted to stay at home and watch this new world all day, but Pembe and Fatma, who

44

were up now, were restless. They were determined to go out into the town to begin the voyage of discovery.

They pointed to the Swiss francs which their father had left under the jar of strawberry jam on the breakfast table. Turgut Bey must have put it there before he and the boys left for the factory. He must have left it for them to spend.

'What shall we buy?' asked Pembe. 'Just think . . .' The possibilities seemed to her to be limitless.

'We don't need to buy anything, we'll just look. That's what people do,' said Sevgi Hanım cautiously.

'Why did Father leave all that money then?' Fatma was always the straightforward one.

'Girls, that's for the housekeeping.'

'Then we'll buy food and things. It'll still be fun. Oh, come on,' cried Fatma.

'But it's still raining.' Pembe looked out at the close, grey sky with some horror. It never rained in Izmir in the summer. They had last seen rain there in April. When it did rain, in the autumn and winter, people hardly went out unless they had to. The roads and pavements in their part of the town always filled with deep, muddy puddles, which made walking unpleasant. In Izmir, people never set out on shopping trips in the middle of a downpour. They waited until the sun shone.

'We could go when it stops,' she suggested.

'That could be days.' Fatma was already getting her coat. 'You know what they say about Switzerland.'

'It'll spoil my hair,' wailed Pembe.

'Oh, come *on*!'

'All right . . .' Pembe got up and stretched.

'We're not made of sugar,' encouraged Fatma, 'so we won't melt!'

'If my hair gets soaked . . .'

'It needn't,' said Selda, looking away from the window, 'we can buy an umbrella.'

They turned to her in admiration and gratitude, for she had found the perfect solution to all their problems.

The rain-water raced down the street beside them. From time to time, it poured into great grilles in the road. Then they heard it roaring and thundering through the drains, deep underground. The pavements were as sleek and dark as a dolphin's back. Here and there the rain had dashed down a few crimson petals from the geraniums in the window boxes and they lay on the washed stone like new splashes of paint. A long curving flight of stone steps joined the upper and lower parts of the little town. Selda, who counted all 137 steps noticed that there was not a trace of mud on them. They shone as did the people they passed. Nearly everyone seemed to have an umbrella, and even the grown-ups wore shiny macs. Men on a building site were all dressed in bright yellow waterproof jackets and hats, as though they needed to stay dry. In Turkey they would have worked on, even in a hail storm, in their shirt sleeves. The rain was certainly heavy and by the time they reached the big supermarket, they could all feel the dampness on their shoulders.

The shop was enormous and bright. It was as though a whole bunch of narrow streets had been broken up and put inside this vast, illuminated hall. There had, of course, been supermarkets in Izmir, but none had been like this. They wandered around amazed, looking at everything. They examined things that would normally have held no interest for them. Everything was the same and yet different. Sevgi Hanım picked up a rolling pin that was as thick as her arm and as short as two hands, whereas a proper Turkish rolling pin was almost a metre in length and as thin as your finger. She looked at the price and shook her head and put it back. Other people were walking around, taking this and that from the shelves, filling their trolleys and chatting to each other in the wide aisles. Selda's family kept on trying to work out how much everything would have cost in Turkish lira and they

46

were horrified. Everything was so expensive here. They were paralysed and confused and after an hour, all they had managed to buy was one loaf of bread. Then they tried to choose the umbrella. It took more time, but finally they settled on one of the cheapest. It was pink and purple and not very big when they opened it up. Walking home they had to huddle close together to avoid the drips. Halfway up the steps Pembe screamed.

A huge, brown slug, as plump and soft as a sardine, was creeping peacefully over the step, and had paused just at the place where Pembe had trod.

'That's nothing to be afraid of,' said Fatma, kicking aside what was left of the creature. She looked up the steps and saw several more and started to do the same.

'*Was mächst du denn, so blöd?*' shouted a small, fair-haired boy who was running down the steps in the opposite direction. He shouted something else, shrilly, and it was clearly at them. He pointed to the slugs.

They stared at him in astonishment and Fatma said: 'What are you shouting at?' in Turkish, and flicked another slug out of the way with the toe of her shoe. The little boy knelt down on the wet steps and held his hand over the others as though to protect them.

When he looked up at them he asked: '*Sind Sie Türken?*'

'*Ja, ja,*' said Sevgi Hanım eagerly. She had recognized the last word.

'*Blöde Kuh!*' the boy cried and, picking up a twig, he began to try to right one of the squashed slugs.

'Poor little fellow,' said Sevgi Hanım, kindly, 'left out on the street by his mother in all this rain. Look at him playing with all those dirty, dangerous things, he might catch some disease. Some mothers don't deserve to have children.'

She gathered her daughters around her and ushered them on up the steps, looking back a couple of times to smile encouragingly at the little boy. But Selda, who had seen the

47

expression of hate and scorn on the child's face, wondered what he had really said. She had a sharp sense of their having done something wrong, but she did not know what it was.

That evening, while the others watched television, she pulled a double page from the middle of one of her Turkish exercise books and finally began the letter to her grandmother. In the excitement of that first shopping trip, she had even forgotten to buy the postcard. She wrote the new address carefully at the top and then began:

Dear Grandmother,
    Since we arrived in Switzerland, it has hardly stopped
raining. It is as cold as winter and as green as the bottom
of the sea. You never saw so green a place. The trees
and gardens look as if they have been painted. It does
not seem quite real at all. Perhaps that is just because I
am so new here, but . . .

'You can't write like that,' protested Fatma, leaning across and reading over her shoulder.

'Why not?'

'You've never been at the bottom of the sea, for a start.'

'It doesn't matter. I've looked down into it. I bet it is like that, down at the bottom, when you dive. Isn't it Ahmet? You've been out fishing.'

'Isn't what?'

'Isn't the sea all green, very deep down?'

'Possibly.' He was following the match and was clearly not interested in her letter.

'Anyway,' said Selda, 'Grandmother will understand.'

'You think so?' Fatma snorted with laughter.

'Look, tell her what we've been doing. That's much more interesting. She'll understand that. Tell her about the umbrella.'

'Tell her about the clean streets,' said Sevgi Hanım.

'Tell her about that revolting child and the slugs.'

'Yes, do. That will make her laugh!'

'No, don't do that. She'll worry. Don't tell her anything, that's always best in a letter. Just say that we are all well and that we hope that she is well. That's what a proper letter should be like. Especially when somebody else has to read it to her. Just tell her . . .'

They all had their ideas and their messages. Selda listened to them and was unable to write anything. She folded the letter away unfinished and went into the bedroom to lie down on the new, white bed and listen to the rain. She heard both the near tap and drip of water falling off the roof into the gutter and the distant rush and roar of more water running underground. She recalled Izmir. She remembered the dry, dusty corners of her grandmother's garden. There, the eyes of the cats would be glowing like golden jewels in the warm night. The white jasmine would be releasing its sudden, drifting scent and the crumbling stones would be warm to the touch like the skin of a person who sleeps. People would be passing to and fro in the streets of Izmir; the sounds of their voices there would drift in through the open windows, and the sounds of the lives lived in the rooms would float out into the evening streets. Here, apart from the rain, it was very quiet, as though the pavements had been washed clean of all traces of life.

She unfolded the paper and tried to continue the letter: 'It is all very neat and tidy here and I have not seen any rubbish but . . .'

Somebody passed her open door and she called out softly: 'Ahmet?'

'Goodnight.'

'Ahmet? Wait.'

'What is it?' He poked his head round the door but she could tell that he did not want to stop and chat. After their first, happy reunion, he had hardly spoken to her.' I'm on the early shift this week, so I'm off to bed now,' he said.

'Ahmet Abi, what does *"blöde Kuh"* mean?'

'Don't you ever say that again!' He came into the room now, looking cross.

'Who said that? Did they say it to *you*?'

'It was just a boy, in the street.' She wished that she hadn't mentioned it. Ahmet looked so angry.

'You show him to me and I'll break every bone in his body!'

'Not *that* sort of boy! This was a very little boy, a kid. He shouted at us when we were coming back up those steps.'

'Perhaps he said it to someone else.'

'No, there was only us. I'm sure he said it to us. What does it mean, Ahmet Abi?'

'It means . . . oh, forget it! It's, it's just swearing. Don't *you* ever say it! Just you show me who talks to you like that and I'll make sure they never do it again. Now, forget it and don't worry.'

But she did. She lay on the bed tense with worry. Later she awoke in the chill, dark dawn, struggling in a nightmare of endless flights of steps.

She lay awake and listened to the noises of her brothers and father as they got up and left the flat in the dark. Then she heard the sounds of the other families in the block, banging their doors and going out down the echoing stairwell. Soon she would be joining them. As soon as the official letter came from the school authorities, she, too, would have to set out to school in the morning.

Pembe and Fatma had expressed mild indifference to the new school. They did not seem to mind if they started at once, or had a long wait. Fatma, as the eldest, had finished primary school in Turkey. Privately, she did not see why she had to go to school at all. She treated the whole thing as a bit of a joke. Pembe was more eager to go to school: she wanted her father to buy her one of the pretty, pale anoraks which she saw girls of her age wearing on the street. Neither of them seemed to suffer from the doubt and fear which consumed Selda. Or, if they did, they did not say so. Selda, in contrast, waited for that letter about the Swiss school with all the passion with which she had once waited for the letter that was to bring the air tickets.

This time the waiting was over in three days. A pale blue envelope arrived and was torn open to reveal a white, printed form. They could not understand what it said although they recognized their three names. When Ali came home at lunchtime he confirmed Selda's suspicions. The girls were to be at the local primary school at ten o'clock on the next Thursday morning. When it finally came, their father took time off from the factory to go with them. It seemed that that hour between eight and nine would never pass. Then, suddenly it did, and there they were hurrying along the road, having left it almost too late.

They pushed open the huge glass doors of the school. At that moment, a bell, like a giant telephone, blared out. Several brightly painted doors burst open and the children began to pound out. Selda and her sisters were engulfed by the shouting, pushing crowd, making for the playground. Their father stepped to one side. The girls followed him. More children came running down the stairs, sparring and tossing things at each other. Their cheerful excitement made one imagine that a holiday had been declared. It hardly seemed like a proper school at all. In Izmir, the caretaker had always positioned himself in the hall at playtime and was prepared for anything, his stick held at the ready. He would soon have dealt with any student who dared to fool around.

A young man in a T-shirt, with shoulder-length hair, smiled at them as he hurried past. He did say something, but he didn't stop, and ran at the stairs, leaping up them two at a time, like a child himself. Selda felt her courage draining away. Her father still stood timidly to one side, looking around. He looked at the letter again, then vaguely after the disappearing children, but he still did not do anything.

'Father, shouldn't we look for an office or something, the Headmaster's room maybe,' said Fatma helpfully.

'All in good time,' said Turgut Bey, crossly, 'and you can stop telling me what to do. I can see that everybody is very busy at the moment. That's why I'm waiting.' He looked at the letter again.

Pembe, who had moved away to look at some children's paintings which were pinned up on the walls, now stopped in front of a huge, green model animal. It looked as though it had been made out of rubbish: rolled-up newspapers and plastic bottles and things, all painted bright green. She giggled and pointed it out. Then she must have seen somebody for she stepped through an open door into a classroom. They heard her speak Turkish to someone.

'Go on Father,' urged Fatma but Turgut Bey folded away the paper in annoyance. It was just what he expected: Adnan Bey had already warned him that the children were allowed to run riot in the schools in Switzerland.

Pembe reappeared with a tall, fair-haired young woman who seemed to understand who they were. She held out her hand to Turgut Bey but he stepped back and held out the letter. She read it and looked pleased and beckoned to them to follow her. Selda did not understand why her father was still silent. He had lived in Switzerland for years and had always told them that he spoke this language better than his own. She so wanted him to speak now, to talk to this teacher and to help them, but he didn't.

He followed the woman into another classroom where they met another teacher and again he just listened and nodded and glanced at his watch several times. He did not translate a single one of Selda's questions. Then, hardly looking at them, he said: 'Well girls, I can see that everything is going to be fine with such nice lady teachers to look after you. So, I'll be off now. Work hard and don't disgrace us.' And he was gone. He almost ran. Selda could hear him going tap, tap, tap, back

down the shiny marble steps. She looked after him in desperation. She could not have felt more abandoned if she had
been flung out of that plane in mid-air. She was sick and
giddy. Why was it that fear always made her feel sick? That
really was the last straw: feeling sick and not knowing where
the toilet was!

The other teacher, a small, pale, sandy sort of woman with
fluttering white eyelashes claimed Pembe and Fatma and
walked off with them. Selda followed and then found herself
not wanted. The sandy teacher had actually taken Pembe and
Fatma by the arm and, as they walked, Selda could see that
they were both a head taller than she was.

She waited alone in the empty corridor. Perhaps she really
was going to be sick. There must be a toilet somewhere.
Downstairs, probably. Something seemed to be catching at
the back of her throat. She swallowed. It looked as though the
teachers weren't expecting her – had no place for her, perhaps. She pretended to be examining a wall map with great
concentration. In fact, she couldn't see a thing. If she had
been the sort of girl who cried, she would have cried then but
she reminded herself that she wasn't going to let them make
her shed a single tear. The bell rang again. All the children
came rushing back. They swarmed around her as though she
weren't there. She was not going to cry. She might be sick
though, and it wasn't her fault. It was the Swiss food . . . One
or two children buffeted against her and they all shouted
across her as though she were invisible, or worse, no different
from that painted rubbish.

She would pretend that she wasn't really there. She shut
herself away from everything so fiercely that, for the moment
at least, she heard and saw nothing. How could her father
have abandoned her like that? 'Work hard.' How could she,
even if she wanted to?

Then somebody touched her arm. It was the fair-haired
teacher, come to find her, it seemed. Now she steered Selda

into a large, bright classroom where all the children fell silent and stared as they entered. On the carpeted floor, the desks were arranged in a half circle and from each a child began its own inspection of the new pupil. Selda saw one, a red-haired lad, pull a face. The teacher said something which ended with her own name 'Selda'. Then the class repeated it, 'Sel-da, Sel-da', and somewhere at the back somebody sniggered and Selda hated them for it. The teacher sat her down in an empty desk at one side. The children whispered to each other and watched her out of the corner of their eyes. Something else was said. Books were opened. Pages turned and the teacher's chalk wrote up a sentence in beautiful, clear, flowing script. It was neat and straight and, to Selda, entirely incomprehensible. The teacher smiled at her kindly, and another pupil tried to help, but Selda could understand nothing.

That first morning in school was endless. Selda listened until her head ached. Sometimes she thought she had actually caught a word. It was like trying to catch in one's hand a single, particular drop from all the torrents of water that rushed down to the lake. If she had not felt so sick, she was sure that she would have understood at least something. But as it was she couldn't even hear properly. Things had gone better for Pembe and Fatma who were together in the sixth class. They had had Handicrafts and both the teacher and the other girls had been astonished by their skill in knitting. Some Swiss children, it seemed, could not even cast on!

They walked home with Selda, chattering in excitement. No, it had not been at all bad. A girl had shared some sweets with them and the teacher, Frau Steinman, had given each of them brand-new pencils, rubbers, exercise books and even a fountain pen. They couldn't believe it.

'Free?' asked their mother anxiously as Ali translated.

'Oh yes,' he said and everybody was very impressed. Pembe and Fatma actually said that they thought school was quite fun: they were looking forward to returning.

Selda, in contrast, could only long for Saturday, when there would be no school in the afternoon. Sunday, with no school all day, would be almost perfect and then she could forget that Monday ever had to come. And for Selda, that next Monday morning almost didn't come.

On the Saturday afternoon, their father insisted that the whole family come down into the town to do the weekly shopping. Adnan Hoca and his wife and daughter were expected that evening. They were coming to say 'hoşgeldin' and welcome the new arrivals and would expect to be well entertained. There would be extra food to buy and carry back. Even as Turgut Bey was speaking, Ahmet was stretching out on the sofa, preparing to watch the football match on the television.

'And you, Ahmet,' said his father, 'I'll need your hands.'

'Not this week, Father,' said Ahmet settling himself with a cushion behind his head.

'I'm not asking, Ahmet, I'm telling you,' said Turgut Bey, holding the door open for his son.

'And I'm telling you that I'm *not* coming.'

'What do you mean, "not coming"? Of course you're coming! Now get up off that sofa and come along. If I'd spoken to my father like you speak to me!' Turgut Bey was shaking with anger but Ahmet did not move.

'Well? I'm waiting!'

Ahmet changed channels on the television.

'I've had about as much as I can take from you, young man.' Turgut Bey had stepped back into the room. 'You'll do what I tell you as long as you live under my roof and eat my bread''

'Do you mean that?'

'Yes!' Turgut Bey spoke quietly now, as one might to a silly child: 'Now *do* hurry up Ahmet.'

So Ahmet got up and switched off the television. He thrust his feet quickly into his shoes and snatched his jacket from the hook, then, without a backward glance at the others, he left the house in front of them. They heard his running steps becoming fainter and fainter. Nobody spoke. They finished getting ready in complete silence and went down the stairs singly, not looking at each other. Selda expected Ahmet to be waiting for them at the bottom, but he wasn't. Turgut Bey strode ahead with Ali, pretending not to notice that anything was wrong. The rest of them trailed along behind. Their joy in the trip was gone. Selda slouched at the very back. She kept looking round to see if Ahmet was coming. She stopped and pretended to be looking at something because she thought it would give him a chance to join her. He didn't. Then, noticing how far ahead the family had got and not wanting to cause more trouble, she started to run.

She never saw the car. She ran into the road and would have taken a second, fatal step if someone had not shouted loudly in Turkish 'stop!' Somehow she checked her movement. The car braked sharply. Its wheels screamed. Her family, safely on the other side of the road, screamed too. She had flung out her hands, trying to stop as she ran and now she stumbled and clutched at the bonnet of the car, but did not fall in front of it. The driver inside, who was as white faced and frightened as Selda, shouted too and pointed to the traffic lights. Selda was clearly in the wrong. She leant against the car seeing but not recognizing her reflection in its polished paintwork. She could not move. Other cars had stopped and now they hooted impatiently.

'Come over here!' her father cried angrily. 'Come here at once, you stupid girl!'

She still could not move. If someone had not shouted out that warning, she would have run on into the road and the car would have hit her. It must have been Ahmet. He must have realized what was going to happen and called out, to save her. She looked around, but, in her confusion, she still couldn't see him. There were only two people behind her on the pavement, two men who stood watching her. One wore a cloth cap and an odd, yellow, patterned scarf around his throat. The other was younger. They watched her, almost coming to help, but she did not want strangers to help her. She wanted Ahmet and looked round for him again, but he wasn't there. Eventually, she managed to stand up straight and let go of the car and, seeing this, the men walked away.

Fatma came over and took her by the arm and led her safely to the other side of the road.

'You could have been killed!' said her mother, with tears running down her cheeks.

'That was a near thing,' said her father. 'If that car had been damaged, it could have been very expensive for me. These Swiss take such good care of their things. They get furious if anything is spoilt. I'd have had to pay. You'll have to be more careful if you want to live here, my girl. You'll have to watch your step, won't you?'

She nodded and rubbed her sleeve over her eyes and looked back one last time, but there was nobody there.

Four

As that first week changed into a first month and then into her first autumn season in Switzerland, Selda did 'watch her step'. She had never thought that it would be like this. When she was in her grandmother's house in Izmir, she had always tried to be so careful: to think before she spoke and to avoid doing the many little things that had annoyed the old woman. She had not always succeeded, but she really had tried.

She had looked forward to leaving Izmir because she had thought that once her family was together again, they would all accept her and love her for being just the person she was. They would let her be impulsive, outspoken Selda, a person who did not, naturally, 'watch her step'. Selda had expected to be as happy as she had been when she was a little girl back in the village, helping in the village shop. She had known, of course, that this foreign country would be different, but she had not realized that everything about it would be *so* different. Now she felt that she had been foolish. She had thought about 'settling down in Switzerland', only in terms of learning the language and doing well in school. She had never realized that she, Selda, would be expected to change or that her own family would already have changed.

She had never dreamt that her own father could speak to her as roughly as he had done on the Saturday of the near accident. It was almost as though he had cared more about not upsetting the Swiss driver than about his own daughter. Selda wished that she did not think like that, but she did. She thought it and was sorry and guilty, all at the same time

She often thought of Kemal Amca in Istanbul. Just before

they left, he had given them a present: a wall plaque, of 'Istanbul by Night'. Now Selda often sat in the kitchen and looked at it and wondered if Kemal Amca would have acted differently if his daughter, Alev, had run into the road. She was sure that he would. Kemal Amca would have dashed over and gathered her up in his arms. He would have made sure that she was all right first and only then would he have bothered to shout at the man in the car, even though it wasn't the driver's fault. Instantly, he would have regretted his anger, he would have shrugged and smiled his apologies to the driver and opened his arms wide to the world, in that tolerant way of his. He wouldn't have blamed anyone and, she was sure, he would have acted just the same if it had been she, Selda, who had been involved.

But not her father – for he had changed. He was a different man here in Switzerland. He was irritable and unsure of himself. At home he grumbled constantly about the Swiss and repeated every bit of factory gossip as though it were certain truth. He was particularly fond of quoting his 'good friend' Adnan Hoca's poor opinions of Switzerland. Yet outside the house, this pompous, blustering man, her father, was as uncritical and obedient as a sheep. He did exactly as he was told.

It made Selda very uneasy. It also made her watchful and cautious. She began to watch everybody and everything as though she were a detective. It was as though her eyes must do twice the work, because her ears were useless, now that she could not understand all that she heard. So Selda watched: at school, in the street, out shopping and at home. She watched unceasingly. By day her favourite vantage spot was her high, fifth-floor balcony. Then, in bed at night, she shut her eyes and could recreate the outlines of the little town laid out before her. She knew it all by heart and she had actually drawn a simple map of it and sent it to her grand-mother.

If she had not been watching everything with such care, she would never have recognized the two men whom she had seen on that first Saturday afternoon. As it was, she often saw them about the town. One, who was much older than the other, always wore that yellow scarf wound around his throat, so they were not difficult to recognize. The younger of the two often seemed to pass along their road in the early evening. He walked with a slow, swinging stride and did not look around at all. He usually carried a couple of loaves of bread. They were workmen of some sort, she guessed, for their appearance was poor and neglected. They could have been from any country, Italy, Spain, Romania or Albania. There were workers from all these countries up at the factory, her brothers said. Yet for some reason Selda was convinced that these two men were Turks. There was something about them: the way they walked along the road; the way the elder always wore a neat, old-fashioned jacket over his work clothes, the way the younger didn't wear jeans and trainers like other teenagers in the town. It was difficult to explain, but she felt it strongly. They could have been any two men in any small country town in Turkey. Yet she never saw them speak to the other Turkish families. In fact, she never saw them speak at all. As the time went by, Selda had got to know most of the small, local Turkish community but nobody ever mentioned these two strangers.

She wanted to ask someone about them, but couldn't. Her father would have been furious to hear of her, a girl, asking questions about two strange men. Nevertheless, she found herself watching out for them and wondering if, after all, one of them had cried out 'stop'. If they had, she owed a great deal to these two strangers who seemed to be silent observers like herself. She would have liked to say 'thank you'.

Selda was thinking about them when the school bell rang for the long, mid-morning break. When kind Fräulein Altmann, her teacher, said that the class could go, everybody else dropped their things and rushed for the door. Selda dawdled and pretended to be finishing a piece of work. It had become a habit for her to be the last pupil in the room. Very often Fräulein Altmann spent a few extra minutes helping her with her German. The teacher had been wonderful, so kind and helpful and so full of praise and encouragement.

Today Fräulein Altmann was busy with a pile of marking. Selda began to pack her things away very slowly, hoping that the teacher would call her over to her desk. It was one of the few opportunities Selda had to speak to anyone. If Fräulein Altmann did not chat to her, then Selda was sentenced to endure break-time. If school here felt like prison, break-time was like having to endure the trial several times a day. It was always the same. She was always alone. It was like being cast adrift in the Bay of Izmir. It was like drowning when the shore was in sight. Even the sick cats in her grandmother's garden could creep to some safety behind the jasmine root, whereas she was condemned to be turned out, three times a day, to pace this concrete playground, all alone. She must walk round and round, with no place to hide.

She waited on at her desk. Fräulein Altmann did look very busy. She would wait one moment more and, if the teacher looked up, she would catch her eye . . .

'Now run along, Selda, and play with your friends. Even my most hard-working children must have some fun and games!' Fräulein Altmann closed one exercise book and picked up another in a very efficient way. Selda knew that today she did not want to talk to her.

'All right, Fräulein Altmann,' she nodded and went out miserably. Could Fräulein Altmann not see that she wasn't a child and that she did not want to play childish games?

For the first two weeks she had thought that it was just her 'foreignness' that made her feel so different and so much older than her classmates. They seemed like little kids, with their blue eyes and their fair untidy hair, their fashionable, bright clothes and their hoards of fancy rubbers and special pencils. She watched them comparing collections of stickers and badges. She stood on the edge of groups who excitedly swapped pocketfuls of toys and trinkets and plastic models. She saw them line up toy cars along their desks and actually fiddle with them in class. Back in school in Turkey, Selda had had a pen, some pencils and a rubber and had shared poor Demet's German pencil sharpener. It had been enough. Nobody had brought toys to school. If anyone had fooled around like that in class they would have been punished. No, she was not envious of these children who tied little, furry animals to their belts and satchels and who played with expensive leather footballs in break. She actually thought them rather silly. She watched them scrambling into their mothers' cars at the end of the day and she secretly despised them. Couldn't they walk? Couldn't they spend a day without games?

Then she began to realize that the fourth formers with whom she was in class were only ten years old, whereas she was twelve. And would be thirteen. In Turkey she would have been in secondary school. In Switzerland she now had to finish the fourth, fifth and sixth years before she could start secondary school. She felt as though she were an innocent prisoner who discovers that her sentence has been increased.

Last week she had asked her father why he had agreed to her being put back into a class of ten-year-olds. He had been awkward and bad tempered.

'They said that it was best like this,' he muttered, not looking up from the television.

'Who said that?'

'The school. The Authorities said it, before you came. I went to see them with Adnan Hoca. They all said that it was the best thing, as you didn't know any German. And those teachers at the school said the same. You heard them didn't you, when I took you that first morning? You didn't make a fuss then!'

'Father! How could I? I didn't understand a word, then.'

'Well! There you are! How could you go straight to secondary school when you didn't understand a single word?'

'But . . .'

'You see! I *did* do the right thing. They said . . .'

'But what about me? Why don't you listen to what I say? You didn't even ask me.'

'You?' He looked up then, surprised.

'Yes. Me. Why didn't you ask *me*?'

'What's it got to do with you?'

'It's got everything to do with me. I don't want to go to school with such babies! I'd have worked day and night in secondary school. I would have caught up. You know I would!'

'That's not what they said. They said that in all their experience, the Turkish children never caught up. They don't expect them to. They said that lots of "foreign" children here don't go to secondary school. They have to go to special schools for children who learn slowly . . .'

'Like poor Demet. I know all about it. But I'm not like that!'

'Well then,' her father glared at her now, his face pale with anger, 'well, my clever daughter, if you know all about it you can go and tell your precious Fräulein Altmann.'

'I will.'

'Yes, Miss. You go and tell the wonderful Fräulein Altmann to put you in the secondary school tomorrow.'

'Father, she can't!' Pembe had interrupted unexpectedly. 'You mustn't let Selda do that, Father. She's younger than us. She can't go to secondary school before us. It isn't fair.'

'I can,' said Selda, 'I can and I will.'

'You can't,' Fatma joined in now. 'Anyway, you only want to go to another school because people don't like you at this one. And it's your fault. You don't try to be friendly. Why do you always stay by yourself at break-time? I've seen you, always walking around on your own as though you're too good for the rest of us.'

'So have I,' said Pembe, stretching her arms lazily above her head. She smiled at no one in particular. 'I can't see why you make such a fuss about school. I don't. It's fun, but then, I'm happy there. Everybody likes me, anyway.'

It was true, too. People did like Pembe. She had become friendly with an Italian girl called Ramona who lived in the same block of flats. They called for each other on the way to school in the mornings. Now, as Selda stepped out into the playground, she saw the three of them, Pembe, Fatma and Ramona, sitting close together on a wall, sharing a packet of crisps. They nibbled, passing the bag to and fro, and watched the football match that was being fought out just in front of them. Sometimes, with a smile of superior indifference they tossed the ball back to the players. Sometimes they were so busy whispering, they let it lie right under their feet so that the boys had to come and get it themselves. Most of the girls in Selda's own class were already walking round and round with their arms linked. She saw one or two glance at her, but nobody called her over to join them.

She began to walk around the edge of the playground, all on her own. She did not even try to catch anybody's glance, because she did not want to be ignored. If only there had been someone she could talk to. Then she could have told them about her favourite brother, Ahmet. He had hardly been back to the house, since that first Saturday. She missed him so much. She had tried to talk to her parents about it, but neither of them would say anything. They just repeated that he was 'very busy at work' and that he was staying with friends. Selda knew that the first part wasn't true because both she and her sisters had seen him around the town in the day-time. He hadn't looked at all busy. Pembe and Fatma had giggled and gone red and said in shocked, but admiring tones, that 'perhaps he had a girlfriend and was staying with her . . .' Ali had finally admitted that Ahmet had quarrelled with their father several times before, but had never left home. He told her not to worry but, of course, she did.

She did another lonely circuit of the playground and stopped by the concrete fountain. She thought about the fortune teller's riddle:

> Plant pretty roses in your garden,
> Plant sweet herbs by your door,
> But bury secrets in your heart,
> To keep them safe for evermore.

It wasn't as though she had any 'secret' to bury, anyway. She knew that her family were ashamed of Ahmet, but it wasn't really a 'secret'. No, she wasn't planning to reveal any secrets, but she would have so much liked to have had somebody to talk to.

She trailed her hand in the water beneath the fountain. It wasn't really allowed, but it took up a few more minutes. She wondered what Ahmet did all day, if he wasn't working. Once, last week, she had tried to tell Fräulein Altmann about him, but she had not managed it. She had used the 'wrong' German. She had said: 'We was a family of seven, we was now a family of six . . .' the teacher had heard her, but not understood. She had corrected Selda's German and had written out some little grammar exercises, but she had missed what Selda had been trying to tell her.

She should have tried again, but she didn't. It was not only that she was shy. Nor was it courage that she lacked; well, not entirely. No. It was words. It was German words. Without them confusion and doubt hung around Selda and threatened to cloud her meaning and hide her thoughts. They were like the white mists which rose up from the still, dark lake. You saw them drifting up the sides of the valley towards the forests. Then they lingered there for days on end and even the mountain peaks were hidden from view. If only she had had the words, she could have swept away these mists of doubt. She could have talked to Fräulein Altmann about her brother Ahmet, and about other things. As it was, all she could do was write down some of her thoughts and send them to her grandmother, who could not even read them. Sometimes Selda felt as dumb and helpless as if she had been struck down by paralysis.

She walked away from the fountain and went to the far end of the playground. There, a group of the youngest children were burrowing in the sand-pit at the end of the long-jump run. The children seemed to be searching for something in the sand and so Selda sat down beside them and pretended to be looking for it too. This way she avoided having to speak to anyone. She could hear the football game roaring on behind her.

Suddenly, one of the little children, a boy in a red jumper and white trousers, threw sand full in the face of another. The victim rubbed his eyes furiously and threw sand back. The attacker leapt up, knocked the other over and began to rub his face in the sand. The watching children paused. Their hands were still under the sand as they watched the conflict and wondered whether to interfere. Selda, afraid that the boy in the sand might choke, caught hold of the other by the belt of his white trousers and pulled him off. It was not difficult to do. He was only seven or eight and as thin and skinny as a spider.

'Nein,' she said and set him back on his feet and gave him a push intended to send him off to play somewhere else. Unfortunately he tripped on the edge of the sand-pit and fell flat on his face.

For a second he lay still. Then he screamed. He writhed and yelled and shrieked until a crowd had gathered. Even the footballers strolled over to see what was up. One of them, the red-haired boy from Selda's class, pulled the child to his feet and several others began to dust the sand out of his face and

hair. He howled on through sandy lips and pointed accus-
ingly at Selda. Then the other little boy reached into the
pocket of his jeans, brought out a two-franc piece and handed
it over. The boy in white trousers sniffed, stopped crying and
pocketed the money and wiped his face. Then he looked
down at his white trousers which were split at the knees and
yellow with sand stains. He started to cry again. The watching
crowd had shifted and eddied around so that Selda now
found herself quite isolated on one side of the sand-pit. The
boy said something else, still pointing at Selda. The whole
crowd stared at her. She knocked the sand from her skirt and
stared back.

'Why . . . sand?' someone asked. Selda had only been able
to catch the beginning and end of the sentence, but she
recognized that its tone was angry.

'Why . . . little children?' She tried to walk away but
somebody leapt over the sand-pit and stood in her way,
grinning nastily.

'Turks are maniacs! Turks are maniacs!' There was no doubt
now what had been said. Suddenly the whole playground
was chanting: 'Maniac, maniac, maniac!'

Selda's face burnt. A nerve near her mouth twitched and
she thought that her whole face must be shaking and
trembling. She would not cry. They were nothing but a
stupid, rotton mob. Then Giselle, one of the girls from her
own class, stepped from the crowd. She was tall and fair with
eyes as pale as ice. Selda could smell the sickly strawberry
smell of bubble gum as Giselle blew a large balloon and let it
burst in Selda's face. Looking for a way past the crowd she
glimpsed her sisters' faces at the back of the group, on the
other side. Giselle came closer and then closer still and Selda
stepped back but shouted as loudly as she could: '*Blöde Kuh!*
Blöde Kuh!'

Giselle hesitated and wiped the bubble of gum from her
chin and turned away, scowling. Luckily the bell rang for the

end of break and everyone trooped into class. Selda made sure that she was the last person in through the glass doors.

At lunch-time Pembe and Fatma forgot to wait for Selda. They walked on home up the hill with a group of classmates and they did not seem to hear Selda calling to them to wait. They were talking excitedly about some letter that they had all been given to take home. When Selda joined them the group fell silent and exchanged glances. After the traffic lights, only Ramona continued with them and then the three older girls walked together, shoulder to shoulder, across the width of the pavement, excluding her. They laughed about something and Selda, trailing behind, wondered if they were laughing about her. She was jealous and hurt.

That evening Selda did cry, but as she was alone and nobody knew about it, she felt that somehow it did not count. Pembe and Fatma had gone into Ramona's flat to ask about some homework. Her parents were visiting Adnan Hoca's family and Ali was on the late shift at the factory. Selda sat on her bed and fought with History. The history map had gone all right at the beginning but the problems began when she had to copy down the place names. In the end the page looked as though a battle had been fought over it. In her own language, she could have guessed when something was wrongly spelt. One knew, instinctively. Now, in German, she had to check every letter. She had altered some words three and four times. She remembered poor Demet and she shuddered. A tear fell on the page and smudged the ink. Her pen stuck on the damp patch and the nib tore out an ugly blue gash. She had not even started to answer the question. How right the fortune teller had been: her's was going to be a black fortune.

She looked at the ruined page in despair. Fräulein Altmann liked work to be neat and tidy. She was very patient with students who had not understood something, or who made mistakes, but untidy, dirty work made her brown eyes cold and disapproving. There was no one whom Selda could ask for help. She would have to do the map again. She went into the kitchen and began to cut out the spoiled pages with the bread knife. It would take her an hour at least, to re-do it, and by then the family would be back. The television would go on. Fatma would be listening to her favourite tapes of Turkish singers. Ali would be back, full of the latest factory gossip, and her father would be loudly praising Adnan Hoca and Adnan Hoca's house and Adnan Hoca's dull daughter. Only her mother would be silent. If Ahmet dropped by, as he did occasionally, there would probably be another argument. The last time that Ahmet and her father had quarelled there had been so much noise that the neighbours had banged on the walls and finally come round to complain. Selda would have to block her ears and work steadily through. She almost hoped that Ahmet wouldn't come round.

If only there had been someone to ask. She did not want anybody to do her homework for her, that only made you feel more stupid. She just wanted someone to say: 'Yes, that's right, do it like that.' Somebody like Kemal Amca would have been fine, he would have cheered her up. Back in Izmir her classmates had often come round to her. Mothers had advised their children stuck on their homework to 'run over and ask that Selda'. In her street it was generally believed that Selda would know what to do. And usually, she had. She had been able to help people then. She had been the one to say: 'Yes, that's what the question means.' She had been so sure of everything then. Whereas now, she floundered.

While she was still in the kitchen the key turned in the front-door lock. She dropped the knife and fled for her room, but did not get there in time. Someone had come in quickly and quietly and without putting on the light.

'Is there anyone in?' It was Ahmet, but his voice was strange, breathless, as though he had been running.

'Ahmet?'

'Selda? Is anyone else at home?' He still had not put on the light.

'No, just me. But they'll be back soon.'

He clicked down the switch then. The glaring, bare bulb in the cramped little hall lit up the coats and the tumbled row of winter shoes and it picked out the tears which had not yet dried on Selda's cheeks. It also showed up lines of blood which had run from Ahmet's nose and mouth and stained the collar of his shirt. One side of his face was badly grazed and muddy and there were leaves or something in his hair. He was still panting, as though he had been running fast. She looked at him in horror and could see that he was swallowing, trying to get his breath back. For one second she thought that he was going to talk to her but he didn't. He shrugged, coughed and pulled a face and then looked away and she was sorry.

'I walked into a lamppost,' he said, avoiding her eye. 'Have you got anything to put on a cut?' He laughed unevenly. 'How could I be so stupid?'

Selda wondered. She found a bottle of Cologne and watched over his shoulder as he cleaned his face up in the bathroom. She saw that one hand was muddy and scratched and that his jacket had several rips in it.

'You won't mention it, will you?' he asked, looking at her reflection in the mirror.

'Why not?'

'You know how Mother will fuss and we don't want to worry her, do we?'

'But . . .'

'Look, let it be our secret, Selda. I can trust you, can't I? Don't tell them that I had an accident – had a beer too many and ran into a lamppost, you know how Father goes on about drinking, these days. Then I won't tell them that I came home and found you crying over your homework.'

'How did you know about my homework?'

70

'Selda, what else is there to cry about at your age? Remember, I had a short spell in a Swiss school too. I know all about it.'

'Then, you can help me. Please Ahmet Abi, please.' She was ashamed to be asking for help when he was clearly in trouble, but she couldn't stop herself.

'Of course I'll help you, any time,' he said gently. 'But not right now. I've got to go. Okay? And don't *worry*. Take my advice: don't *do* the wretched homework. Just say that you don't understand it. That's what I always said. I mean, they don't expect you to understand it. You're a foreigner, see? Foreigners aren't supposed to understand. Now, that's my clever girl. Smile.' He was already at the door, but turned back and said, more seriously: 'You promise you won't mention it Selda? Promise?'

'I promise. Honestly, Ahmet Abi.'

Then he nodded and was gone. She listened to his running footsteps growing fainter on the stairs, then she slipped quickly out on to the dark balcony to see where he went. Two people were waiting in the shadows opposite. She leant cautiously over the rail and saw Ahmet come out of the stairwell below. He paused and looked all around and then joined the waiting people. All three walked quickly up the road in the direction of the forest. When they passed under a street lamp she saw that he was accompanied by two men. One had something yellow tucked around his neck. The other, slighter one seemed to be wearing something red. So she was right. Those men were Turks. She watched them with a beating heart until they disappeared from her sight.

'Selda!' Pembe and Fatma, returning suddenly from Ramona's flat, startled her.

'What are you doing out on the balcony? You'll freeze!'

'I was just watching –'

'You and those mountains! You can't see anything, anyway, at night. Come on in before you catch your death.

71

Ramona says it may snow soon.' Fatma pushed her back into the flat. She was right, it was bitterly cold.

'Oh! I hope it doesn't snow,' wailed Pembe.

'Why not?' asked Selda. She was curious to see the snow.

'If it snows, we won't be able to go on our trip.'

'What trip?'

'The school trip. It was in that letter we brought home. The trip is on Thursday, but only if the weather is good. That's what Ramona says.' Pembe hung up her coat and looked at herself in the mirror.' I'm so excited!'

'So am I,' said Fatma. 'Ramona says that these trips are terrific, you know, no lessons for the whole day. We're going to ask Father for something new to wear. It'll be a long walk. Ramona says that sometimes you walk for hours and hours and that Frau Steinfeld is the fastest walker in the school. She says . . .'

'Ramona said all that?'

'Oh yes. She said . . .'

'And you understood it all?'

'Of course I did. I'm not stupid, you know.'

'I didn't mean that.'

'You did. I can tell. You think I'm too stupid to ever understand German!' Fatma was defiant. 'Well I'm not! I speak better German than you, because I talk to people. You'll never learn because you're too afraid of saying the wrong thing. I don't care about trying to prove I'm clever all the time. I just like to chat.'

'So do I,' said Pembe, not to be outdone. 'And I understand everything that *Zeki* says.'

In the awkward silence which followed this remark, the three sisters did not look at each other. Fatma, instantly regretting her ill temper, joked mildly: 'Well, you would understand him, wouldn't you Pembe? I mean, he was speaking to you in Turkish.'

Selda looked from one to the other of them.

'Look, Selda,' began Fatma, 'it doesn't mean anything. You won't tell Mother will you? There's no harm in it and you know how she'll worry. Zeki is just a friend. He's a friend of Ramona's sister. Ramona's parents were out and so they had school friends round and Zeki was one of these friends. He was good fun and he and Pembe chatted. He's from near Izmir, I think.'

'Why should I say anything? I'm not interested in who Zeki is.' Selda wished that they wouldn't insist so. They had gone into the sitting room and Fatma turned the television on. In silence they began to watch a film that they did not understand as it raced and flickered on the screen. It seemed to hold them captive and Selda only remembered her unfinished homework after several minutes.

'I've done mine,' said Pembe languidly, leaning back on the sofa with her hands behind her head.

'What? All of it?'

'Oh, yes. Zeki did it for me. He's been in Switzerland since he was a baby. He knows everything . . . But you won't tell, will you?'

'No, of course I won't tell. Why should I anyway?'

'Thanks, Selda.'

But Selda had already left the room. She did not want to hear anymore secrets. She crouched over the little bedside table and began to copy the map anew. She heard her parents come back and she called out a greeting, but worked on. She wanted the map to be perfect and to lie as cleanly and clearly on the page as though it had been printed there. When Pembe and Fatma came in to bed she was still only halfway through. They grumbled about her bedside light but were soon asleep. Selda shaded in the last bit of mountain and looked at it with pleasure: it wasn't bad. She felt much happier, even though her legs had got dreadful pins and needles. She got up to stretch them and crept to the window. The flat was quiet. The street below was dark and still. No cars passed and no steps

73

could be heard. There was not a light in any of the houses. She pressed her cheek up against the glass and was startled by the chill that seeped through from outside. Perhaps Ramona was right. Perhaps it would snow soon.

She had never seen real snow. Once, during their first winter in Izmir, it had actually snowed. Their teacher had let them out of class especially to see it. They had raced around, holding out the skirts of their black overalls and catching a flake here and there. She remembered the bitter wind that had dashed the tiny, vanishing stars into her face. She had tried to keep a few to take home to show her grandmother. The old woman had mocked and teased her when the hand-kerchief in which she had folded the snow flakes had turned out to be merely damp and empty. She still remembered what her grandmother had said: 'I suppose this clever grand-daughter will fetch me water in a sieve, tomorrow.'

Her grandmother had always had a quick, cruel tongue. It was as though she took pleasure in other people's foolish-ness. She was such an obstinate old woman and Selda, think-ing about it now, was glad. She knew that her grandmother would be too proud and too obstinate to show the letters which Selda had written to anyone else. They would be quite safe. Indeed, she was not sure that she could have written them at all if her grandmother had been able to read them.

As Selda watched, the clouds parted. Suddenly, startlingly, the full moon hung before her in the night sky. In the white light the little town looked as though it too was drawn upon a page: as fixed and still as any picture in any book. Even the firs in the forest were undisturbed by the winds that blew the clouds swiftly by. Then she remembered the mountain. She must see it by moonlight. She felt her way through the shadowy flat, opened the balcony door and stepped out into the bitter night. There they were: the two mountain peaks, snow covered, certainly, shadowed briefly, then, suddenly, clear in the moonlight. They were like hands, thrown up to the sky and then held there, frozen and for ever apart.

Selda's stockinged feet ached with cold. She crept back into her room thinking that she would slip back into bed, just for a minute to warm up again. Then she would tackle that question. She thought it wouldn't hurt to rest her head on the pillow for just one comforting minute. . . .

The next day, Saturday, was a black day. It even started badly and Selda, as it were, had caused it all. She had awoken suddenly at about five in the morning. She was too hot and fully dressed in a tumbled mess of bed clothes and books and pencils. She remembered the unfinished homework instantly and switched on the light in a panic. Then she discovered that her fountain pen had leaked a great pool of black ink on to the new pink bedspread. Pembe and Fatma, disturbed by the light, complained loudly. Their mother, woken by their voices, came in half asleep, with her hair standing up on end. She saw the ugly ink stain and burst into tears. Selda hunched herself up over the bedside table, fitted a new cartridge into her pen and began to finish her homework, regardless of all. She did not even say that she was sorry.

Then Sevgi Hanım loosed upon her all the anger and worry that she had felt and tried to keep hidden during these difficult weeks of settling in to this different country where she seemed to have no place. You would have thought, listening to Sevgi Hanım, that a spoiled bedspread was pretty well the end of the world. Selda was reminded again of her grandmother. How she had gone on and on about dripping taps and banging doors and chipped cups and tiny bits of wasted food! Surely they weren't things that truly mattered so much? Now, here was her own mother, acting in the same way over a wretched spoiled bedspread. You would have thought that it was more important than her homework!

The bad atmosphere persisted at the breakfast table and it

seemed unwise of Pembe to ask her father for 'something new to wear' just at that moment when he was drinking his tea, but she did.

'Why?' he asked, with the glass still at his mouth.

'For the trip.'

'What trip?'

'For the class trip that we have next Thursday. It's a trip to somewhere . . . I've forgotten the name, but it's an all-day trip with Frau Steinfeld and we have to take lunch.' Pembe, breathless with enthusiasm, smiled at her father as he sipped his tea. 'Please, Father?'

'Well, I'll see. It's the first I've heard of it.'

'But we gave you the letter last night. Look, here it is again.' Pembe jumped up and took it down from behind the Istanbul plaque, where he had slipped it.

'All right, all right girls. I'll think about it.'

'But we have to tell our teacher today,' insisted Fatma.

'Tell her today that you'll let her know on Monday,' said Sevgi Hanım sharply. She wanted to restore the peace so that the problems could be forgotten. In these three months she had hardly been outside the flat, except to go shopping or visit other Turkish families. For a woman who had been used to running a shop and a small-holding and looking after her family in the village, her world seemed to have shrunk and shrunk. All she expected was a little peace in this small, enclosed world. Nobody had asked her if she would like to go on a trip. She did not expect to, naturally, but she did not see why these girls should either, especially if it involved scenes like this.

'How do we know it's safe?' she asked, hoping to scare the girls off.

'Exactly, that's what I meant,' said Turgut Bey, gratefully. 'I mean, you do hear such things. Adnan Hoca has told me all about what goes on here! Your mother is right, girls. It won't be safe. Another time.'

Pembe wept helplessly but Fatma was not so easily defeated.

'Really father, we have to go. If we don't go on the trip, we still have to go to school, to another class on Thursday. We can't just "not go".'

'What if you pretended to be ill . . .' suggested Sevgi Hanım, weakly.

'Father,' continued Fatma, ignoring Sevgi Hanım, 'do you really want us to be the only girls not to go? Ramona says that the Turkish children often miss out on things . . . because their parents can't afford to pay . . .'

'Pay?' said Sevgi Hanım irritably. 'I didn't know you had to pay. I thought everything was free in school. You didn't tell me you had to pay.' She picked up the letter and looked at it vaguely, trying to find a figure which she recognized.

'Mother! I don't care how much it is!' Turgut Bey was offended and angry. 'Who says I can't afford to send my girls on an outing!' He looked reproachfully at his daughters, aware yet again that they were no longer the dear little girls he had left behind in the village.

'Go on this trip, then, if it's *so* important!' He got up from the table and handed a large Swiss note to his wife.

'Get them what they need, whatever it is. I'm going out to meet Adnan Hoca.'

They stared at him in surprise but at the last moment he spoilt his generosity by muttering: 'But don't blame *me* when things go wrong! And don't forget, *I* never wanted them to go!'

Pembe, whose tears had vanished, only to leave her eyes brighter than ever, laughed and chattered with Ramona all along the road to school. She did not seem to think that anything of consequence had happened, whereas Selda, who had only been an onlooker at the breakfast table, felt upset. She felt responsible for the ill tempers displayed. Still, perhaps it wasn't important. Perhaps she was just too tired

77

because she hadn't slept properly. Nevertheless, she felt as though a shadow lay over her.

Near the school, a large, sleek car slowed down just in front of them. Selda was aware of a familiar face turning back to look at her. The car stopped. A tall, very smart woman got out of the passenger's seat. She did not close the car door but held it open across the pavement. She stood beside it, barring the way. The four girls looked at each other and had to stop. Selda knew instinctively that the woman was going to speak to her. For one, desperate second, she thought that she should just run. Run away, run anywhere . . . but, of course, she was too old for that. And she remembered the fortune teller's advice. No, she wouldn't run.

'Which of you is "Selda"?' Though the woman looked at all four of them, Selda was sure that she already knew the answer.

'I am.'

'So.' The woman stepped away from the car. Inside it Selda saw the pale faces of the little boy who had fought in the sand-pit and of Giselle, the girl whom she had called *'blöde Kuh'*. A man in a uniform sat like a statue in the driver's seat and did not turn round.

'So. You are the Selda. You are the great big, foreign girl who hurts little children!' At first the woman spoke very slowly and clearly. Then she seemed to lose control of herself. She began to shout. Children going into school loitered to watch. Selda could only catch a word here and there. Then the woman darted back to the car and brought out a small pair of white trousers, torn at the knees and still stained yellow with sand. She shook them close to Selda's face. She pulled the boy out of the car and held him in front of Selda, shouting excitedly. She must be his mother. Somewhere in the background the school bell shrilled.

'Well, did you hit him? Did you?' the woman was a little calmer now and repeated again and again: 'Did you? Did you?'

'Yes but . . .' Selda wanted to get into school to escape.

'Yes? Good! That is very, very good. Now "Selda" we can go into school and talk to your teacher about what you have done. You must not forget that you are in Switzerland now. We, in Switzerland, do not spoil our things.' She shook the trousers again. 'We are very careful people. And you, Selda, must learn to be a careful girl.' She spoke so slowly now, and loudly as though talking to someone who was deaf. The little boy jerked his arm away from his mother and made a grimace, as though he thought all this was rather stupid. Then he suddenly ran off, across the road and into the school yard.

'We keep things very, very nice, here in Switzerland. And we keep our children very, very nice too,' said the woman, smiling fondly after her son.

'Fatma? Whatever shall I do?' In panic, Selda turned back to her elder sisters but they were not there. They had followed the crowd into school.

'I'm sorry,' she said, and meant it.

The woman put her head on one side and looked at her with her exquisitely made-up eyes.

'I'm glad that you are sorry, but that is not enough. These trousers are spoilt. I must buy my son a new pair. Trousers like this cost fifteen francs.'

Selda looked at her and thought that she understood.

'I? I buy?' She would have offered anything to have kept this dreadful woman out of the school and away from Fräulein Altmann.

'Yes. You must buy them! Good. If you bring fifteen francs to school next week and give it to my daughter Giselle, then I do not have to speak to the teacher. It was an accident.' And she actually smiled. Her beautiful face came alight in a radiant smile as thought all were well.

'Fifteen francs?'

'Yes. That is not too much?'

'No.' Selda shook her head. Since she had no money, it did not make any difference.

'Good. Now, hurry up. You don't want to be late for class.'

Giselle had got out of the back of the car and the woman now climbed in and drew down the window and waved, as though they were old friends. The car pulled slowly and smoothly away.

Everybody had gone into class. The only person still hanging up a coat was the tall, pale Giselle. Selda tried not to look at this enemy, this traitor. She must have gone straight home to her awful mother and told lies. One day she would get even with her. Nobody was going to treat her like this. She was glad she had called her a 'stupid cow'. She deserved it. Selda pushed her hair out of her eyes and held her breath. She would walk straight past the girl, just as though she weren't there.

Giselle left off fiddling with her coat and looked suddenly and openly up at Selda and Selda saw that her enemy was not at all triumphant, but bitterly ashamed.

Five

Selda did not tell anyone about the curious request for fifteen francs. It was so extraordinary that she did not know what to make of it. At home, in Turkey, when you had an accident and broke or spoilt something, even her grandmother would, in the end, have made peace and said: 'better that you should be healthy'. That was what people did: in the end Sevgi Hanım had washed the bedspread and had agreed that the stain wouldn't show that much. Selda remembered that once in Izmir, poor Demet had slipped on the newly washed kitchen tiles and dropped a whole tray of tea glasses. Her grandmother had scolded her and said that she was careless and clumsy and should have seen the floor was still wet. But that was all. Never in a thousand years would her grandmother have wanted the glasses replaced. Even her grandmother, who loved her money, would have been deeply insulted.

Selda could understand that the Swiss woman would be angry that her son had been pushed over and annoyed that his trousers had been torn. There were plenty of mothers like that in Turkey too. They were anxious, interfering mothers, eager to fight the playground squabbles anew, long after their children had forgotten about them. This, however, was quite different.

This mother had been so strange, especially when she smiled at the end. Selda suspected that, for her, everything would be put right when Selda had paid up the fifteen francs. The problem was, she didn't have fifteen francs.

No, she could not explain at home and she did not want to.

She just wanted to hand over the money, if this was the price of keeping Giselle's mother out of the school. So it was with this worry in her head that Selda found herself trailing around the supermarket after her family on Saturday afternoon.

She had not wanted to come at all. She had pleaded tiredness, which was true and extra homework, which wasn't, but her family had insisted. Sevgi Hanım had said that the 'fresh air' would do her good. Fresh air! In this stiffling shop! Selda had tried to remind them all that she did not like shopping, but Fatma, who was feeling guilty about having deserted her sister that morning, now wanted to make amends. She suggested to her parents that Selda should have something new too. There was no escape. The family united: of course Selda should not be left out just because she was not going on a school trip. That would be unfair. Turgut Bey, unable to resist the temptation of watching his money spent, decided to come down with them after all. Selda, anxious to avoid further trouble, said nothing more.

Now she leant against the racks of clothes under the hot, flickering lights and listened to her father's excited voice rising above all the others in the crowded store.

'Well? Doesn't it suit her? Doesn't it?' He was holding a pale blue, woolly dress up against Pembe.' Isn't that a lovely elegant colour for a young girl?'

'Yes, it *suits* her, but . . . '

'Then we'll buy it. Now, Mother knows about sizes and things. Let her look. Unless you'd rather have pink.' He snatched another from the rail, like a child unable to resist the goodies. 'Try this, oh, do, Pembe.' He tried to hold it under Fatma's chin, but she moved away, scowling.

'Now what could be nicer? Sisters in matching dresses. That's how we dressed you when you were little girls. Do look at yourself, Fatma.'

He was very pleased. He really did love his daughters. He

82

had missed them too, during those years of separation. Now, he liked to spend money on them, to prove how much he loved them. He was proud of them. They were such a pretty pair. And Selda, of course. Though she would be prettier when she was older and less obstinate. It showed in her face, he thought. A girl should look, well, compliant.

'Well, girls?' He was looking at the price tag, proud of his ability to spend this money. His daughters had probably been right, though he would never admit it to them: they did need something new for a school excursion. Pembe smiled into the mirror and thought how well she looked in powder blue, and was tempted. Fatma, who had firmer ideas, was not impressed.

'Father, we don't want dresses. Nobody wears dresses.'

'Skirts, then skirts and blouses. Now that's smart too.' He was determined to be patient. Adnan Hoca always said that the fathers of daughters must be extra patient and extra vigilant. Women and girls, being less intelligent, took longer to make up their minds. Fathers must therefore be patient.

'That's what we want!' Fatma pointed to a row of jeans.

'Don't be ridiculous.'

'I'm not. That's what we want, Father. And they're not expensive, look . . . '

'Put them back.' He felt his patience slipping away fast.

'Or these! They're wonderful!' She held up some blue jeans which had artificial patches sewn on to them.

'Don't be stupid. Do you want to look like a beggar in patched clothes? This is what comes of leaving you girls too long in Turkey. You don't even recognize nice things when you see them. Tell them, Mother. Tell them to put those shameful trousers away.'

'Your father says you're to put them away.'

'But nobody will wear a dress! It's a walking trip. We're going to walk for *hours*.'

'Can't you walk in a skirt?'

'No! You don't understand, Father. Everybody else will wear jeans . . . '

'I'm not having my daughters dressed up like men.' He was red with anger.

'It's disgusting and you should be ashamed of yourselves.' How right Adnan Hoca was: as soon as nice Turkish girls set foot in this country, they began to forget themselves.

'I suppose you'll be wanting to shave your heads next and paint your faces!'

'Father! Of course we won't. Even the teachers wear jeans.'

'They don't!'

'They do, don't they, Selda?'

'Yes.' She was reluctant to say so and remembered that, to be honest, both she and her sisters had been surprised to see this. Now they were used to it.

'You see, Father? So we do need jeans! I'm right, aren't I Selda?'

'Why don't you buy something else then?' suggested Selda. She was aware that they were blocking up the aisle in the shop and that people were staring at them. She longed to escape. 'Buy . . . buy shoes or something.'

'Now that's a good idea,' cried Sevgi Hanım. She too wanted to avoid a dispute. She beckoned them over to look at the shoes.

In the end, this compromise was struck. Two pairs of elegant black shoes with little buckles on top were chosen. Pembe was enchanted. Fatma, who had remembered Ramona's secret offer of the loan of a pair of jeans, was reconciled. After all, they might not even go on the trip if it snowed, whereas one could always use pretty shoes.

While they had been choosing the shoes Selda had suddenly and guiltily realized how she might get hold of the fifteen francs she needed. When the family, grateful to her for the suggestion, turned to her to ask her what she wanted, she had her answer ready.

84

'I'd like a dictionary, please.' She remembered how useful the dictionary had been on the plane. She had wanted one ever since.

'Where will you get that?' Her mother looked uneasily around the shop.

'Why do you want one?' said her father. 'I thought they gave you your books free in school.'

'They do. But not a Turkish–German dictionary. That's what I need.'

Her parents exchanged glances. There was not a single book in their house, apart from the Koran and school books. They did not know much about things like that.

'How much would this "dictionary" cost?' her mother asked suspiciously.

'Only fifteen or sixteen francs. But you can't get them here. I've seen them in the book shop. Look, you finish your shopping and join the queue at the check-out, while I run over to the book shop. I'll get it and come straight back. I'll find you in one of the queues.' Even as she spoke the plan formed more clearly in her mind. She would tell her parents that the book was out of stock and that she had ordered it and had had to pay the fifteen francs in advance. They would never know. Really, she would just keep the money in her pocket and have it ready to give to Giselle on Monday. She would worry about getting the dictionary later.

Her plan worked as well as she had hoped it would. When she returned five minutes later her family were still in the queue with their trolley now piled high. The two pairs of shoes were perched carefully on the top. Selda squeezed through the crowds to rejoin them and hurriedly told them her 'story'. Two men were waiting in the line in front of them. Their trolley only contained some large loaves of bread, some soap powder and several packages of damaged goods that had been marked down in price. There was a bag of oranges that was no longer so fresh. When Selda had finished explaining she glanced at them and instantly recognized the two men whom she had kept on seeing around the town and who had waited for Ahmet last night.

Now, at close quarters, anybody could surely have seen that they were Turks. The elder one restlessly passed his prayer beads round and round through his fingers as he waited. The younger, who must have been about fifteen or sixteen, wore black rubber over-shoes on top of his ordinary shoes. She had never seen anyone here wearing those. She remembered them perfectly from her childhood. All the poorer men and women in the village wore them in wet, muddy weather. She had actually sold them in the shop: they had hung in pairs on a white string, near the door. She had thought them rather odd, even then, because they had the eyelets and shoe laces printed on top of them in moulded leather. It was as if they were pretending to be 'real' shoes. And now, here was this boy, in the middle of a small town in Switzerland, wearing a pair.

She forced herself not to stare at his feet. Yes, anybody would know that they were Turks. Anybody, that is, except Pembe. She glanced into their trolley and said loudly and brightly in Turkish: 'Poor things, look at that. They've only been able to buy the rotten things,' and she giggled. Selda nudged her but it was too late. The men had heard and understood. They did not turn around, but they moved sharply. The elder stopped passing the white plastic beads through his fingers. He just wound the string up and dropped it into his pocket. The younger shifted his position and leant forward, drumming his fingers on the trolley.

Selda was ashamed. When they moved forward towards the cashier, she guessed from their faces that they were a father and son. They were dark, slim men, with the same thin face and straight, dark brows. Their skin was sunburnt, yet the older man did not have the deeply lined and weather-beaten appearance of one who has always worked outside.

He started to pay the cashier, then, shaking his head, started to point to a difference between the reduced price on a packet of lentils and the price that the machine had registered. The cashier looked at him and, maybe understanding that he was a foreigner, began to explain very slowly and clearly that what looked like a 'three' was really an 'eight'. She said that if they did not want the lentils, that was fine, she would put them aside. As far as Selda could understand, the woman was being very pleasant and agreeing that the numbers were poorly written. The two men listened in total silence. They did not say a word to each other or to the cashier. She repeated herself. The long queue behind was restless. The two still stood there, silent. Selda saw the confusion in their eyes. Then, realizing that *she* had understood, impulsively, she began to translate what the cashier had said in German into Turkish. The younger of the two looked sharply at Selda and his glance was cold and unfriendly. They still did not speak, yet she knew that they had understood her. She looked right into his face, but his eyes remained blank. Once she thought he might have been about to say something but then his antagonism returned.

'Selda, whatever are you thinking of?' said Sevgi Hanım. 'Don't interfere like that. They are not Turks.'

The older man bent down quickly and took a thousand franc note from inside his sock. The cashier looked very annoyed. She shook her head at the ever-lengthening queue and began to count out a great pile of change. The man and his son packed their things away impassively, as though they didn't care, yet Selda saw that the younger one's hand shook as he drew the handles of his bag together. She had seen something else too: there had been several of these large notes fastened around the man's ankle with a rubber band. She watched them, packing away the bread. The two shopping bags were of the type poor people sewed from animal feed sacks in Turkey. Of course they were Turks. How could people be so blind?

She watched them leave the shop, vanishing silently

through the crowds and into the evening, as though they had never been there at all. But as they passed in front of the shop window, the younger swung his bag up over his shoulder and glanced back and then his eyes met Selda's.

That night there was a frost. When she looked down from the balcony on Sunday morning, the world was touched with white and was different. The tiles on the pointed roofs glittered and sparkled. The black pavements were paler and the bright, green autumn lawns had yellowed and withered overnight. There were no boats out on the lake, but the seagulls now swooped and wheeled and turned inland. They cut through the thin air above Selda's head and they called harshly. The bushes in the nearby gardens seemed suddenly to have dropped their leaves and taken up coverings of shivering, gleaming cobwebs. Selda had never seen anything like it. Her indrawn breath froze her lungs. She had not known that it could be so cold. Once or twice in Izmir ice as thin and brittle as cheap glass had formed on the edges of puddles. The winter winds had blustered in from the bay and the air had been raw and wet. But this was different. This brilliant, frozen world excited her. She wanted to go out. After breakfast, when Turgut Bey had gone to meet Adnan Bey and other friends, Pembe and Fatma grew restless. When they said that they needed to go to Ramona's to ask about the homework, Selda suggested to her mother that the two of them should go for a Sunday walk.

'Walk?' Sevgi Hanım looked puzzled. 'But the shops are shut.'

'Not to the shops.'

'Where else?' Her mother could not see the point.

'We won't go anywhere special. We'll just walk, you know, like the Swiss.'

'Like the Swiss?' They had all seen them, certainly. They were energetic people, striding out with sticks in their hands, special boots on their feet and even special trousers and socks, it appeared. Selda had watched them going purposefully and cheerfully up the road which led to the forest. She had seen white-haired women in knee-length breeches and red knitted socks climbing the hill with those little bags over their backs, and with all the energy and excitement of children.

'There won't be any proper roads up there,' objected Sevgi Hanım. 'It's a forest. I don't want to go up there. There might be animals and things.'

'Well, we could walk straight along if you're scared. Not up or down, but just along.'

'Why?'

'Oh, Mother! You're the one who says she never gets out of the house. Well, you *can* now. I'll go with you. We'll go for a walk.'

'Whatever will your father say?'

'Oh, he won't mind. Go on,' urged Fatma. She was eager to get away to Ramona's.

'Whatever will you girls suggest next,' said Sevgi Hanım, but she got up and brushed her hair, and took out her best coat.

In five minutes the two of them had passed the station and were walking along a quiet road that seemed to lead out of the town. In ten minutes more Sevgi Hanım had stopped and undone the top button of her coat. She put her hand up to her glowing cheeks. They had walked too quickly and had not expected the sun to be so warm. The road which they had been following now curved downhill, back towards the lake, but a footpath apparently continued through two fields. One had been ploughed recently and gulls strutted along its furrows. You could smell the clods of earth which had been split open by the frost that night. It reminded Sevgi Hanım of the village.

On the right-hand side was pasture land and there, rooting about under an old apple tree, were three enormous pigs. Above them, a few apples had defied the frost and clung, red and round, to the black branches. The pigs busily thrust their pink snouts into more piles of apples, heaped up on the ground. Selda and her mother could hear the wet crunching of their jaws.

'Well!' exclaimed Sevgi Hanım. One pig, a vast sow, had a row of teats hanging down under her that swung and flapped like flags as she moved. She looked towards them with little, feeble eyes, then turned nimbly around and trotted briskly away. Her ridiculous, curly tail bounced about against her massive, muddy flanks.

There were several low concrete buildings on the far side of the field and from them came a distant chorus of squeaking and squealing.

'Dirty, unclean brutes!' Sevgi Hanım sniffed the stale air and stared at the animals in guilty horror. Selda, who had also never seen domestic pigs before, found them funny and laughable as they nudged and pawed and grunted around the apples. They reminded her of country women crowding in on a bazaar stall that sold cheaper goods. She was fascinated at the way their neat little feet and legs carried their awkward, bloated bodies.

'Do you think we should turn back now?' asked Sevgi Hanım who felt bad about looking at the pigs. She did not turn round, however, and they went on through the fields. Other people, out for their Sunday walks, greeted them. At first Selda and her mother stared in astonishment at this approach by total strangers, but Selda, filled with a sense of adventure at being out on so fine and sunny a morning, plucked up her courage and when a friendly, elderly couple drew near, she said: '*Grüezi*.' They said the same back and stopped and she held out her hand to their little dog who jumped up at her.

'He's very quiet, usually,' the lady said, 'but he's been a naughty boy. He barked at those rabbits.'

'Rabbits?' Selda wondered if she had misunderstood.

'Yes,' said the old man, 'old Bauer's rabbits, down by the barn. Perhaps you don't know them? Perhaps you are not Swiss?'

'No, we're Turks . . . '

'Ah, so you wouldn't know. You must go and see them.' The lady took Selda gently by the arm and pointed ahead. Speaking more slowly, she explained that if they walked on to the next group of farm buildings, there, just near the path, they would see the rabbits.

'Lots of rabbits,' added her husband and he made movements with his arm as though the rabbits were piled up in the sky.

'You'll like them,' they said. Then they smiled and the old man raised his hat to them as they parted.

Selda translated to her mother what had been said adding that wherever she went, she seemed destined to see rabbits.

'I don't know what's so special about rabbits,' said Sevgi Hanım. They were a real pest, back in the village. I remember one year when they stripped the fields bare. Lettuce, parsley, beans, they had the lot. I think I planted out three times that spring. I'd poison those pests, if I had my way.' Sevgi Hanım was still a country woman at heart and could never be romantic about animals.

'These rabbits will be different,' said Selda, hopefully.

'Ah, you young girls,' said Sevgi Hanım. 'You think that everything here will be different. And better, don't you?'

'Not everything . . . but . . . that's why we've come, isn't it? So that things will be better?'

'Yes. That's why we've come.' Sevgi Hanım repeated the words mechanically, as though not believing them. Selda did not know how to answer her mother and so she pretended not to have heard. They walked along to the farm buildings in silence.

'Look!' cried Selda, running over. 'These rabbits *are* different!'

They certainly were. She understood now that the old man had been trying to describe the rows and rows of cages which stood one on top of the other, against the side of an old barn. Through the open barn door she saw yet more cages. They all contained rabbits. Some had single rabbits in them and some had families. Some rabbits were very small and some were average sized. Some were simply huge: as big as small dogs. There were fluffy white rabbits with pinky red eyes; there were jet-black rabbits, with jet-black eyes; there were brown rabbits and grey rabbits and rabbits with dabs of colour on them as though they had been softly touched with a paint brush. There were rabbits with upright ears and with drooping ears, but most startling of all were the giant grey-brown rabbits with black, lopped ears that fell down into their straw bedding.

Even Sevgi Hanım was impressed. They peered excitedly into all the cages and noticed that many of the rabbits had metal clips in their ears.

'Poor things,' said Sevgi Hanım unexpectedly, 'all caged up like that.'

Selda looked at her mother in surprise.

'I thought that you didn't like them, that they were just pests.'

'Yes. They are. But all the same,' she shook her head, 'at least they had their bit of freedom. These . . .' but she didn't finish her sentence. Instead she turned away and picked a handful of grass and, after glancing guiltily over her shoulder, poked it through the bars of one of the cages. Selda did the same. A minute later they were both pulling up the frozen grass and weeds and hurrying from cage to cage, trying to be fair and to give each a little taste.

Then, someone banged sharply on a window. They jumped as though they had been shot at. Looking in the direction of the noise, they saw a face at the window of the farmhouse. A man banged and shouted again, but Selda could understand nothing. A dog barked in the house. They dropped the grass, and, like children caught stealing flowers in the park, they ran. They rejoined the path and made for home as quickly as they could.

They had been away longer than they intended and Turgut Bey was already back. He looked displeased.

'If you had told me you wanted to go out,' he said, 'I'm sure that Adnan Bey and his wife would have taken you for a run in their car. They're always offering. Then you wouldn't have to go wandering about in the country.' His eyes rested on the fronds of grass that had stuck to his wife's new coat. There was silence in the flat. Then he said, less crossly: 'Well, you might at least tell me what you did.'

'We saw some rabbits, on a farm.' Selda spoke first hoping that her mother would not mention the pigs.

'Rabbits? Is that all? And what was so special about this farm, that you had to go and see it?'

'It was . . . clean.' She couldn't think of anything else to say. His disapproval had killed all her pleasure in the walk.

'Clean? A farm?'

'Yes, really. Look.' She pointed to her stockinged feet which were not even muddy. 'You won't believe it, but it looked like a picture. It was like walking through a beautiful, painted landscape, which wasn't quite real.'

Her father was not listening. He had already turned the television on. Selda and her mother exchanged a brief glance.

'Those cages were real enough,' exclaimed Sevgi Hanım quietly and went into the kitchen to prepare the lunch.

That evening Selda wrote to her grandmother again. She described the rabbits and the pigs and the couple who had been so pleasant. Then she mentioned the old man who had banged on the window.

It's like being deaf, this not being able to understand what people say. I was so scared that I wanted to run away and hide. Of course we couldn't. We ran like kids,

93

but we couldn't hide. I never thought I would be such a
coward . . .

She remembered that her grandmother had often banged
on the windows of the old house in Izmir. She banged to
frighten off children who were stealing apricots from the
remaining tree, but she also banged to catch the attention of
street sellers and neighbours . . . So she added to her letter:

But you know, Grandmother, he might not have been
shouting anything bad at all. He might have been saying
'thank you' because we were feeding his rabbits. I just
didn't know. I suppose one day I will, but at the
moment, I feel quite lost. Pembe and Fatma seem to be
settling down better than me. They have friends at
school, while I just seem to have made enemies . . .

She wondered how truthful she should be, then she
reminded herself that after all, her grandmother would not be
reading the letters, so she might as well write exactly what she
felt. She wrote about home and the dispute between her father
and Ahmet and about how sorry it made her, but she kept her
promise to him and did not write about the secret, night-time
visit which he had made. She wrote about school and about her
sisters' coming trip and then she wrote more about the rabbits.
She was just going to end: 'your loving granddaughter, Selda,
who misses you very much', when she realized, with a shock,
that she did *not* miss her grandmother at all. Now that they
were separated by a distance which no bridge could span, she
felt nearer to the old woman than she had ever done before. For
the first time she understood something of her grandmother's
bad temper and bitter tongue. Perhaps her inability to read and
write all these years had made her secretly unhappy. Perhaps it
had made her feel foolish and helpless in a world where,
nowadays everyone else could read and write. Perhaps one
became very fierce when one wanted to keep one's secret
weaknesses well hidden.

She sat up writing many pages of the letter and when it was finished she fell asleep. She woke to the Monday morning which she had so dreaded, feeling almost cheerful. Even the coming encounter with her enemy, Giselle, hardly worried her. She would pay her debt and that would be that. Perhaps life was like that in Switzerland. Maybe it wasn't even so bad. One just had to learn. And she was learning.

Six

Giselle was sitting by the playground fountain flicking the water so that it nearly splashed the other children, but not quite. When Selda approached her she scowled, took the fifteen francs and hastily stuffed them deep into the pocket of her jeans. She said thank you in an awkward, nervous voice and put her hand back into the water so carelessly that her sleeve got all wet. One or two children who had been standing around in the playground saw the transaction and whispered amongst themselves. Selda thought she saw scorn in their faces and she wondered if this had all happened before. Giselle got up and walked away whistling defiantly with her hands stuck in the pockets of her anorak. A couple of girls followed her, mimicking her walk and making loud remarks about the greed of some people. In a second, Giselle was involved in a furious slanging match. Selda did not understand it all, but watched puzzled, as Giselle defied the growing band of hostile children. It was a scene that Selda now saw regularly repeated.

There Giselle would be, in break-time, one girl at bay against the rest. She wasn't being defeated, however. Often she would be winning and when her tormenters withdrew defeated, Giselle was left alone with her victory. Selda wondered why she had not noticed Giselle before. She had always thought of the rest of the class as 'them', and she had not been interested in them. She noticed now that Giselle had no proper friend. One day she roamed with this group and later with another. The only certain thing about her was that wherever there was trouble, there you would find Giselle.

Each morning Giselle and her little brother were driven to school in that car. Selda realized that it was extremely luxurious even by Swiss standards. Sometimes the mother sat by the chauffeur, sometimes she didn't. She was always so beautifully dressed that she reminded Selda of a picture in a fashion magazine. The little brother seemed to bring an endless supply of new toys into school. Now it was a green skateboard, then a much bigger blue one, then roller skates, then a new football and then a series of radio-controlled cars. One day it was something that flew and the children let it off and it soared with a mighty crash into a nearby window. Selda had learnt that his name was Anton. A group of the younger boys was always waiting for him and as soon as he arrived they began begging to play with his toys. There was always some small boy declaring himself to be Anton's 'best friend ever'.

Giselle and Anton obviously came from a very rich family but while Anton was always at the centre of an admiring crowd, Giselle apparently worked hard at driving everyone away from her. Selda found herself secretly admiring Giselle's reckless defiance of the world. Had their family circumstances been more similar, Selda could imagine that in the end, they might have become good friends. There was something about this girl that, almost against her better judgement, Selda liked. Giselle could have been the true friend that poor Demet had failed to be. Why, despite all those promises and tears, Demet had never once written or replied to all Selda's cards and letters. Selda was disappointed.

Outside school Selda continued to watch for the two Turks. She sometimes saw the boy coming back up the hill in the evening with the two loaves of bread slung in the bag over his shoulder. Once she saw him from a distance, standing by himself at the edge of the lake. It was a Sunday afternoon and he was just standing, looking into the dark water. Selda, jammed into the back of Adnan Bey's car, was being taken on a forced visit to the Imam's wife and daughter. She had wriggled round though, to make sure that it was him. She had become so curious about him that she even began to make inquiries. He was obviously too old for their school, but not too old for some other. He must be studying somewhere, for this, after all, was Switzerland. She questioned Ramona and her elder sister carefully but discovered that there were no Turks in the secondary school. She persuaded Pembe to ask the famous Zeki if there were any Turks in his technical school. There were, it seemed, two or three, but none of them fitted the description of the boy in the red shirt.

Selda kept on trying to find out who he was, even though she did not really know why she did it. On the Wednesday evening before Pembe's and Fatma's class trip, Adnan Bey brought his wife to visit. When they came, Selda usually pretended that she had a test the next day and with this excuse she escaped to her room after the first ten minutes. She disliked the family and their superior manners and she hated the way Adnan Hoca, in his neat, black suit and his tieless white shirt, sat on the edge of his chair with his knees pressed tightly together and advised everybody about the proper way to live. He had long white hands with slightly too-long fingernails that were not absolutely clean and the last time he came Fatma had whispered wickedly that she thought he smelt of the dead bodies which he washed. Pembe had whispered back that a patch of his beard seemed to have got the moth and they had all rolled about on their beds, overcome by an attack of giggles which they were sure the visitor must have heard. None of the girls liked him. He frightened them. He was the sort of adult who would never give a straight answer to a straight question. If you asked him if he thought Zurich was a nice city he would pause and rub his fingertips amongst his beard and say: 'And why are you asking that, my dear?'

This evening Selda had asked him if his coffee was sweet enough. He hadn't said 'yes' or 'no' like an ordinary person.

He had looked at the dregs in his cup and said that 'a *good* cup of coffee is remembered for forty years . . . '

She hated the man, but she stayed on in the sitting room, pretending to be pleasant to the wife and the daughter, but really, listening in to the two men's conversation. They were discussing Adnan Hoca's new plan to set up a religious study group for the students in the town. He wanted to get an idea from her father of how many Turkish workers in the factory would be interested to send their children. Naturally, there would be different groups for girls and boys. Selda listened carefully to the names of all the families under discussion. No mention was made of a father and son. It was as if they didn't exist. She sat on, wasting a whole evening of study but did not hear anything.

If only Ahmet had been at home, she could have asked him. She would question him outright, whatever he said. As it was, she had not seen him since that night. All she could do was watch out for the strangers on the street.

And why did she watch? Who were they, after all? Two Turks. Two more Turks. And so what? What was that to her? Hadn't she come here to make a new life in a new land? Yet she still watched for him. It was like a secret. And nobody knew. It was her secret. It was something special which tied her to this different place and nobody else knew of the link. It was foolish, maybe, but that didn't matter. She would continue to watch for this stranger like you watch for some distant landmark to gain a better idea of where you are.

Thursday morning, the day of the long-awaited school trip, was cold and dull but not snowy. Ramona came round early to tell them that the outing was definitely on. She also brought the jeans. Turgut Bey, who was fortunately on early shift, had already left the house and so did not see his daughters dressed up and ready to go. They had no long mirror at home and so they had to wait until they passed the window of the Co-op on their way to school, to get an idea of

99

how they looked. There Pembe stopped and gazed at herself amongst the pyramids of soap powders and soft-drink cans. She was entranced, twirling round slowly and smiling as she pushed back her hair.

'Everybody thinks I'm Swiss, anyway, with my fair hair,' she said. 'I mean, you wouldn't know, would you?'

'Know what?' asked Selda.

'That I'm a Turk.'

'Of course you would!'

'No you wouldn't. Not if I didn't speak. Not if you just looked at me . . .' Pembe was begging but Selda wouldn't agree. Her sister did not even look slightly Swiss. Dressed in the ill-fitting jeans and bright, flowered jumper that had been bought in the bazaar in Izmir and wearing the new but impractical black patent shoes, Pembe looked exactly what she was: a hopeful stranger in a foreign land. She jumped excitedly from foot to foot but did not appear ready to walk along the mountain paths of this new home.

The news of Pembe's accident came to Selda at the end of afternoon school. People had already tried to phone home, but Sevgi Hanım had not understood. Now, Fräulein Altmann took Selda to one side and explained that Pembe had tripped on a narrow mountain path. She had lost her balance and fallen down on to rocks below. It had all happened several hours ago.

Selda was so shocked that at first she could not speak. This was the sort of thing that happened in films. She could almost see her sister's face down on the rocks with her fair hair spread out and the pretty shoes flung off. The soles of Pembe's small white feet would be quite cold . . . The children in her form crowded round her, suddenly upset and concerned. Somebody even patted her shoulder.

'Is she, is she . . . dead?'

'No, no, Selda, nothing like that! Oh dear, I thought you'd understood. It's not that serious. She has cut her leg deeply and they think that she's damaged her knee. That's why she's in the town hospital. They brought her by ambulance. Your other sister, Fatma, is there with her.'

That at least, was a relief. Then she thought of her father, and of how angry he would be.

'Come along then.' Kind Fräulein Altmann was insisting on driving Selda home to fetch her mother and then on taking them both to the hospital. Poor Sevgi Hanım cried all the way: partly for Pembe's sake and partly for her own. If only she had not let them go . . .

Pembe, looking very small in a white hospital gown, was sitting up in bed, with a huge cage thing holding the blankets off her legs. Fatma was sitting beside her turning the pages of some Donald Duck comics. Frau Steinfeld, the sandy-haired sixth class teacher who had been in charge of the trip, was standing by the window talking to a nurse. Seeing them she strode over and, after greeting Sevgi Hanım very briefly, she immediately turned to Selda.

'You must explain to your mother how sorry I am, but you must tell her, Selda, that I am not responsible. I've been taking children on these class trips for twelve years, and this is the first child, ever, to end up in hospital! I really *cannot* be held responsible.' She looked to Fräulein Altmann for some support. 'The school is not responsible either. I sent written instructions home with all the children. Look, I have a copy here. Look, it says 'old clothes and sensible footwear'. And what do these two girls turn up in? Brand new shoes with little heels! If Pembe had been wearing proper walking shoes this accident would never have happened! I must say I think it very thoughtless of parents to send their children up into the mountains dressed like that. If Pembe had been wearing proper shoes, this accident would never have happened!'

Selda translated as much of this as she was able to. Sevgi Hanım listened in growing outrage.

'Those were perfectly good shoes!' she cried. 'Your father

only bought them on Saturday! Pembe put them on new this morning. You tell that woman, Selda.'

Selda did, miserably. Then Frau Steinfeld and Sevgi Hanım stared at each other across a cold sea of total incomprehension. Pembe, whose knee had begun to throb again, now let the tears trickle down her cheeks.

Fräulein Altmann, who alone seemed to understand, pulled a chair up to Pembe's bedside and sat down there. She stroked her hand and said: 'I'm sure you'll soon be well. It's nobody's fault. You won't believe me, but years ago when I was in school, I went on a trip and I climbed up a tree which I had been warned not to climb, and I fell out and broke my wrist.' She pushed up the sleeve of her jumper and showed them a small white scar, where, she said, a piece of bone had actually come through the skin.

'Accidents do happen,' she said,' especially when we stretch the rules.'

Selda thought that it was the nicest thing anyone could have said, under the circumstances. Fräulein Altmann was clearly trying to make the peace. She felt disappointed with her mother and with Frau Steinfeld. She wanted to avoid both of them, so that neither of them could use her in their battle.

'Do you know,' continued Fräulein Altmann cheerfully, 'in a few days' time, when you're home again, Pembe, you'll find that you've learnt more German here in hospital, than you would have in weeks of school.'

'How?' Pembe's smile was still rather watery.

'Nobody can speak Turkish here. You'll have to speak. You'll come out better than you went in and I'm not just talking about your knee.'

'In that case, I'll break both my legs,' said Selda in quiet desperation.'

'Don't talk like that.' Fräulein Altmann smiled and put an arm around Selda as if she really cared.

Turgut Bey arrived soon after they got home. He looked pale, upset and angry.

'You see! Didn't I warn you what would happen! I knew that they wouldn't look after the children properly. I told you, but you wouldn't listen. Adnan Hoca never let his daughter go on school trips. What do these teachers think they're doing, running around the country when they should be in school, teaching lessons? These people don't know what "proper" school is. They think studying is a joke. Nobody ever took me on a trip and look at me now!'

'It wasn't like that,' protested Fatma, boldly. 'It was part of our Geography lesson, I think. We have been studying the maps and things at school and now the teacher wanted us to see what the lakes and mountains really looked like.'

'There!' snapped Turgut Bey. 'What did I say! An utter waste of time when you've got it all there on a map. And why did your poor sister fall down and hurt herself? Now, tell me the truth. Did somebody push her?'

'No, of course not. She tripped.'

'There! You see! She wouldn't have tripped if she had been in the classroom.'

'It wasn't that. It was her *shoe*. The heel caught in a crack and she tripped. Even the doctor said that it's easy to trip in shoes like that.'

'There! I knew it: you should have bought dresses. Nobody would have fallen down on to rocks if you'd been wearing dresses. You should have listened to me. Children shouldn't think they know best.' He suddenly turned round to Selda. 'It's your fault! Now do you see what trouble you've caused? You always think you know best. Now look what's happened. You put ideas in their heads and they never even needed shoes!'

'But . . .' Selda stared at him in utter disbelief. How could he speak to her like that. It was so unfair.

'That's not true, Father,' cried Fatma, who also felt the

103

unjustness of what Turgut Bey had said. 'And the doctor said that ... that ...' She was unable to go on. The doctor had actually said that if Pembe had not been wearing the jeans, her leg would have been far more seriously injured.

'What's not true?' asked Turgut Bey, suspiciously.

'Nothing.' Fatma had changed back into her skirt as soon as she got in. She did not want to tell her father what she too had been wearing, so she shrugged her shoulders unhappily and let Selda take the blame.

Selda went into the white bedroom and lay down on the bed. This was all too much. She wished for the first time that they had never, ever come. She turned over and sobbed into the pillow. How could he have said that to her? Didn't her father know her at all? She felt as though her head would split open: there was so much to say and yet no one to say it to. She hated them. She really, truly did. Even stupid, hurt Pembe. Why couldn't she have looked where she was going? It had only been bad luck. Fräulein Altmann had said so. Why did her father seek to blame her? She had never imagined that one could hate one's family at the same time as one loved them. But she did. She thought of her grandmother: that old woman got so cross so often but if anyone else criticized her granddaughters, she would tear them to shreds. Selda cried and cried until her face, pressed into the pillow, was swollen and burning.

Later that night, long after Fatma had come to bed, Selda awoke. This time she shaded the bedside light carefully. She found paper and pen and began another letter to her grandmother. Only when it was finished could she sleep again.

It was a strange thing, but, after the crisis of Pembe's accident, things actually seemed to get better for the family. Pembe's leg healed well and she came home from hospital and hobbled around on crutches. She was so full of praises for the doctors and nurses in the hospital that, for a time at least, Turgut Bey stopped complaining about everything Swiss.

Several girls from the sixth class came home with Fatma to see how Pembe was and they enjoyed these visits. Even Frau Steinfeld came. She would only come in as far as the hall and then she stood there, looking all around and fluttering her strange, thick eyelashes. She had brought Pembe a present of chocolate and though she wouldn't stay and sit down, Sevgi Hanım felt very honoured by the visit and forgot that she had once 'detested' that woman. Pembe accepted all the attention as a proper tribute to her beauty and her suffering. It was the nearest Pembe had come to being a heroine and she enjoyed it.

For Selda, one of the great advantages of the accident was the reappearance of Ahmet. He had come hurrying back as soon as he heard of it and was even persuaded to stay on to supper that evening. Then, soon after Pembe came home from hospital, he seemed to patch up his quarrel with his father. There he was, one morning at breakfast, teasing his sisters, making his mother laugh and hopping around on Pembe's crutches. Turgut Bey was calmer perhaps helped by the fact that Adnan Bey was away from the town on a trip to Saudi Arabia. It was wonderful not to have to listen to his second-hand opinions on every matter under the sun.

Then, unexpectedly, Selda got the second-highest mark in Mathematics. She had hoped, but hadn't dared to expect it. There it was, however, in red biro, at the top of the test sheet and she was aware of the other children looking at her in disbelief. She felt wonderful. When she told Ahmet he was delighted and, recalling his promise to help her with her History homework, sat down with her to look at the books. As they turned the pages together she gradually realized that she actually understood almost as much German as he did. He spoke the Swiss–German dialect fluently but he admitted that his written and spoken German was not so good.

'It's not as if I need it. Not in my work,' he said, defensively.

'Which is?' She looked up at him, preparing to ask more questions.

'Restaurant work. At the moment. We have a restaurant in town.'

'What, here, in this town?'

'No, in the next village. But we've got plans, me and some friends. We plan to save a bit and rent a place and open a proper Turkish restaurant in one of the villages. It would be very popular with the Swiss, I know it would. They love eating, especially foreign food. I'd do *doner kebab* and *pide* and *baclava*, you know, all the popular things. It'd be a great success.'

'I'm sure it would.'

'Do you really think so? Father doesn't.'

'Why not?'

'You'd better ask *him*.' Ahmet spoke with sharp bitterness.

'All right, I will.'

'No. No Selda, don't mention it. It was a joke. Don't say anything.'

'Why not?'

'You'll be wasting your breath. At one time he thought it was a good idea. Then this Adnan Hoca came to the town and everything started to change for the Turkish families here. You do know what Adnan Hoca is, don't you?'

'Yes, he's an Imam.'

'He's not just that. He's a Selametçi, you know, the sort who wants a return to Islamic law, who wants to destroy all the reforms of Ataturk. He's encouraging the Turks to keep themselves separate from the Swiss. He'd like you girls to go around in head scarves! I've head him talking and he's a real reactionary. He sees everything Swiss as a threat. That's how he's persuaded Father that the restaurant idea would be a sin. You know, we'd sell alcohol and maybe cook pork sausages and he says that that would be wicked.'

'But what's that to you Ahmet? There are always cranks like

that. There certainly were in Izmir. I can remember Grand-mother getting really annoyed, saying that it would be like the bad old days, if people weren't careful. Why can't you just ignore him?'

'It's difficult in a place like this. An Imam has a lot more power in a little Swiss town. People find it difficult to stand up to him. They think that if they do, people will say that they are not true Turks. Look at what's happened to Father. Adnan Bey persuaded Father that it would be a sin to run a place that sold beer and sausages when he could be using his money for something else!' Ahmet's voice shook with fury. 'Selda do you know what Father's done?'

'No.'

'Adnan Hoca has persuaded him to give a large part of his savings for the building of a new Mosque! And it's not even here in the town. It's in the capital, Berne.'

'That's stupid. Grandmother always says that all you need to pray is a clean heart.'

'I know.'

'Has he really given his money away?' She thought of the long, long wait for the plane tickets.

'Yes, and it wasn't all *his* money. Some of it was *my* money!' Ahmet got up and opened the window and leaned out. She felt the cold air stream into the room. 'I never imagined anything like this. From the day I started work, I gave all my wages to Father. Ali and I both did. I kept a bit for myself, of course, as pocket money, but all the rest, Father put in the bank.' He shook his head bitterly. 'Do you know, Father even persuaded me to leave school and start in the factory as soon as I was able to. "Get a wage, get some Swiss francs behind you," that was what he always said. And I believed him. We both did. We worked like slaves, did double shifts, worked at the weekends when other people wanted to be with their families. We just had that month off in the summer when we used to come and see Mother and you girls. It was work,

work, work, and "You'd better do as you're told or you'll lose your job". If you lose your work permit, then you have to leave the country. How we worked, Selda. I'm not saying that Father didn't, that's not the point.'

He buried his head in his hands as if he still could not quite believe it. 'All those years, working and planning, he and Ali and I. We were planning for the family, for all of us. That's what all we Turks do here. We dream of going back with enough money to start a little business. I thought that we could start a restaurant here and after we'd made a bit more money, sell up and go back to Izmir and start a small motel. You remember Husein, the fisherman's son? His family have a bit of land by the sea which they want to sell. I even talked to them about it last time we were back. Then, just before you all arrived, I discovered quite by chance that there were hardly any savings in the bank. Father had given it to Adnan Bey for the Mosque.'

'Can't you get it back?'

'What? Take my own Father to court? Not even I could do that and anyway, how could I prove it? No, there are some things that you can't do.'

'But why would Father do a thing like that? Was he like that back in the village?'

'No. He's changed here, he's afraid.'

'Afraid? What of?'

'Adnan Hoca, but not only that. You know it makes you afraid, coming here. From the moment you step off that plane, people are ordering you about: "Do this, do that, that's not allowed." And you do as you're told. You have to. You don't understand any of it, anyway. And in the end, it becomes a habit. You do what you're told and it takes away all your courage. You become afraid, and suspicious, like Father is. You fear that you'll lose your job and be sent back. You're afraid that you've broken some law you didn't even know about. And all the time people, not everybody but a few, call you a "filthy Turk". And it hurts. And you wonder. And you get so that if someone laughs in the street you think "Are they laughing at me?"'

'That's how Father is . . .' said Selda quietly. And wondered if she was changing, too.

'And then someone like Adnan Hoca comes along. He's a Turk. He speaks your language. He says that he's come to this country just for your sake. And he starts to tell you what to do. Now, don't get me wrong, there are some really nice Imams. I've met a couple. No, it's the *man* that's rotten. So, he starts to tell you what you can think and what you can't and what you can do and what you can't. And you listen and you believe him. And you do what he says because it's a habit. And Father never was the sort of person to say "no", was he? He never wanted to stand out in a crowd.'

'I do,' said Selda shyly.

'Don't worry. You already do.'

'What about your restaurant, then? The one you have in the next village?'

'Well, I don't really "have it".' He looked away out of the window again.

'What do you do there then?'

'Well, at the moment . . . I haven't been there long, you see . . . well . . . I wash up.'

Selda stared at him. So this brother, her hero, who did not even carry his used plate from the table to the sink, stood in a kitchen somewhere and washed up other people's dirty plates. She couldn't believe it. She stared at him, letting him see her astonishment. Nothing in this country was as she had expected it to be.

'So now you know: your big brother, who planned to open a motel in Izmir, actually washes up.' His voice was harsh and cruel. 'So! It's not much good asking me about History, is it?' He came over and slammed the books shut. 'But I'll tell you something else, Selda, I'm not letting him get his hands on these wages. Not a franc of it. And, if Adnan Hoca was starving, I wouldn't throw him the scraps from the plates!'

He spoke so wildly that Selda wished that she had never started the conversation. She opened her Maths books, pretending to study and shivered in the cold draught that still blew in through the window. It was early on Sunday morning. Selda had got up to study while the house was quiet and Ahmet would soon go to work. She looked at the numbers on the page and they danced mockingly. She had wanted to ask him about the two Turks, but the moment had gone. Tomorrow, perhaps.

'Selda!' Suddenly he called her, and his voice was kind again. 'Selda, come and look!' She went to his side and stood very close.

'Look. It's snowing!'

They smiled at each other and he stretched out his arm trying to catch one of the dancing snowflakes for her.

She looked out and saw the morning sky very low and very grey and there, speckled in it like dust, floated tiny, darker flecks. It didn't even seem extra cold. She too reached out and caught one and then another on the palm of her hand.

'Is that all?' she asked, disappointed.

'Don't be so impatient. You must wait.' He seemed to have recovered some of his good temper. 'Look at the sky on the other side of the lake.'

He was right. The air was still and damp and the flakes by the open window still fluttered and flickered aimlessly, but on the far shore of the lake, the upper ridges were already white. The lower fields were bathed in a pale glow that seemed to be filtering down from the low-pressing, golden-edged clouds. While the two of them watched, more and more flakes swirled more and more closely. The light behind the distant ridges faded. The snow began to fall more thickly. Endlessly, closely, it fell and fell and, as Ahmet and Selda watched, a white line began to form slowly, then more and more thickly along the balcony rail. It was as though an unseen hand brushed to and fro and painted layer upon layer of glistening, perfect white. It reminded her of something, this standing with Ahmet and watching. Then she remembered. Years ago, back in the village, he had taken her to see the first chicks tapping and beating their way out of the shell. She was shy to remind him now so instead she held on to his arm very tightly and she leaned out to capture more frozen crystals of snow.

It snowed all that morning. Ahmet went off to work and Selda, watching from the balcony, saw the snow quickly cover his footprints. The family got up. The girls crowded together at the window. Pembe shivered and was hopeful that they might be snowed in and not able to get to school the next morning. Ali laughed at her and said that all the pavements would be cleared in a few hours. They sat down to a late breakfast in an atmosphere of excited anticipation. They could hear the calling voices of children already out on the streets, playing. Fatma kept jumping up to see how deep the snow on the balcony was.

'Why do you want to know?' asked Ali.

'For the skiing. Ramona says that *everybody* goes skiing in winter.'

'Everybody may,' said Turgut Bey, looking at her severely, 'But *you're* not. I've had quite enough accidents, thank you.'

Fatma kept quiet, but did not agree. The snow fell more thickly. Selda could not help herself: she fetched a handful in from the balcony. This time it didn't vanish. She squeezed it into a hard lump and then the girls passed it from hand to hand, gasping at the cold. When nobody was looking, Selda tasted it quickly, with the tip of her tongue.

Even Sevgi Hanım marvelled at the snow. As she washed up she kept on pausing to stare out of the window. Selda joined her and they saw the dark fir trees patched with white and the curve of gulls which wheeled and called as they turned inland from the lake, and they both remembered the walk.

'Do you think those rabbits will get cold?' asked Selda. She wondered if they were left outside and whether the snow blew into their cages. She imagined them, trapped behind the bars, unable to scamper around and get warm. Then she thought of the fortune teller's rabbit and she wondered what happened to that in the winter winds that swept in off the Bosphorous. And the man himself, where did he go, in the winter?

Suddenly, desperately she wanted to go out and see that the rabbits in front of the barn were all right. Sevgi Hanım had gone out on to the balcony. She was supposed to be cleaning Turgut Bey's shoes, but really she stood there with a shoe on one hand and the brush poised in the other and her eyes fixed on the falling snow, as enchanted as any child. Selda mentioned the rabbits and this time Sevgi Hanım didn't scoff.

'You go, dear,' she said. 'Go with Fatma.' She inclined her head to where Turgut Bey sat in his chair in front of the television. 'You two run along and get a breath of fresh air. It does look lovely out there.'

It did. The sun had come out now and it was wonderful: a white world with ridiculous patches of summer blue breaking out in the sky above. The sun shone with increasing brilliance and the ribbon of snow on the rail blazed.

'You could come too,' encouraged Selda. She knew that her mother wanted to.

'Another time dear, I've got things to do.' It wasn't true. The little flat was as neat and tidy as a prison cell. For Sevgi Hanım who had once run a shop and a small-holding and raised five children, a small box on the fifth floor was not really a challenge.

When Fatma and Selda stepped out into the snow they looked back up and saw their mother still standing on the balcony. She waved the unpolished shoe to them and they waved back.

It seemed that half the village had come out on that Sunday morning to enjoy the snow. What was more surprising was

112

that they were all dressed up. They must have been waiting, ready for the snow. It looked as though there was a uniform: mittens and knitted hats, thick padded snow-boots and then colourful, nylon suits such as small children wear. There they were, men, women and children, dressed up like toddlers! They were even doing special things: neighbours cleared the snow from their drives with big, long-handled shovels which Selda decided were kept just for the snow. Several parents were already out pulling their children on sledges and one small child sat in a push chair that had been fastened on to runners. Selda actually saw a couple of dogs firmly buttoned into little jackets.

Within five minutes of leaving the house, Selda and Fatma, who wore everyday skirts and shoes, felt their toes begin to freeze. Both kept quiet for it was worth it: the world was transformed. Children were out building snow castles with red, plastic spades and their voices carried clearly and happily in the quietness. Everybody out on the street smiled at them or greeted them. The air itself tasted different and sweeter. As they approached the path which led between the fields, Selda turned and looked back at the mountain. Its peaks were now entirely covered with snow, but, magically, they were not white.

'Look!' She caught Fatma's arm and pointed.

'At what?'

'At the mountain!'

'What about it?'

'It's changed colour, look. On that side it's almost blue, but there, where the sun shines, it's gold and on that point, the right one, it's pink.'

'Pink?' Fatma squinted into the sun, but could only see the snow lying thickly on the peaks, shaded and shadowed, maybe, but still white. Selda, narrowing her eyes against the dazzle, had spent so many hours staring at those summits, that now she could see where the low, round, winter sun had stained the mountainside. It was coloured like a late, unopened winter rose. To her, whatever other people might say, it was magical, a transformation.

'What's that smell?' Fatma sniffed loudly and looked around her and then gave a little scream. 'Pigs! Ooh, how horrible!'

Selda laughed. The pigs had already churned up the snow by the fence. Now, a couple of massive, solemn sows stood ankle deep in the slush and watched the passers-by hopefully. Other pigs were rooting around at the base of a snow-covered pile in the distance. A man, who had his back to them, balanced on top of the pile and shovelled off the snow. He worked quickly, unclearing a patch and then bending down to toss something to the pigs who pushed and shoved and grunted with pleasure. He bent and straightened and bent again, with a swift, mechanical movement. He must have been working for some time and got too hot, because a jacket was hanging from the lower branches of the apple tree.

The girls, who were feeling very cold, stamped their feet and swung their arms and went on towards the rabbits. Selda was delighted to see that they all looked fine. She hurried up to the cages and poked her fingers through the bars, trying to stroke them.

'Do they bite?' asked Fatma, nervously.

'No. Look what I've brought them.' Selda gave her sister some of the dry bread which she had put in her pocket. The little animals pressed their quivering noses up against the wire as the girls began to feed them. Selda wished to be fair: to give a piece to each and to miss none out. It was not easy. In the more-crowded cages there was often one who pushed to the front while another crouched timidly at the back. Once or twice she looked nervously towards the farmhouse window, but this time nobody banged.

One brown rabbit stood right up against the wires. He was smaller than the rest and had the most beautiful eyes she had ever seen. One of his tiny paws, which was white underneath, came through the wire as though he were reaching out to her. She stroked him with two fingers and he did not pull away and she remembered the fortune teller's rabbit in Istanbul. They could have been brothers.

'They don't look cold, do they?' said Fatma. To be honest, they didn't. Someone had recently put in thick, fresh straw and many of the feeding dishes still held uneaten slices of carrot and oats and corn. Several were nibbling on bundles of spinach and cabbage that looked newly cut.

Selda had to admit that even animals were well looked after in Switzerland. Whoever owned these rabbits spent time and money on them. She was impressed. She could remember families both in the village and in Izmir, who endured their winters shivering with cold in rotten, dirty hovels which you could hardly call houses. The children from such families were always hungry and never left their food unfinished.

'I wonder why they have so many,' mused Fatma.

'I expect they love them. They must treat them like part of the family, like they do their cats and dogs. Haven't you seen all those shelves and shelves of pet food in the supermarket?'

'Yes. And those other things, toys and leads and dishes and even chocolate for dogs. Ramona showed that to me.' Fatma laughed. 'Do you know what I saw last week? It was that very frosty morning, when all the puddles froze. Well, I saw an old lady with a little dog and that dog had boots on. Really! It had a checked jacket and boots to match, four of them. But it still shivered, poor little thing. I expect its paws ached.'

'Like mine,' said Selda and tried to stamp some feeling back into her feet.

Looking up from the cages they were aware of someone trying to attract their attention. A group of people on the upper field was waving and calling.

'Fa-t-ma! Fa-t-ma!'

'Whoever is it?'

'It must be somebody from school.' It was. Ramona, dressed from head to toe in purple, was shouting to them as she flew down the slope on a bright red sledge.

'Fatma! Come and have a go!.

'I couldn't. I don't know how!'

'Oh, come on, I'll show you, come on!'

'No . . . really . . .' answered Fatma as she scrambled up the bank and through the wire fence.

Selda, uninvited, stayed by the rabbits and watched her sister struggle up to the top of the field. There, with much laughing and protesting, she was persuaded on to the back of the sledge behind Ramona. Several people pushed off together and some way down the field two sledges collided and their riders were thrown off in a heap. One was Fatma. She picked herself up, shrieking with laughter, brushed the snow from her hair and raced back up the field with the sledge jerking and bouncing behind her. Selda watched as she began to come down again. It was cold, waiting. Her feet had begun to ache and throb with the cold and, looking for shelter, she stepped through the half-open door of the barn. It was definitely warmer in there. She jumped from foot to foot and then realized that she was not alone. There were other animals in there in the half dark. She remembered the atmosphere from far-off childish days. There was the smell of warm, animal fur, of urine trampled into straw and of seeds and corn stored and dried. All around her was the restless movement of creatures held in captivity.

On her left-hand side she made out more rabbit cages, some occupied and some not. On her right, bales of straw were stacked higher than a man stood. Farm machinery was stored there as well and, at the end, out of sight, something moved and stamped inside a boarded-off stall.

She knew that she should not go in alone and look, but it was so much warmer in the barn and she was so curious. And had not Fatma run off to join the others without giving her a backward glance? Looking up she saw windows set in the high, pointed roof, but they were covered with a layer of snow, so that the barn was as gloomy as a high cave. She noticed a pitch fork, which someone had left thrust into a broken-up bale, as though they meant to return to it. The creature behind the boarded stall stamped and scraped at the concrete floor. Surely it was a goat. She knew that sound, that irritable scraping. Her mother had kept a bad-tempered white nanny goat back in the village. She had been a difficult animal, unwilling to let down her milk. She had smelt too, just like this animal.

Selda took a step further into the barn. She would just peep over the planks then hurry back to Fatma and they would run home. They had already been out too long. They'd have to be quick . . .   'Hey!' The door at the far end of the barn opened suddenly. Somebody, a man, was outlined there, against the doorway. He was bent under a sack, but stopped, steadying himself under the weight, staring at her.

He had frightened her so much that she thought she would faint. She thought for a second that she was going to fall down there, amongst the trampled straw. The smell of the goat stifled her and made her sick. If she could only have drawn one deep, fresh breath, then she could have escaped and run out into the clean, white, winter snow, but she couldn't.

And he muttered, breathless under the weight of the sack:

'You! What are *you* doing here?'

Then she realized that he had spoken in Turkish.

'Me? I . . . I . . . I came with my sister. I came to look at the rabbits . . . '

He swung the sack down awkwardly and she heard him gasp at the weight of it. Then he closed the door behind him and rammed the bolt home.

'My sister's waiting . . .' she said, wishing Fatma was there with her.

'Don't go. Please.' He almost moved towards her, but didn't.

'I must go. I only wanted to look at the rabbits . . . '

It was the same boy. She had recognized him instantly. He walked very slowly, knocking dust and bits of straw from his hair and shoulders. It was the same boy in the same red checked shirt.

'I know you,' he said. 'Really I do. You're Ahmet's sister, aren't you? You must be Selda. He told us about you. He told my father and me that he had three sisters, and that you were coming here. I guessed it was you from the very first time I saw you . . . '

'In the supermarket?'

'No. No it was on the road near your flat. Don't you remember?'

'That was *you* then?'

'Yes. I'd seen you running. I saw you start to run across.'

> 'Dogs are fast
> And men may be faster,
> But watch where you run,
> Or you'll run to disaster.'

It was stupid to say it, but she did, *hating* herself.

'It's true,' he said. 'We shouldn't run, really. Well, sometimes.' And he smiled at her.

The goat, which she could see now, butted its head against the planks and the claws of a rabbit rang on the wires and she knew that she ought to go, but instead she put her hand over the stall to try and stroke the goat.

'I've got sisters too. Back in the south. Near Alanya.' He spoke very quickly, too quickly, and he glanced back over his shoulder although the door was bolted. 'My sister, Gül, she must be about your age. She's started secondary school.'

'And you?' She had not meant to ask. He was not so old, she was sure, certainly not as old as Ali and Ahmet.

'Me? Oh, I'm working now. I'm farming . . . '

'Ferhat!' Somebody called from the other side of the bolted door. They looked at each other. Somebody rattled it and tried the lock, then shouted: 'For the love of God, open this door, will you?'

'That's my father. I have to go.'

'Yes. I must go too. My sister will be waiting. She'll worry.'

'Don't tell her.'

'Tell her what?'

'Don't tell her that you spoke to me. Don't tell her that you even saw me. Don't tell anyone, please.' The door rattled again.

'Why not?'

'Please Selda, please.' He went to open the door, but did not move the bolt and was waiting for her answer.

'I won't tell anyone,' she said.

She didn't want to anyway. Now she just wanted to get away. As she ran past the rabbit cages she heard him draw back the bolt and push open the creaking door and then she was free to step out into the dazzling snow and be dazzled by its brightness. She shaded her eyes and saw Fatma and Ramona coming down the slope yet again. They were shouting with pleasure and their hair streamed out behind them as they skimmed over the icy white slope.

Seven

Several days after the visit to the barn, Selda was crouching close to the shaded light and re-reading what she had written. Pembe and Fatma slept peacefully beneath their pink coverlets, like two fairy princesses.

My dearest Grandmother,
  It has snowed on and off for most of the week. Watching the snow is like watching a film and I do so wish that you were here to see it with me. Each morning, when I draw the curtains back, there is a new scene outside. Each morning the snow has hidden something else. Although it is so cold here, both our house and the school are beautifully warm. You won't believe this, but when it's not actually snowing, the sun shines quite brightly. We thought that the school might close here, after the heavy snowfall, like the schools do in Turkey, but it's not like that here. Life goes on with hardly a change. Early in the morning, while it's still dark, workmen are out, clearing the roads and pavements. We walk to school along a cleared path, with the snow banked up high on either side. Father has bought us all a pair of 'moon-boots'. You'd laugh if you could see us. We look like clowns at the moment. We've got these giant feet and then whoolly hats and clothes and scarves. When I'm out in the snow, you can only recognize me by my red nose.
  Sometimes, Grandmother, I think that I'll wake up and find that this is all a dream, and that we were just playing at being here. It's difficult to explain but I'm

sure that you understand: the town still doesn't seem to be part of the real world. It's too pretty and too perfect. Nowadays, I wonder what I will find underneath, after the snow has melted.

You'll be glad to hear that we are all well. Pembe does not need her crutches any more, but the doctors told her that she must be careful with her knee. She has to do special exercises. Fatma goes out with friends every day after school. She is learning to sledge. Everything is like that in Switzerland, Grandmother. You don't just 'do' things. You have to learn to do them 'properly'. Even sledging! Fatma would like to learn to ski, but I don't think she'll be able to. None of the Turks here ski. Pembe is getting on so well in school and she said to tell you that she is really happy. She has a lot of friends, especially since the accident. As for myself . . .

That was as far as she had got with the letter. She chewed the end of her pen and wondered what exactly to say about herself. Pembe and Fatma breathed so quietly under their covers. She opened her pencil case and felt carefully down between the pens and colours. She did not want to make a noise and disturb them. Her fingers felt the roll of black paper. She drew it out. In the dim glow she could hardly make out any of the words written so faintly on the black. It didn't matter, because she knew them by heart:

> Plant pretty roses in your garden,
> Plant sweet herbs by your door,
> But bury secrets in your heart
> And keep them safe for evermore.

She read the last line of her letter again: 'As for myself . . .' Should she tell her grandmother about Ferhat? No, not yet. She would tell her about school instead. There was more to write, anyway, for school was still a struggle. Sometimes Selda's head ached with the pain of concentration. Now, although she often understood the questions, she still could not answer all of them. She did not have the German words to express herself. She regretted that she still did not have the dictionary. In Maths, things went better, but it was all a struggle. Nevertheless, she knew that slowly, slowly, she was climbing up the slope. She also now had some idea of where she was climbing to. It was to the high school in Zurich. Fräulein Altmann had suggested it. She had been so surprised by Selda's progress that she had explained to her that in the sixth year, a few of her outstanding pupils would sit an examination to get a place in this best school. She had suggested that Selda might attempt this and now Selda was determined to do so. She hadn't talked about it at home because she knew they would object. Her grandmother, in contrast, might grumble, but really she would be very, very proud.

That was what she would do: she would tell her grandmother about these plans and about Giselle. It had been the oddest of things. Giselle had been really nice about Pembe's accident, asking how she was, and once offering to carry books when Pembe was on crutches. Little by little, they had got talking. They were not real friends, naturally. Just sometimes they walked around together at break-time. Fräulein Altman had encouraged it, making them work together in pairs. Giselle was very good at German, but Selda was better at Maths. Giselle was a prickly, difficult person, but secretly Selda had to admit that she was more fun than poor Demet had been. Poor Demet had not had an original idea in her head, and had always agreed with whatever Selda had said. It had got boring, after a time.

'As for myself, I've made a sort of friend at school. Her name is Giselle and she is Swiss . . .' It was the best thing to do to write of Giselle and school. Her meeting with Ferhat joined the growing list of things that she must bury deeply in her heart. Otherwise, day by day and week by week, she had been writing continuously to her grandmother. It had become a habit. She wrote to the old woman just as she might have written in a diary.

One day, when she was back in Izmir, when none of the family was around, when the cats slept in the shade of the jasmine root and the few people who were out on the hot street walked very, very slowly, then, she would re-read these letters. Perhaps her grandmother would be sitting on the balcony, watching the street, her rough old hands busy shelling red beans. She would pretend not to be interested, but really, she would be listening. Her fingers would move more slowly when Selda read out an interesting part. Selda thought that on this second reading, she could alter bits that she did not like. She could leave out whole sentences and her grandmother would never know. Or would she? The old woman was no fool. She did understand things, which, after all, was why Selda had written to her. It was difficult to admit it, but Selda knew that she owed her grandmother a great deal. Sometimes she thought that she could not have struggled on in school if she had not been able to come back and write all about it. But she wouldn't write about Ferhat. Not yet. It was not as if there were anything to say . . .

All that week after school, groups of children went up to the field to sledge. Selda learnt from Fatma that it was an 'official' sledge run: cars were not allowed up there in the winter. The Swiss and their children slid on the snow with the same seriousness that they expended on everything. They practised until they were perfect. The boys shot down head-first on small, high sledges with metal runners. The girls preferred to sit one behind the other, with their legs stuck out and flailing like beetles, then down they went, shrieking and laughing. Although Fatma had no sledge of her own, she went up regularly with a group of girls from the sixth class. Selda, still uninvited, had to go too. This was at her mother's request. It was called 'keeping Fatma company'. Selda knew,

123

of course, that Fatma would much rather have been alone, but she still went. She stayed down by the rabbits and watched her sister go on up the hillside. Most afternoons that week, at about four thirty, Ferhat came into the barn to feed the rabbits and the goats. When this was done they walked up and down together and looked into the cages and talked. She did not like to follow him too closely. Instead, she lingered in front of the rows of barred door, putting her fingers through the wires, and stroking now this one, now another and she listened to his story of this other world. He talked and talked and talked as though he had been silent for too long.

He had been in Switzerland for nearly three years and during all that time had never been back to see his mother and younger brothers and sister. He was here just with his father.

'Perhaps you'll go back this summer,' she had said once and paused in front of a big, white rabbit which looked at her with gentle, dark red eyes. She wondered briefly if the world looked different, with eyes like that.

'I can't go this summer,' he said, 'nor the next. Or ever.'

'Why not?' She could not have waited three years. 'I know it's expensive, the plane tickets and things, but some people go by coach, don't they? Ahmet told me. Three years is a long time.'

'It isn't the cost, really.' He looked about him. He was an anxious person, she could tell. He was always looking back over his shoulder, always restless as though expecting somebody to shout at him. It was almost as though he were ready to run off. She secretly wondered if his father was cruel to him, beat him, perhaps. You did hear of such things. Her own father was all blustering bad temper, but you did read in papers of men who beat their children dreadfully.

'My father managed to come back every summer,' she said. 'Doesn't the farm close down for a month? He said that

124

all the foreign workers went home for that month. Why don't you?'

'We're different, my father and I . . .' He fiddled with the catch on a cage.

'Why? How different?'

'We're . . . You won't tell anyone, will you?'

She shook her head.

'We're in Switzerland illegally. Nobody knows we're here. We're not like you. We don't have permission to be here. If the Swiss police knew that we were here they would send us back. And we can't go back, ever. If we don't work here and send back money, the whole family back in Alanya would starve. I've got a younger sister there, the one who is in secondary school now, the one who's a bit like you, and two younger brothers, and there's my mother and her parents and an aunt who is a cripple and so never married. We look after them all. You know what it's like there. There's no work and we don't have any land. My father was a primary school teacher. You know what that means.' Selda did. One teacher's salary in Turkey would let a family like that quietly starve.

'Then there's my little brother's illness. He has to have this medicine from abroad all the time and we just couldn't afford to buy it there. That's when my father decided to come. I was thirteen then, so he thought that I could work too. A friend of my father got us to Italy on tourist passports and we worked there in a summer café, illegally. When we had saved up enough money to pay them, somebody guided us secretly over the border into Switzerland and then helped us to find work here. We've been here ever since, illegally. That's why we work with pigs. It's dirty, hard work and the Swiss won't do it. They always pay foreigners to do it. The Turks who have work permits won't touch it either, so it's always people like us. We can't refuse. I'm not complaining not really. Old Bauer, the farmer, is not a bad man. He was desperate for help. He's almost a cripple himself now, and can't manage

125

alone. He loves his animals. Somebody fixed the job for us and we came up secretly from the south, travelling at night through the mountains, and we've been here ever since. He's happy with us and needs us, so he doesn't tell the police, of course. Nobody else knows. We're safe for the moment. So long as nobody tells.' He looked at her then.' Only you and your brother know.'

'But . . .?'

'But what?' His face changed and she saw that hostile, defiant expression that she had seen at the supermarket. 'But what?' he repeated.

'But some people must know . . .' She didn't really want to say it. She didn't want to upset him, but it was such an awful, impossible story that she found herself trying to make it less impossible.

'Who knows?' His voice was anxious.

'Well, you say that Ahmet knows and I know. So other people must have seen you too. I mean, I saw you.'

'When? At the supermarket?'

'Not only. It was one evening, outside our flat. I wasn't spying or anything, honestly. I was on the balcony and I saw Ahmet go across the road and join you and when you walked under the lamp, I recognized you. You went up the road to the forest. So, what if somebody else had seen you?'

'Oh, just seeing, is all right. But knowing us would be different. That's why we never speak in the town, so people won't know we're Turkish and start asking questions. To the Swiss, we're just another couple of foreign workers. And Ahmet is one of us.'

'How's that?'

'Didn't he tell you? He's one of a group of people who help the illegal immigrants here.'

'You mean that there are other people like you then?' It was hard to believe. Here in Switzerland she had thought that everything was done so carefully and properly.

'Other people like us?' He laughed. 'There must be thousands. And we're all the same. We have no future in our own countries and other countries don't want us, so we have to steal in secretly. We're all the same. We all say that we'll just stay for a little while. We say that we'll save a bit and then we'll go to the police. We'll ask to be given a permit. Perhaps the police will make a bit of a fuss, but, if you've been a good worker and your employer needs you, then you hope that they'll let you stay. But it doesn't work out like that. You wait a bit. You start to send money home. You wait a bit longer. You hear from home about how grateful they are, how they need the money. You wait. Winter's coming. You know they need to buy some wood to burn. You think: "I'll wait till spring, just in case." Then the fear starts. You think: "What if they send me back?" So you decide that you'll do another year. Then it will be different. And it is. You get more afraid. You can't take the risk. You're caught.'

'But . . . '

'But what . . .?'

'But how long will you stay?'

'Don't ask me, Selda. I don't even let myself think about that question.'

'But?'

'Please, Selda. Don't. Just tell me what you would do. Suppose it was your little brother who needed the medicine, your grandparents with no income, your sister with no dowry?'

'I'd . . . I'd . . .' And she would, if she were brave enough.

'You see. You'd do the same. Do you know, I've met men who have been here for fifteen years. They've educated their children. Sent them to university even. Their parents have died and their children have been ill and they never went back. There's a man in the next village like that. He's got two grandchildren he's never even seen. He just has photos. He always says: "Next year, if God is willing," and do you know,

I don't think he really wants to go now. It's been too long. He's afraid to return as well as to stay . . . '

'But you can't do this for ever, can you?'

'Why not? If that man can, I can.' But he didn't look into her face. He kicked at the loose board on the goat's stall.

Selda had no answer either. She scuffed the toe of her new, white moon-boot amongst the straw on the barn floor and wished that she had not been wearing such unnecessarily extravagant things. She wished that she had never come into the barn and never ever seen Ferhat. But most of all she wished that she had not heard his story. She had not known that people could be trapped here, as surely as the rabbits were trapped in the cages. It hurt, knowing, and it made her feel so helpless. It made her regret coming to Switzerland. She should have stayed there, in Izmir, watching the cats scratch and skirmish over the fish heads, watching her mother and grandmother arguing over who had left the tap dripping, and who had used up the last match and not bought any more. She had not liked those battles, but at least she had known what most of them were about. And at least most of them had ended. Here, she had discovered that beneath the dazzling surface, there were hidden things that you had not even dreamt of when you first looked upon the perfect whiteness. It was as though the distant mountain peak had been torn away to reveal a rotten core.

She trailed the sledgers home and thought constantly of him, this stranger who had shouted out '*dur!*' He had saved her from a certain accident and she knew that she owned him something. It was not that she liked him particularly. After all, she didn't know him and was not likely to, under the circumstances. What was he to her? But she went back to the barn. Each afternoon, as soon as Fatma started to pull on her boots and gloves, Selda did the same.

The next time she and Ferhat walked up and down the barn together he did not mention his life in Switzerland. It was as though he knew that she had been upset. She too took care not to question him. They talked about Turkey instead and about all the things that they had both done as children. They laughed about primary school, about how they both had hated the stiff, white collars that had scratched their necks. They remembered the strictness of the teachers and the rustle of the dark blue and red waxed paper with which they had covered their books. Though he had grown up in the south and she in the west, they had much in common. They talked of the festivals and of the street sellers and the dancing bears. Ferhat told her that nowadays the gypsies took the bears down on to the beaches to perform for tourists. She told him about her grandmother's love and hate for such things. They talked of the seasons and of the endlessly hot summers and of the July afternoons that passed so unbelievably slowly, when it was too hot to play out in the sun. Sometimes he spoke of his family and though he never complained about his long separation from them, it lay there between them like a wound. She was glad to be distracted by the rabbits and paused in front of the cage in which 'Brownie', her favourite, was kept.

'You're just like Gül, my sister. She likes animals. When she was little, she was always bringing home baby kittens, tiny, half-starved things, covered in fleas and filth. My mother would get angry and warn her that she'd catch things, but, she still did it.' He smiled to himself and shook his head and then said, half under his breath: 'Maybe she still does.' And that was all.

Two weeks later, when the sledgers had worn the snow away so that the metal runners sparked on the bared stones and when the milder weather saw the pigs out rooting under the apple tree, Fatma remarked that as the season for sledging was over she did not want to go out there any more. Selda looked out at the yellowed winter grass and found herself telling her mother that one of the rabbits, who had got to know her and was really tame, would now miss her if she didn't go and visit it. She must, she said, go and see if it was all right. It was a shy rabbit, whom the others would push to the back. She offered to take some of their stale bread and feed it to the animals. In this way, she reminded her mother, she could help them avoid the wickedness of putting useful bread in the rubbish bin. It was something Sevgi Hanım felt strongly about.

Ridiculously, the 'rubbish bins' were one of the few things about which the family held a united opinion. These bins, almost as big as a small car and running on four black rubber wheels, stood in front of every house and flat. When opened they revealed, not only rubbish, but the most incredible surprises. When Selda had raised the lid of theirs, she had seen perfectly good shoes and clothes, saucepans that were slightly chipped, frying pans with scorched handles, flowerpots and rolls of old carpet, and all manner of treasures laid carefully amongst the plastic bags of rubbish. Other people had thrown out a bedside lamp and several small pieces of furniture that were still quite good. In their very first week the girls had watched with horror as the dust cart slowly crushed up what appeared to be a set of coffee tables. When they told their father, he shook his head and shrugged and said: 'That's the way it is here. It's a rich country. Even Swiss rubbish is better than ours.'

The girls all secretly planned to rescue some of the good things and use them, but as yet they had not dared to. Sevgi Hanım particularly hated throwing out bread. She had been a careful housekeeper all her life and anyway it was considered to be a sin to waste food that others could use. Bread was too precious to be wasted. In Izmir they had put the dry bread aside for the milkman, everyone did. At the end of his round the milk cart would often be piled high with polythene bags of food which could be given to the cows. Her grandmother had always done the same: pieces of pie or left-over cake were set on clean newspaper and left out on the wall. It was really for the children from the shanty town, if the cats did not get it first. It was the same with clothes. Her grandmother grumbled at the beggars at the door but she never sent them away empty handed. It seemed to be different here in Switzerland. All the children were tall and straight and strong and there were no old men with their feet wrapped in rags, going through the rubbish bins. Nobody seemed to be hungry, but it still felt wrong to throw out good food. Sevgi Hanım was therefore very pleased when Selda said that she would take the stale bread to the rabbits.

'Yes, that's a good idea,' she said, 'we can go together.' It was a Wednesday, which meant that there was no afternoon school and Turgut Bey was still at the factory.

'But . . .' Selda wanted to tell her mother that she could quite easily go alone, it wasn't far away. 'Anyway, you said that you would go shopping with Pembe and Fatma. That'll be more fun.'

'Oh no,' said Fatma instantly, 'we'll be fine. You go with Selda.'

'See Mother,' smiled Pembe, innocently, 'nobody is a nuisance today. You can have a nice, quiet afternoon, all to yourself.'

There was a moment's silence in the room.

'I see,' said Sevgi Hanım, in a different voice, 'yes, I do see, Pembe.' She got up and went round the room straightening this and that. 'A nice, quiet afternoon. All by myself. I am lucky, aren't I?'

She went into the kitchen where everything too was in perfect order. Then they heard her go into the bedroom. The door shut and, looking at each other guiltily, the girls thought they heard her beginning to cry.

'You shouldn't have said that!' accused Fatma.

'Me?' cried Pembe. 'I didn't say anything. We all said the same. I didn't mean anything bad.' And she jumped up and, ran into her mother and the two of them must have started to cry together.

Selda grabbed her anorak and the bag of bread and escaped before anything else could be said. She ran down the steps and over the road and up the street. The snow now remained only in the shady hollows, but it was very cold again. Ice had formed at the edges of puddles along the footpaths. It shattered with a shrill sound when she stamped on it. She saw that the mud in the pigs field was set in pale, hoary ridges. She ran quickly. She wasn't going to stay long. She might even get back before the girls set out. She would just hastily poke the bread through the wires and be off. That was all. Ferhat would still be at work, somewhere out on the farm. If she got back in time she'd even go shopping with her mother, to make up. Of course, she would have to check on Brownie, her special rabbit. If she saw Ferhat in the fields, well, she could wave, nothing more. She ran faster. She would just stroke Brownie, to keep him tame, then she would hurry home. She did not have anything special to say to Ferhat, anyway. She was only thinking of the rabbits.

This afternoon, there was no one in sight. Now there were no sledges on the field above. No one was out walking on such a chill, sunless afternoon. It was quiet, very very quiet. Her own gasps of breath were loud as she ran. There were no birds calling in the hedgerows and no yachts cutting the grey waters of the lake below. The mountain peaks were once again hidden in low cloud and the forest beyond was dark and still and thick. She almost wished that she had not come. Maybe she would not go into the barn at all. Maybe this time, she would leave the bag outside the barn door and run back. Ferhat would see it and understand. He would feed Brownie. He knew that it was her favourite. Last week he had taken it out of the cage for her and offered to let her hold it, but she had not dared, not then. Next week, perhaps.

Then she stopped running. The rows of cages outside the barn were empty. Their doors were propped open. She moved from one to the other, now bending down, now stretching up, looking in all of them. Her heart pounded. They were all empty and had been swept out too. There were the feeding bowls, scrubbed clean and left in a pile, so it could not have been a fox or anything horrid like that. Or could it? She shivered. She had run out of the house without her scarf and gloves and now her ears were beginning to ache. It was bitterly cold. And that must be it: they must have moved the rabbits into the barn because of the weather. It was just what she always said. People here in Switzerland looked after their animals as well as other countries looked after their citizens. After all, the old farmer must be very fond of his rabbits, to keep so many. Ferhat had said he was. Of course, that was it. He didn't want them to catch cold.

The barn door stood ajar. That was where the rabbits would be. But she had to know, to be sure. She stepped inside. There was something moving in there. From the dark, warm interior, she heard the sound of claws on wire. So the rabbits were there. But something was different. Something smelt different. She half recognized it from far back, from long before Izmir days. It was a warm sickly smell, like salt and sugar mixed and dampened and left. She stepped further into the barn, blinking in the darkness.

The far door was half open and someone was working there. Then, in the gloom, she saw the yellow eyes of the farm cats. They were crouched in the shadows and they too watched the worker. She knew that it was Ferhat's father. She recognized that scarf. As she watched, he straightened up and flung something out of the barn door and the cats leapt after it, mewing and shrieking. Then he took something else from the crate on the ground and laid it on the bench and she saw the knife flash as he cut down and she heard the pulled skin part.

She understood what he was doing. And then she was overwhelmed. She was so blinded by her tears, so completely plunged in misery, that she had walked back as far as the pig's field before she was aware of what she had done. And she was still clutching the wretched bag of bread. She leant over the gate, crying hopelessly, helplessly, feeling her face get red and swollen. She felt again like very little children do when they know that they have been wronged and something that they have dreamed of has been denied them. It was just like imagining a wonderful birthday for oneself and then, everything going wrong, and nothing being special at all. Yet it was partly her fault. How could she have been so stupid? What was so different about those rabbits? Why had she imagined that they were 'pets'? It wasn't as if she didn't know about things like that. She'd grown up seeing chickens killed and plucked and gutted. She'd helped. They all had. She'd been interested, to be honest, watching the steaming coils of gut and all those tiny, tiny eggs as pale as bunches of unripened grapes. At New Year she had fed the turkey by hand and then eaten its flesh and only felt the meerest pang. It was the same with the lambs which they had bought in the spring and fattened up for the sacrifice at Korban. She had watched it all. She had seen the sharpened knife at the throat and later carried the plates of meat around to the neighbours.

Why then was this so different? Why was she so upset this time? Was it just that she had not expected it in this picture-postcard world, where dogs wore boots and cats were fed on chocolate treats and supermarkets sold special food for wild birds? Or was it that she was older now? Was this what being grown-up was like? Did other people feel such anger and sadness and helplessness, all at once? She thought of her grandmother. Had she felt like this as she stamped around the house? And her father and Ahmet? Did they feel trapped? And Ferhat?

She wiped her eyes and looked briefly over the fields, but there was no sign of him. Was he keeping out of sight on purpose? Had he known that the rabbits were to be slaughtered? And why, then, had he not told her? Why had he let her think that they were pets? Why had he offered to let her feed Brownie? Why had he let her get fond of the animal? Why hadn't he warned her? He should have. He'd warned her once. He should have done it again. He had tricked her. She found a handkerchief and blew her nose and pushed her hair out of her eyes.

She wouldn't go back and see him again. Not ever. After all, who was he, that she should worry about him? He was obviously well able to take care of himself. He'd managed all right for the last three years. And what could she do anyway? Nothing. That was the truth of it. Nothing at all. She began to tip the bread out on to the frozen mud. At least the pigs could have a treat. She couldn't see what was so unclean about pigs anyway. Pigs, rabbits, sheep, it was all the same. Maybe the Swiss were right. She looked down at the ground and saw that she had made a dreadful mess . . . She glanced guiltily around her, but luckily no one was about to see the litter that she had thrown down. The Swiss were certainly right about that: they kept everywhere so beautiful. Even her mother had admitted that the streets were so clean that you hardly needed to take your shoes off when you came into the house. She wished that she had not tipped the bread out. No wonder children at school whispered 'dirty Turk' behind her back. Perhaps she deserved it.

She sniffed back the last tears and began to walk home briskly. On the way she rammed the empty bag into a litter bin. That was the proper thing to do. It was the only thing to do. If you were going to live here, you had to live by the Swiss rules. People like Ferhat just shouldn't have come. She wasn't going to worry about him a moment longer. She wasn't going to worry about anything that she couldn't help. She was just going to look after herself.

The first thing she was going to do was to ask Ahmet to give her the fifteen francs so that she could finally go down and get the dictionary. Then, at least, that problem would be solved.

She was going to learn perfect German, and she was going to be 'more Swiss'. She had learnt from Giselle that there was a public library in the town and that, on their free Wednesday afternoons, many of the Swiss children went there. She would go too. Perhaps Pembe was right. One needed to become Swiss. If you didn't, you ended up like Ferhat and his father. Selda did not want to be like that.

She hurried up the echoing stairwell of the flat to be greeted at the door by her mother. Sevgi Hanım no longer looked sad, but was bright eyed with excitement.

'At last, Selda!' she cried. 'I'm so glad you're back. You've got a visitor. And I just don't know what to say! The girls went out shopping and there was just me at home. Oh, it's been so embarrassing! But such a nice person, such a good family, you can tell at once. Oh do hurry Selda. Do go in and *say* something!'

'Who is it, Mother?'

'Hurry, Selda, she's been waiting for ages.' Sevgi Hanım was pushing her into the salon. 'I've made her tea and given her Cologne, but it's been so awkward, not being able to talk. We could only smile at each other, and we have, of course, but it's not the same. Go in and talk, Selda, and I'll make more tea!'

It was Giselle.

'Am I glad to see you Selda!' She laughed. 'You're poor mother has been feeding me with tea and biscuits as though she thought I was starving. I think she even tried to tell me that I was thin! Me!' Giselle laughed again and tossed back her silken fine yellow hair. She was too thin.

'It's because you're a guest in our house. Guests are very important . . .' began Selda. It was not easy to explain.

'Does your mother like guests, then?'

'Yes. Of course.' Now Selda smiled in surprise. In Izmir, in the afternoons, when housework was done, there had always been visitors. Her mother had grumbled but always enjoyed it. It was a way of life. No one was ever turned away. Not to have visitors was considered a great insult in Turkey. 'We have lots of guests . . . in Izmir.' She wanted to be accurate.

'Aren't you lucky?' said Giselle, rather sourly.

'Lucky? Why?'

'My mother won't have guests, apart from business guests, that is. I'm not allowed to invite friends home. Or I'd have invited you. Really I would. Mother says that guests make a mess and get in the way . . . '

'In the way of what?' asked Selda, and they stared at each other and were glad that Sevgi Hanım came in with more tea and biscuits.

'Tell her,' said Sevgi Hanım, 'tell her that she's *very* welcome. Tell her that I'm sorry I don't have anything better to offer. If you had told me that she was coming, I would have prepared things. Tell her, Selda, that I've made the *pide* and put it in the oven but that she'll have to wait a few minutes . . . but there are chocolate biscuits in the meantime . . . '

Selda, embarrassed by her mother's excesses, translated some of it. Giselle smiled and took another chocolate biscuit and did not seem at all embarrassed.

'You tell your mother that this is wonderful. It's not what I expected, and do say thank you, Selda.'

Selda saw with some surprise that Giselle meant what she said. She noticed with more surprise that when the *pide* arrived from the oven with its cheese-and-tomato top still sizzling, Giselle ate up more than half of it. It was almost as though she were hungry.

When the visitor had finally gone, Sevgi Hanım could not stop talking about her: 'What a nice girl! What a friendly girl. Oh, I have enjoyed myself. You must ask her again, but with her father and mother, next time. Who ever said that the Swiss were unfriendly? They were quite wrong, just look how pleasant she was. I wonder if her father is at the factory too. Perhaps you could find out. Then you and I could visit her mother next week.' Sevgi Hanım looked so cheerful as she gathered up the dirty tea things that Selda did not breathe a word about the strange behaviour of Giselle's mother. She did not mention the chauffuer or the huge car with the white leather seats, nor did she mention that Giselle was famous in school for her bad temper, but she thought it.

Later, as she lay in bed, she wondered what Giselle had meant by their home not being as she had expected it. What had she thought they ate? Bread and onions? And why had she come? They weren't real friends, yet Giselle had acted as though they were. And yet, why shouldn't they be? She needed a friend. She needed somebody else to talk to, now that she wouldn't be going to the barn any more.

Eight

Despite her firm resolution, Selda did not ask Ahmet for the fifteen francs for the dictionary. When it came to it, she was ashamed. She was ashamed of having lied in the first place, so she kept quiet. Then, unexpectedly, Giselle produced the wretched notes.

'I never wanted the money, anyway,' she said. 'It was mother who forced me to take it from you. She's like that . . . I mean, she doesn't need it, it's just her way . . .' She shrugged awkwardly and held out the money.

'I can't take it.' Selda was dreadfully embarrassed.

'Yes, you can.'

'I can't. Whatever will your mother say?'

'She won't know, will she? This is my money, so it's different.'

'I can't take your money, either.'

'But I've got heaps of it. My father is always giving us money.'

'But . . .'

'All right! If that's how you feel! I thought you'd be pleased!' Giselle scowled. 'Who wants to be friendly with a Turk, anyway? All my Swiss friends think I'm crazy.' But she did not walk away. She still held out the notes, waiting. And Selda took them. She folded them up very, very small, as though this made them less. She shouldn't have taken them. She knew that really, but she also knew that she did not want to walk the playground endlessly alone. She needed Giselle, so she pushed the money down into the deepest corner of her pocket and smiled. Then, remembering Kemal Amca, she opened her arms wide as though finishing something off.

'Hey, come on then,' cried Giselle and it was almost as though everything had been put right, now that the money had changed hands. 'Come on, they're starting a new game. They're going to play "elastic" over there, and I've got a new one in my pocket. It's a terrific one, I only bought it yesterday. Come on, they'll have to let us join in with this new elastic!'

Her face shone. It was a playground game which Giselle, who was tall and very thin, played brilliantly. Selda was hopeless at it and hated it. Now, however, she knew that she must follow Giselle and join in. She must try to jump and get tangled up and endure being laughed at for her clumsiness. She mustn't mind, either. She would let them laugh at her: maybe they didn't mean anything so bad. This time she would laugh with them, if that was the price of not being alone.

After school, Selda went straight down to buy the dictionary and then, guiltily, keep up the pretence to her family that the shop had only just got the book in. Her parents were mildy disapproving and uninterested. Her father said that he had learnt his German without needing a dictionary. Her mother remarked that since Selda got such good marks at school, it all seemed to be a waste of money, now. Nevertheless, Selda was pleased with it, for she needed it more than ever. It took time to discover how much one did not know. The several hundred simple words which her father and brothers used to get by were not enough. She wanted to do more than 'get by'. She listened to them repeating the same sentences all the time and she realized that it was not because they were stupid, but because they were starved of new words. They had never learnt any more and so still stayed behind the bars of their early, wordless days in the country. Turgut Bey, especially, had become a man for whom the world which he dreamed of would always lie just out of his reach. All he could do was grumble and complain, or seek some comfort in the rules set by men such as Adnan Hoca. Selda did not want to be like her father.

She did join the library. She went one afternoon and borrowed her first four books. Carrying them back home she felt like a small child who has been given a present. That evening she wrote to her grandmother about it. She was glad now that she had never mentioned Ferhat. It made it easier to forget all about him. She decided never to think of him again and would have done so, she was sure, if she had not kept on seeing him.

Now that she was no longer trying to catch a glimpse of him, it seemed that she was unable to avoid seeing him. If she was helping her mother hang out washing on the balcony, there would be, strolling up the road with the bread under his arm. One bitter evening, when she had just started to hurry up the steps on the way back from the library, she thought she saw him, up ahead, near the top, where the path curved. She wasn't quite sure, but she waited, shivering, at the bottom, pretending to be looking for something she had dropped. She stayed there until he, or whoever it was, had gone away. Then she climbed slowly up, step by step, but towards the end she ran, leaping up the steps two at a time, in a sudden desperate attempt to see if it really had been him.

No, she was not going to think about him. She had enough problems, hadn't she? She was going to pretend that he didn't exist. After all, that was what he wanted, wasn't it?

But she kept on seeing him . . .

It was the infamous Saturday afternoon trips that were the worst of all. Turgut Bey insisted that the girls accompany him on these shopping expeditions. He enjoyed it so much, this spending and even wasting a little of his hard-earned money. On these Saturday outings, he always chose some little extra thing for the house; last week it had been a butter dish, this week a bigger mirror for the hall. In the future he planned to buy new knives and forks, better furniture, pretty things for the girls, clothes and tools and gadgets, there was no end to it. He demanded that they all gave their opinions, but the final decision was naturally his.

One afternoon they were looking at torches. It was not quite clear why they needed one. The electricity in Switzerland never went off as it did in Turkey, but that was not the point. The point was that Turgut Bey wanted a torch and, for the first time in his life, he could afford to buy one. Now, they all watched as he finally picked out this week's bargain: it had an extra, free battery in the pack! Selda, bored, looked away and immediately saw Ferhat. He, apparently, was looking at tools. Actually, his eyes, which were intense and unfriendly, never left Selda's face. She stepped closer to her mother, daring him to continue to stare. He did. Then he walked right over to them. He reached past her shoulder and took down a torch himself. He acted as though she were not there at all. Her mother had moved out of his way but Selda stayed where she was, as though paralysed. She only bent her head slightly so that his hand did not brush against her hair again. But she half looked up and saw his left hand moving clumsily, trying to hang the packet back on the hook again.

'Come along girls.' Turgut Bey ushered his daughters away from the ruffian who had pushed amongst them. 'Rude lout,' he muttered as soon as they were out of earshot. 'Did you see him pushing aside a decent family, like that? Some people never learn how to behave! It's peasants like that who give us foreign workers a bad name.'

'Wasn't he a Turk, then?' asked Pembe, turning round to stare.

'No, not he,' said their father confidently. 'I know every Turk in the town now. I expect he's a Bulgarian. We've one or two in the factory, I'm afraid. They're not like us, they're uncivilized. I'm not saying that they are bad people, oh no. It's just that they don't know any better. They can't help it. "Uncivilized", like I said. That's how Adnan Bey always describes them. They're not ready to come to a country like this. They don't appreciate it here. Not like us. And they make life very difficult for people like us.' He picked up the torch again and examined it with the satisfied smile of a civilized man.

'There's something wrong with him anyway,' said Pembe, and sniffed. 'Look at him!'

Selda turned round then and looked. Pembe was right. He walked oddly. He had not walked like that in the barn. He was lame. And not just that: the right arm of his jacket swung free. She watched horrified as he limped away and disappeared through the busy crowd.

The next Saturday she saw him again. His arm was in a sling of sorts and he looked quite ill, but still he limped determinedly over to where her family stood. Once again he looked at the things they were looking at. Selda saw her father go red with annoyance, though he had not the courage to say anything outright. She knew that Ferhat wanted to speak to her and it filled her with panic.

Selda started to hate these shopping expeditions more than ever. She dreaded seeing Ferhat. Then, suddenly, one Saturday, he was not there. Instead of being pleased and relieved, she missed him. She watched for him with even greater care than before. She did not see him all week. Nor did he appear in the shop on Saturday. She saw his father, so guessed that he must still be around the town. If she could have only known, known that he was all right, nothing more, then she would have been happier.

Then she saw him. A week later, in the busy Saturday shop, he stood beside the trolley while his father went to and fro taking things from the shelves. He looked different. His normally pale face was altered by red marks that flamed on his cheeks. His eyes were sunken and dark. There was something else that was different: he was normally such a restless person who could never be still. He used to look around him,

143

glance back, rattle things, kick things and, even while he stood, shift from foot to foot. But not now. He slouched against the shelves looking at the ground. He did not seem to notice her or anyone else. He just stood there in everyone's way, resting his head back against the shelves of bread.

Selda could see that other customers were irritated. They had to reach past him for what they wanted. She saw them stretching eager hands to take down the plaits of soft, white milk bread, the wholemeal brown loaves, the buns and fruit bread, the black bread, the long French sticks and the golden-crusted farmhouse loaves. There was bread to meet all tastes and yet there he stood, in the way. He shut his eyes and, for a moment only, stumbled, as though one could, standing still. Then he put out his hands and clutched the trolley to regain his balance and, looking up, saw her. And smiled. She started to move towards him, then remembered her family and looked back. They were not interested in her but were clustered around a stand of reduced jumpers. She stepped towards him and saw that his right hand was wrapped in a dirty bandage and that the fingers were discoloured and swollen. But he had smiled when he saw her. He had smiled the open, kindly smile of one friend to another. He pointed to his right arm and pulled a wry face that she guessed hid pain, as he tried to raise his arm. He was trying to say something to her. She knew it. She saw his lips moving as he repeated it, trying to tell her something without drawing attention to himself in the store.

Behind her, Pembe seemed to have found some treasure. Selda heard her sister's voice, low and sweet and persuasive: 'Oh, Father, dear Father, oh it's only half price, oh please . . .'

Selda took her chance. She went over to where he stood and pretended to be looking at the bread beside him.

'What happened?' she asked, meaning his hand.

'I hid it.'

'What do you mean?' She looked up at him in astonishment. Had he gone mad?

He did not seem to find his answer at all strange, but continued to look pleased. Close to him she could see how the pallor of his face contrasted with the flushed crimson patches. His lips were cracked and beads of sweat stood out of his forehead. He looked like somebody with a fever. The bandage on his hand was rotten with old blood and mud stains. Then, out of the corner of her eye, she saw his father returning with a bag of oranges.

'Your hand?' she whispered.

'Come tomorrow,' he replied and then his father was back. Selda turned aside and pretended to be reading the information printed on the bread bag. She sensed rather than saw that the father and son had moved away without exchanging a word, as was their custom. She did not look up but read the same words again and again.

'Look, Selda, look!' It was Pembe, dancing across with a jumper held up in front of her. It was purple and orange and, to Selda's eye, quite horrible.

'Everybody at school has one of these.' Pembe was delighted.

'But . . .'

'Don't you like it? Doesn't it suit me?'

'The colours are odd.'

'But it's only seven francs. It's half price!'

'That doesn't make the colours all right.' She saw doubt flicker in Pembe's eyes and she wished that she had not said anything. Pembe glanced at the label again, saw the unbelievable price and shrugged and said: 'you never like anything, anyway. And the price of things is very important. Everybody knows that!' Then she walked off, hugging the jumper to her.

When they came out of the supermarket, it was already as dark as night and the temperature had fallen unexpectedly. Moonlight shone on the frosty edges of the 137 steps as they

145

toiled back up them. They went in single file and panted in the cold. When they were almost at the top, where the way curved and there was a small slope without steps, there, Sevgi Hanım slipped. She grabbed at the rail and so did not fall completely, but she grazed her knees and laddered her stockings and some of the lemons and oranges on the top of her bag shot out. They went bouncing back down the steps before anyone could stop them. Selda offered to run down and get them but her father shook his head.

'Don't worry, dear. My family won't be struggling up this hill like donkeys for much longer.'

'How's that?' asked Fatma.

'I'm going to buy a car!'

'Oh, Father! How wonderful!' Pembe ran up to him and kissed him.

'Turgut, how can you talk like that.' Sevgi Hanım sounded disbelieving.

'I don't mean tomorrow,' he said defensively. 'But sometime. Soon. We need one . . .'

'But we don't go anywhere,' protested Sevgi Hanım.

'We will, when we've got the car. Look at Adnan Hoca. His wife and daughter don't tramp around the streets. He doesn't let them get on buses and things.'

'Why not?' asked Fatma.

'He's a careful husband and father. And you can't be too careful, these days. Look what happened down there in the supermarket! Do you think I'm blind? Do you think I didn't see that same wretched foreign lout standing in Selda's way on purpose, when she was trying to get the bread? I'm no fool. I see what I want to see. No, girls, this is a dangerous place and you can't be too careful. Adnan Bey has taught me that. No, Sevgi. I need a car. Not for myself, of course, but for you and the girls.'

Selda listened to her father and drew in long, cold breaths of night air to steady herself. She gripped the rail and felt its crust of ice stick to her hand. It stung, like held fire. At the top they all stopped again to sort out their bags and catch their breath before their final climb to their flat. Looking back, Selda saw where the lights of the far shore sparkled and the cars on the lakeside road drew brief, white streaks with their headlights. It was a very cold, clear night. The stars were beginning to come out, and the moon, full and low had not yet risen above the mountains. It lit a path along the waters of the dark lake, as though a silk carpet had been gently smoothed by a passing hand. She thought of Ferhat and wondered if he had reached the farm safely.

As they took a fresh grip on the bulging, awkward bags, a large car slid silently past them.

'Father, will you get one like that?' asked Pembe, excitedly.

'Well, who knows?' said Turgut Bey. Selda, who had recognized Giselle's sleek fair head against the soft leather seats, said nothing at all. The car glided away into the night and the only sound on the street was the crunch of their feet as they broke the ice in the gutter.

Giselle had given no sign of recognizing Selda but she clearly had, for there she was, early on Sunday morning, on the doorstep of their flat. She was dressed in an ice-blue anorak, lined with white fur. Standing there, she looked like a princess. Selda, who was still in her pyjamas, was reminded of the fairy stories of her childhood, where the rich man's daughter visits the poor girl in her hovel at the castle gate. She did not really want to let Giselle in. They were not even up yet. And what was she doing, anyway, out on the streets at this hour?

'I saw you yesterday,' began Giselle, brightly. 'At the top of the steps, you remember? You were with all your family, helping each other carry things. You all looked so cheerful, you know, doing all that together.' She had already begun to unzip the anorak, taking care not to catch the white fur. There was nothing else for it, Selda stood to one side and let her in.

She understood that, in a way. Giselle was making her excuses for being there so early. She remembered the fierce way in which Giselle's mother had once barred the pavement, and the curious alteration in her mood from one of intense anger to one of sudden calm. She wondered uncomfortably what had made Giselle leave her home and come to total strangers, foreigners, on a bitter cold winter morning.

'*Hoşgeldin, büyrun,*' she said and only then realized that she had said 'welcome' and 'come in' in Turkish. Giselle smiled brilliantly and laughed and handed Selda the beautiful anorak to hang up.

At breakfast, Giselle was so charming. Selda's mother fussed over the visitor as though she were a real princess. The rest of the family was woken briskly and threatened with terrible consequences if they did not appear instantly and properly dressed. Sevgi Hanım got out the best table-cloth for this important guest and then she brought out the best and finest from their fridge and cupboards. She even insisted on frying the final quarter of the garlic sausage which had been hanging up, waiting for a special occasion. The girls begged her not to cook it, but she did and Giselle bit into it boldly and rolled her eyes and said 'mmmmm', which the Swiss did when anything tasted extra good. She said that it tasted just as delicious as the dried sausage that you got in the southern part of Switzerland. In fact, she said that everything was delicious and she ate ravenously. She did not seem to be at all embarrassed that most of the family sat around the table and watched her. She ate and ate and laughed and chattered and flattered Sevgi Hanım and praised her cooking. She praised the little, cramped kitchen, she admired the plastic flowers on the window-sill and the picture of 'Istanbul by Night' which Kemal Amca had given them.

There was nothing, it seemed, that she did not like. Sevgi Hanım was speechless with pleasure. She insisted that Selda 'say this' and 'explain that'. Then Turgut Bey, who had been watching cautiously, said, 'Ask her what her father does.'

Selda translated the question and Giselle's happy chatter stopped instantly.

'Tell her,' insisted Turgut Bey, 'that we are all working people here. Nobody should be ashamed of earning a wage, however small. Now Selda, ask her what he does.'

'My father says . . . he says . . . he expects your father does an interesting job . . .' She mumbled, ashamed of not translating the question accurately.

'Yes. My father is a busy man.' Giselle frowned and pleated up the edge of the table-cloth.

'But what does he do?' Turguet Bey continued.

'He . . . he works at Hebels!'

'There! What did I tell you,' cried Turgut Bey triumphantly. 'There's nothing wrong with working at Hebel's! Tell her that I do. It's a good factory. Now, which department?'

Giselle did not reply.

'Go on Selda, ask her which department!'

'Which department?' Selda's voice was low and unwilling. She hated being used like this. Couldn't her father see how the girl felt?

'My father,' said Giselle, in a voice that was equally low, 'is Herr Hebel.'

There was silence. It was as though all of them, squashed into the tiny, hot kitchen, had breathed up all the air. Selda, suffocating, pushed back her chair sharply and jumped up.

'She has to go home,' she said.

'Yes,' said Giselle, getting up too.

'She wants me to go with her,' lied Selda.

'Of course, of course you must go with her.' Her parents nodded in unusual agreement: of course Herr Hebel's daughter must have somebody to walk home with her . . .

They stared at the girl in silence. Herr Hebel was reputed to be one of the richest people not only in the town, but in Zurich. There were Hebel factories all over Switzerland.

'Off you go then, you mustn't keep her waiting,' said Turgut Bey, eyeing Giselle with some horror.

The two girls went down the steps in silence.

'You don't have to come with me,' Giselle said crossly. 'I can find my own way home.'

'I'd like to come with you.'

'You wouldn't. I can tell. You're just like everybody else, you're pretending. As soon as they know I'm Herr Hebel's daughter, nobody wants to be friends with me any more. I though you'd be different. Being a foreigner you wouldn't know.'

'Know what?'

'About my parents and that . . .'

'I don't know anything about your parents.'

'You do. Everybody in the town does. As soon as people know my name is Giselle Hebel, they don't trust me.'

'That's not true.'

'It is. Haven't you seen them at school? Everybody hates me!'

'But that's . . . that's because . . . 'Selda was going to say that Giselle was so quarrelsome in school she was bound to have enemies, but she fell silent. It was too complicated to put tactfully in German and on second thoughts she was not sure if she wanted to say it. She needed Giselle and, against all the odds, she liked her.

'Go on then' goaded Giselle. 'Finish what you were saying: "that's because . . ." See? You don't trust me either! You aren't prepared to say what you think!'

'I am.'

'Prove it, then.'

They had walked quickly up the street and now Giselle stopped at the place where the road branched. One way led up past her house to the forest, the other way ran through the fields to the farm.

'Prove it,' she repeated.

'How?'

'Prove it by being a real friend' Giselle fiddled with the fringe of the beautiful fluffy scarf which she had thrown over her head. She picked the delicate weave into a small hole. 'Prove it by doing what real friends do, you know, tell me something. Tell me something that you wouldn't tell anybody else. Tell me a secret. Then I'll know that you trust me. I mean, I could tell you things too . . . things about my family . . .' She looked up from the scarf, daring Selda, challenging her to speak.

And she really was as beautiful as a picture-book princess, with her eyes the colour of frozen seas and her pale skin glowing in the sharp morning air.

'I don't have any secrets,' said Selda, thinking of him.

'You must have. Everybody does.'

'But . . .' She remembered him, clearly vividly. She remembered how they had talked so happily of childhood days. She would have liked to talk to him again . . . properly . . .

'Well?' Giselle tapped her foot impatiently.

'I could tell you something.' Selda spoke so quietly that Giselle had to step closer. 'I have this other friend. A sort of secret friend. Nobody knows. And they must never know, it's very important. If anybody ever does my friend will be sent away, sent back to Turkey. I'm the only person who knows. It's a secret, but I could take you, if you liked. I could take you to this friend . . .'

'Would you really?'

'Yes. But you mustn't tell anyone, Giselle. It's so important. You *really* mustn't tell.'

'I won't. I promise, Selda. I won't tell. You can trust me.'

Could she? She remembered the fortune teller's warning and her whole body seemed to freeze with fear.

> 'Plant pretty roses in your garden,
> Plant sweet herbs by your door,

151

But bury secrets in your heart,
And keep them safe for evermore.'

She had not followed the advice. She had remembered the concrete playground where everyone played together, except her, and she had betrayed her secret. And it was not ever *her* secret. It was his, Ferhat's secret. Perhaps it was not too late. She could still turn back. She could change her mind and just walk away. But she wasn't going to. She was going to walk on with Giselle towards the farm. She was going to walk on through the perfect, frozen fields where the struggling sun picked out the stretched spiders' webs and decked them with ice-bright jewels. And she was going to look at all this fine brillance and know that in quiet barns, men unnamed and unknown, worked swiftly in the shadows, gutting the rabbits and stripping off their skins and throwing the entrails out to the waiting cats. And she did want to see him now, even though he was a part of that dark world.

So they walked in silence and the cold seemed to touch Selda's bones. She could still have turned back. Just stopped and turned round and walked away, but she didn't. Couldn't, in the end.

'I know all about this place,' said Giselle, as they passed the pig field.

'How? How do you know about him?' cried Selda in astonishment.

'Everybody knows about him,' laughed Giselle, easily. 'Everybody's waiting for him to die . . .'

'No! That can't be . . .' She was shocked. It was like being hit by a hand that one had trusted. She felt urgent, hot tears in her eyes. She saw him again, saw the filthy bandage on his hand, his head resting back as he smiled at her, and she quickened her step. Ran, almost.

'Why not?' panted Giselle, hurrying to keep up. 'He's terrifically rich! People say he's a miser and he's certainly a bit mad. I say . . .'

'Sorry.' Selda slowed down. She had misunderstood. Of course Giselle was not speaking of Ferhat.

'That's better,' said Giselle. 'The "mad miser", that's what they call him. People are just waiting for him to die so that they can get hold of his land. He doesn't have any family, so his land will be up for grabs, my father says. But he just won't die. People say he must be crazy, with all that land and only breeding those rabbits and having those pigs. He gets those awful foreigners to work for him on the cheap . . . Oh, I'm sorry, Selda. Honestly, I didn't mean that. They're not people like you and your family. My father says that they really are the lowest of the low, you know, people who have no education at all. Not much better than animals, themselves. Those are the only workers who'll stay at Paul Bauer's, with all those rabbits and stinking pigs. I feel sorry for them.'

'For the workers?'

'No! For the rabbits, of course. Shut up in cages all day and then, when the price is right, wham! A blow on your neck and that's it. You're torn up to make a fur jacket.' She laughed. 'I can't think why he bothers with them. My father says that if he only sold a corner of his land he'd make thousands more than he ever makes from those animals. People say . . . hey, what's the matter?'

Tears had begun to trickle down Selda's cheeks.

'I've got earache,' she sniffed.

'You should have said.' Giselle looked genuinely concerned. 'Here, have my scarf. It'll keep you warm.' She took it off and draped it carefully around Selda's head. It was very warm, although it was as soft and light as silk. Perhaps it was silk . . . pure, blue silk. Selda blinked back her tears and wondered briefly if she looked pretty in it. Then she remembered that she was not the sort of person people called pretty. She was dark and rather fierce looking, with her black brows and large, bony face. She sometimes hoped that when she was older, she might be what people called 'handsome'.

Now, beside Giselle, who nestled into the fur-lined hood of her anorak, Selda knew that she could never look like that. She was just herself. Just Selda, that was all.

'Is that better?' asked Giselle, actually putting an arm around her. 'Yes? Well, go on then, tell me about this friend.'

'It isn't really a friend. I mean, I hardly know him . . .'

'Him!'

'Yes. He . . .'

'Goodness, Selda, and you a good little Turkish girl. Who would have thought it?' Giselle giggled and rolled her eyes.

'It isn't like *that*,' protested Selda. 'Nothing like that. I just feel sorry for him. You would, too, if you knew. It's awful, Giselle. I never knew that things like this happened, and here, too.'

'Like what? Tell me.'

So she told her. With a fluency that she did not know she had, Selda explained to Giselle all that she knew about Ferhat's situation. Giselle listened in silence and then, in a very small voice, that had no hint of mockery in it, she said: 'But that's awful! I never knew that things like that went on. Not here, in Switzerland. It's like having slaves!'

They had walked right up to the barn. Now they stopped in front of the door. There was no one in sight. Selda stepped inside and breathed in the familiar smell and peered through the warm remembered shadows. There were the rows of cages. Most were empty, but a few it seemed were still occupied. There was the old, white buck, whose ears drooped so low that they swept the straw. He looked back at her with his deep, red eyes and he blinked. There was that black, still all-quivering whiskers and shaking shoulders. It was such a timid animal, darting and starting whenever you approached the cage. There was one of the greys, but most of the others had gone. All those lovely cream-coloured ones and the whites with the patches dappled on their backs as though someone had gently touched them with a brush, they were not there. It

154

was useless to think about it now. It was too late. Brownie's cage was empty too. She'd seen the door swinging free, the moment she stepped inside. She wasn't going to look.

'Well?' Giselle was peering around expectantly. 'Where is he?'

'I'm sure he's here. Or will come, in a moment.' Somehow, she sensed that he was already in the barn. He was watching them, she thought.

They walked along to where the goat stamped and rubbed its shoulder against a post. A cat slithered under the other door and came to them in that careful way of cats, putting its feet one after the other, in a straight line. Then behind them, one of the rabbits suddenly started to burrow frantically, as though it would escape from its cage. Something else moved too. Giselle looked around her impatiently and glanced back at the door several times.

Selda tried to force herself to see into the shadows. He was there, she was certain. He was watching them. He was angry that she had betrayed his secret. That must be it. He was right, too. She should never have brought Giselle. She had betrayed not just Ferhat, but his family too. She had tried to buy Giselle's friendship and the price had been Ferhat's safety. How could she have done it? But, really, truly, it hadn't only been that. She had so wanted to see him again, to talk to this person who liked her just for what she was. She hadn't meant to harm him. It had been a way to see him again. She thought she was going to cry, so she bent down to tie up the lace of her moon-boot and, crouching there, brushing away the tears, she saw Brownie.

The little rabbit was all by itself, in a cage well away from the others. At first glance this cage had appeared to be empty, with a sack and some flowerpots stacked in it. But it was Brownie all right. As always, the rabbit stood up against the bars and poked its paws through. She would have known it anywhere, with that one white sock.

155

'Look, Giselle, it's safe!' She knelt down and undid the latch and put her hand in. At first Brownie hid away in a corner, then, gathering its courage, it poked its head out above the sacks, and finally scrambled over the flowerpots, towards her. Without thinking she reached in, grasped it firmly and lifted it out of the cage. It crouched against her and through its trembling she could feel its heart beating hotly. She pressed her face into its soft fur and she felt all the pattern of the fragile bones beneath.

Then something moved beyond the bales of hay. Somebody moved and trod and coughed. The girls looked at each other. Apprehensively Giselle moved towards the door. Brownie too struggled for freedom and Selda nearly let him go, only just managing to hold on. She felt his claws scratch along her wrist. Giselle had already reached the shaft of light which fell across the floor of the barn from the doorway. Selda tightened her grip on the rabbit and saw Ferhat step out from behind the pile of bales. She saw him look at Giselle and then at her and then again at Giselle, whose hood had fallen back now so that her face and hair were uncovered and radiant in the cold sharpness of the winter light. Selda hid her face in the soft down of the rabbit.

Nine

'You see?' said Ferhat, walking past Giselle. 'I did hide it. That was what I wanted to tell you in the shop. That's what I meant yesterday. I guessed that you must have been upset when you saw what had happened to the rest of the rabbits. I thought that you knew they were no different from any of the other farm animals. But I'd never have let anything happen to this little one. Not when it was your favourite. You should have realized.'

'But . . .'

'When old Bauer told me that it was time for the rabbits to go, I hid this one down there. The farmer is an old man now and he doesn't get around the farm. He just gives orders from the house, and we carry them out. I knew he wouldn't miss one rabbit. And he didn't. Really, Selda, it was quite safe here and still is.' He stood close to her and put out his undamaged hand and stroked the rabbit's head as it lay in Selda's arms. Then he nodded towards Giselle and, speaking more quietly, asked: 'And the girl, that fair girl, she doesn't look like another sister. Who is she?'

'A friend, a school friend. I know I shouldn't have brought her. I'm sorry Ferhat, I know I promised not to . . .'

He did not say anything and, if he was annoyed, he did not show it, but just withdrew his hand and walked away to the goat's stall. He paused there for a moment, looking down at the animal, then he kicked at a loose board, as though getting it back into place.

Giselle, meanwhile, had been slowly approaching, studying them both with curiosity. She examined Ferhat, staring into his face with no sign of embarrassment at all.

'Ask him what he's done to his hand,' she said, continuing to stare. Selda did, awkwardly.

'I had an accident,' he replied.

'What sort of an accident? Ask him, ask him how.' Giselle insisted on knowing everything.

'She wants to know what happened.'

'Does she?' said Ferhat, suspiciously.' She's very curious, your "friend".'

'She doesn't mean anything bad. She's just, oh, you know, she's just "Swiss". They always want to know everything properly.'

He relaxed then and smiled and told them that it was nothing much: he had had an accident with one of the farm machines. It had turned over on a corner and trapped him. He was lucky that it had not been worse, he said.

'It looks ... bad enough,' said Selda shyly, and found herself wondering if he was telling the truth. She thought of her brother Ahmet's accident. She was still sure that he had been lying when he told her that he had walked into a lamp-post. Had Ferhat too been doing something that he did not wish to speak of, and had he got hurt, badly?

'I look worse than I am, really,' he said. 'The accident wasn't so bad. I just got a fever afterwards. Father thinks that the wounds got infected in the pig house. I had to be off work for some time, but it's much better now. This'll be my first day back at work.'

'I'm surprised the doctor allows it,' said Giselle. 'He looks awful still. Tell him.'

Selda did and then Ferhat laughed.

'Doctor? Does she think I can go to a doctor!' Now his voice was bitter. 'Go on, tell her, if she wants to know things "properly". Tell her that I'm an illegal immigrant. That means that I'm not insured. So I can't go to a doctor or to a hospital. I'm not a proper person here at all. I can't go anywhere!'

'But he could have tried to go,' protested Giselle unhappily, as Selda interpreted.

'Oh yes,' he said sourly.' I could, could I? And risk being arrested and sent back to Turkey? No thank you.'

'But you could have died ... you know ... got tetanus. That kills people,' Selda said in horror. She knew that in Turkey it was a very real danger. People did die from infected cuts. Her grandmother had told them lots of stories about it.

'So what?' he cried furiously, but then was instantly sorry for his anger. 'This *is* the one you liked, isn't it?' he asked gently, coming over to stand beside her to scratch Brownie under the chin. He clearly wanted to change the subject.

'Yes. This is Brownie,' said Selda quietly.

'May I stroke him?' asked Giselle, rather sulkily. She stepped over to them and laid her hand on the rabbit's back and Selda watched her friend's slim, white fingers moving through the soft fur beside Ferhat's hand.

'You can have it, if you like,' said Ferhat suddenly. 'Old Bauer will never know now.'

Both girls looked up at him, but only Selda had understood the Turkish.

'Would you like it? As a pet? Perhaps your brother Ahmet could fix up a cage. You could keep it like the Swiss do, in the house. Wouldn't you like that Selda?'

'Oh, yes.' There was almost nothing she would have like more. 'Brownie is just like the one I saw in Istanbul before we came here. Do you remember? I think I told you about the fortune teller. This rabbit, Brownie, could be a twin.'

She cradled Brownie in her arms. She could imagine it already. She'd ask her brothers to make a cage for it and then they could have it on the balcony. Even her mother would like it and would fuss over it, she was sure. She could see Sevgi Hanım putting aside titbits of salad and vegetable. When Selda herself was studying, she would teach it to snuggle down on her lap. The whole family would like it and, at the very least, it would provide a use for the waste bread.

'But . . .' Suddenly, sickeningly, she realized that if she had Brownie in the house as a pet, she would no longer have an excuse for coming to the farm. She couldn't say either that she needed to visit 'her' rabbit, or that she could get rid of the bread for her mother. She would not then be able to come and talk to Ferhat.

'But what?' He sounded disappointed. 'Don't you want it?'

'Yes, I do.' She must think of something quickly. 'I'm sure my mother will say that it's dirty, carries diseases and things. You know how they talk.' She felt very guilty about unfairly blaming her mother.

'Oh well, I suppose you're right. I had a dog back in Alanya, but my mother would never let her in the house. Said she had fleas, which she did, but only a few.' He shrugged and turned away but then looked back.

'What about her?'

'Her?'

'Yes. Her. This friend you've brought. Perhaps she'd like a rabbit. Ask her.'

'Oh no! I'm sure she wouldn't. I don't think she likes animals. I . . .'

'You haven't asked her, Selda. Go on. The Swiss love their pets. They've all got dogs and cats. Old Bauer sometimes talks about it. He says that Swiss homes are full of birds and fish and mice, even. Think of it: mice as pets! If my mother knew that she'd faint. So go on, Selda, ask her.'

Giselle had looked from one to the other as they spoke rapidly in Turkish. She guessed that they were speaking about her and her face clouded with irritation.

'What's he saying Selda? Tell me what he's saying. It's not fair of you both; I can't understand.'

'He asked,' said Selda, slowly and painfully, 'he asked if you would like to have this rabbit, as a pet.' It hurt to say it.

'Me?' Giselle's eyes narrowed. 'He's offering to give it to me?'

'Yes.'

'Oh, yes please. I'd love it.' She looked so very happy and Selda realised she had never seen Giselle look quite that way before. 'I'd love to have it. Oh, thank you. Can I hold it? Please?' She held out her hands.

'She says that she'd love to have it,' said Selda. She tried to make her voice cool and calm but she was sure that it trembled. Why had he offered Brownie, her special rabbit, to Giselle, whom he had only seen for the first time a few minutes ago?

'There! That's all right then. What did I tell you? I thought she looked like a kind girl. It'll be safe, now.'

'But . . .' It wasn't all right at all, but Selda did not know what to say.

She handed the rabbit to Giselle who laid her cheek against it and kissed it and then suddenly thrust it back into Selda's hands. She dusted one or two fronds of hay from her anorak as though disgusted.

'Don't you want it?' asked Selda, her heart pounding.

'I do! I do!' There was real unhappiness in Giselle's voice. 'I *do* want it, but I won't be allowed to keep it. I just know it. I had a dog but they wouldn't let me keep it although it was a very valuable dog, with a proper pedigree and things. It barked a lot and it chewed a chair leg and it made my mother nervous, she said, and one day when I came home from school, it wasn't there. And they never, ever said where it had gone. But I could guess! I don't want that to happen to the rabbit. Anyway,' she tossed back her hair defiantly, 'I don't think I want the responsibility, you know, it would always be there, waiting to be looked after, waiting to be played with. It might even die and I don't want to be sorry for it.'

Selda put the rabbit carefully back into the cage.

'So she doesn't want it after all?' said Ferhat.

'No . . .' It was the simplest answer that Selda could make.

For a minute or two they walked up and down the barn in silence, none of them knowing what to say. Then Giselle began to chatter. She began to ask an endless stream of questions and she got Selda to translate them all. She wanted to know everything. In another ten minutes she had discovered more about Ferhat than Selda had learnt in weeks. Selda expected Ferhat to be annoyed and at first she tried to apologize on Giselle's behalf, but he stopped her.

'It's all right,' he said. 'I don't really mind. I can see that she's just a little kid. Do you think I don't see them all around in the town? These Swiss children don't know what problems are. Life is so easy for them, they don't have to worry about anything. She's just a curious child, she's not like us.'

Although Selda was pleased to hear him speak of her like that, she was not sure that he was right about Giselle. Giselle was certainly rich and maybe younger than Selda, but there was more to her, she thought. Sometimes Selda felt that Giselle's cool, blue eyes had seen a great deal and what she had seen had made her very unhappy.

'No,' continued Ferhat. 'She's a nice girl. I'm glad that you've got a friend. Bring her again, if you want to. Do you know, seeing the two of you, here together, it reminds me a bit of my family.'

He kicked at the corner of a bale so that a chunk of sweet-smelling hay tumbled down in front of them. Selda remembered the warmth of summer fields and the way the wild red poppies, which were called 'little brides' in Turkish, danced amongst the taller grasses. She thought of the yellow jasmine which would be coming into bloom in her grandmother's garden and she thought of the cats. They would be sitting out in the strengthening sun, licking their paws and yawning and watching each other as they sensed the arrival of spring. There, in Izmir, the season would already have changed.

The girls walked back in almost total silence, but it was companionable and not forced. It was as though they had shared a whole day of exploration and experience rather than a short hour.

'Poor thing,' was all that Giselle would say about it. Selda wanted to remind her 'not to tell', but she didn't. It seemed both unkind and lacking in trust, so she said nothing and just nodded.

She knew that her family would be waiting for her and when she looked up, there, sure enough, was Ahmet, looking for her from the balcony. He waved and she waved back, and she wondered for how long he had been watching them. Had he seen them coming from the barn?

'I have to go in,' she said. 'They'll be waiting for me.'

Giselle nodded but did not say goodbye.

'I expect your mother is waiting for you . . .'

'She isn't,' said Giselle flatly. 'Nobody is at home.'

'I suppose they'll be home soon . . .'

'How should I know?'

They had stopped in front of the flats. Giselle's road home went on past a few isolated houses on the forest edge. She didn't take it.

'That's my brother Ahmet, up there.'

'I know.'

'You could come in again, for a bit . . .?'

'Could I?' Giselle sounded tempted then suddenly, seemed to change her mind.

'No thanks.' Her voice was very bright. 'See you on Monday then!'

'Wait,' called Selda, 'I've still got the scarf!'

'You can keep it. I never liked it anyway!' she shouted back and then she was gone, skipping up the street as though she did not have a care in the world.

Selda climbed up the flights of concrete stairs and there they all were, waiting for her in the doorway. Where had she been? Why had she taken so long? Why hadn't she taken that girl straight home? Where had she got the scarf? Shouldn't she run after the Hebel girl and give it back? They made so much noise that a neighbour banged on the wall, but Selda did not care. This time she was glad that her family had been waiting for her. She was glad that they wanted to see her safely home. And she was glad that she did not have to walk up that lonely road to that empty house.

It seemed that February was a particularly bleak time of year in Switzerland. The weeks passed yet the trees and plants in the gardens were still frozen and dormant and black. Mist, both from the lake below and from the forest above, veiled the town in an icy whiteness. The far shore and the mountain peaks were hidden. The lights were kept on all day in school and both pupils and teachers seemed tired and irritable. Then, quite unexpectedly, Selda learnt that a fourteen-day holiday was to begin the following week. Giselle explained that it was called a 'sports' holiday. When Selda asked why they had a holiday in the middle of winter, Giselle laughed and said that was exactly why: people needed to go up into the mountains and enjoy the winter, skiing and playing winter sports.

Giselle's family had a chalet in the mountains where they always went. Ramona was going skiing with a party of child-ren from her church. Others were going to hotels or to stay with relatives in different parts of the country. The talk in the class was all about snow and ski jumps and avalanches and races. Fräulein Altmann was going to do something which translated as 'cross country' skiing. To Selda, how-ever, it was all equally mysterious although there was no mistaking what was happening in the town. Families were packing their cases into the boots of their cars. Skis were being fastened on to special racks on the roofs. The train station and the buses were crammed with skiers and noisy with the crash of their enormous, plastic ski-boots. The town

164

emptied of children and for Selda, the days without school were endless.

She found herself thinking more and more about Ferhat and yet she was unable to go and see him. Pembe did not want to walk along to 'some old farm' and Fatma was sulking because everybody except them seemed to be doing these magic 'winter sports'. Both girls refused to come out and lolled in front of the television for hours on end, watching the ski races. Selda had tried to set off by herself, but each time her mother had offered to come with her. She was trapped.

In order to pass the time, she started going to the library every day. It was curious to walk through such deserted streets. It looked as though some shops had actually closed. In the library, she was often the only person apart from old ladies. One afternoon, she had stayed on reading longer than she intended. As she returned along the quiet street, a crowd of people, dressed up like actors in the theatre, suddenly burst out in front of her. There must have been nine or ten of them, and they rushed noisily from the door of a restaurant. They were laughing and shouting and for one moment Selda thought that they were calling to her. There was a woman dressed up in something Chinese. She must have felt very cold, but she was laughing terrifically. One, who had to be a man because he was so huge, was wearing black stockings and the sort of costume that belly dancers wear in Turkey. He teetered along on gold high-heeled shoes and kept trying to pull the wig of golden curls more securely over his forehead. His face was made up with crimson lips above an unshaven chin. He clung to the arm of somebody dressed up as a gorilla. Two others were dressed as clowns and another couple were wearing some sort of uniform. In their midst paced a slender black cat, with a swinging rope of a tail and fine black whiskers painted on smooth cheeks. They were all shrieking and laughing and throwing handfuls of coloured paper bits at each other, right there, on the still, cold afternoon street.

One had a whistle which he blew shrilly and continually like a child who has been told not to. The cat smiled at Selda and tossed a handful of fluttering paper scraps at her, miaowing loudly and baring long painted nails curved like claws. Selda froze against the wall and held the books up in front of her face. Then the masqueraders ran off. If she had not found the pieces of paper in her hair and had not heard the harsh cry of the whistle grow fainter, as she climbed the steps, she could almost have thought that she had imagined it.

She told them about it at home and her father laughed at her. It was, he said, only something called *Fasnacht*. All over Switzerland, people celebrated the end of winter by dressing up in these strange clothes and dancing about on the streets. For the few days of *Fasnacht* people could do what they liked, he told them with a disapproving sneer. Their town was celebrating *Fasnacht* at the moment and at the weekend there would be a procession through the streets. He promised to take the family down to watch.

'But nobody is there,' said Selda.

'Oh yes they are. The factory is still open, and so are most of the other places. You just don't see working people around so much. *Fasnacht* is very popular with ordinary people, the sort of people who don't go away skiing.' He looked meaningfully at Fatma.

'It's not just factory workers who enjoy it,' said Ali. 'Look at Herr Hebel. They say he stays in town for it. He provides most of the money, at least that's what they say in the factory. He even dresses up for the procession.'

'I bet he's a king, or something like that,' said Pembe.

'No,' said Ali. 'Last year when I watched, I think he was a baby, yes, that's it, he was a baby, dressed up with a huge dummy and a rattle. He got a great laugh.'

'Do you think he'll be in it this year?' asked Fatma.

'I don't know. I heard that he wanted to take his family up

to the mountains, but maybe he'll be back at the weekend. Do you know Selda?'

'Giselle said that she was going to the mountains, but she didn't talk about her father.'

'Or her mother?'

'No. Why?'

'Oh, Frau Hebel is famous around the town. She's supposed to be even keener on *Fasnacht* than her husband is.' Ali laughed.

'Adnan Hoca said that somebody had already seen her, all dressed up. Pretending to be an animal or something,' said Turgut Bey in disgust.

Immediately Selda knew the identity of the sleek, clawed cat who had smiled at her. Yet, surely it couldn't have been. How could Frau Hebel do a thing like that? And whatever did Giselle think? Or did she accept it as quite normal? Whatever was it like to go around the streets pretending to be something else altogether?

When they walked down to look at the procession on Sunday afternoon, the streets were as crowded as her father had predicted. He told them that people from other villages around the lake came in to watch the procession. Huge floats were already moving down the street and the spectators were cheering. Many wore fancy dress themselves. Others had painted their faces or put on a funny hat or a plastic nose. Many hid behind wild masks. As they found a place from which to watch, a lorry, disguised as a boat, was moving slowly between the crowds. The people on board were dressed as sailors and they tossed mandarins down to the crowd who scrambled and grabbed at the bright orange fruit.

After the boat, a brass band marched in a smart formation and played loudly, although all the musicians were dressed as frogs. They even wore masks with bulging frog's eyes which rolled and rattled. Behind them came two men on stilts and then a group of very fat men with barrels strapped to their padded stomachs. They were handing plastic cups of drink out to the crowd. Pembe and Fatma, who had worked their way through to the front, accepted several cups and drank them down eagerly, unaware that it was beer. Another large float passed by, crowded with people dressed as Arabs who squirted the onlookers with what they shouted was 'oil'.

They were followed by men and women in white powdered wigs and elegant, historical costumes. Pembe and Fatma, giggling and enjoying themselves, were becoming slowly separated from the rest of the family. They seemed to have met up with some school friends and Selda could hear Pembe's happy laugh floating up above the rest of the crowd. A group of animals passed and Selda tried hard to see if there was a cat amongst them, but the onlookers blocked her view. The crowd pushed and ebbed and small children ran alongside the procession. Pembe and Fatma had moved out of sight and Sevgi Hanım sent Selda to 'get them back'. She had started to pick her way through the pressing crowds when a troupe of little children dressed as devils and witches hurried by, singing some song in their high, breathless voices. The crowd cried 'Aah, *herzig*' – how sweet – and surged forward to look. Selda was completely hemmed in. Handfuls of small bright objects were thrown pattering and tapping into the throng and the crowd leapt to left and right, pushing and snatching at the brightly wrapped toffees. Selda wanted to escape but couldn't get free, and she too began pushing in her confusion, until someone in a mask held out his hand and offered her the sweets that he had caught.

'Ferhat?'

'Yes.' He nodded and pushed a clear space for her. 'I hoped you'd come. I thought you might.'

'But what about you? Won't somebody see you?'

'What? Like this?' He touched the plastic cheeks of the hideous mask and she could see his eyes shining very brightly through the pin holes in the painted eyeballs.

'I missed you,' he said. 'Why didn't you come last week? I waited, every afternoon.'

'I wanted to, but I couldn't. My sisters wouldn't come and my friend, that girl Giselle, has gone away to the mountains. So I couldn't come. Not alone.'

'Wouldn't your brother, Ahmet, have come with you?'

'I don't know. I never thought of that.'

'You could ask.'

'Yes. I could . . .' She did not want to, but she had heard the tone in Ferhat's voice. 'Is something wrong then?'

'No!' he answered, too quickly. 'Not really.'

There were jugglers now and the crowd twisted and turned, trying to follow the spinning coloured balls.

'Can I . . . can I help?' she asked, at last, just as she had wished to do, all along.

The crowd surged and would have swept her with them in their eagerness to get close to a group of brown, furry bears who marched in solemn lines and handed out biscuits smelling of aniseed but Ferhat stretched out his hand and caught hers and kept her with him. He bent down and began to speak quickly through the mask.

'You could' he said, 'I know I shouldn't ask, but I've been thinking and thinking. When I was ill and couldn't work after the accident, I started thinking about home and about being here, and you know what it's like when you've nothing to do, you can't stop thinking. When I was working hard on the farm there was no time, there was always the next job to be done, and old Bauer, watching from the window. He could sack us, just like that, so we do our work properly. We don't think. But when I was ill, I was thinking . . .'

'About what?' she hardly dared ask. She wanted, desperately, to know and at the same time, she didn't.

'About . . . well, about everything, about being trapped here. About . . . Selda, it's because of you, don't you see? I saw you and your family here, I know that you can all make a new life here if you want to. You're not trapped, like me. You go to school, you can do . . . anything, Selda, anything you want, but not me. Not now or ever. I'm . . .'

'A prisoner?'

'Yes.' He nodded. 'And then last week you brought that girl with you, that yellow-haired girl . . .'

'I wish I'd never brought her,' she said recklessly.

'No, don't say that. I'm glad you brought her. It was seeing the two of you together that made me think even more. There you were, Selda: you could talk to her and talk to me. You could tell her what I said and tell me what she said. You could understand everything. You can talk so well, Selda . . .'

'I can't, honestly.'

'But you can! I saw it.'

'I make hundreds of mistakes.'

'But that's not important. I don't even know enough to make mistakes! Selda, surely you know what it feels like? We understand old Bauer, but we don't talk to him. He tells us what to do and we listen and do it. That's not talking and it's not enough. Suddenly, Selda, it isn't enough, I *have* to learn to speak. That's why I'm asking you.'

'Asking me?'

'Yes. I'm asking you if you can help. If you can teach me German. You go to school, you could borrow some books for me. If I studied in the evenings, I'd learn, I know I would. My father would help, he's an educated man. He was a teacher, as I told you. When I learn German, things will change. I can get a decent job. I mean, who knows, maybe I could go back to school again, night school, or something.'

'Shall I ask at school for you?'

'Yes.'

'But . . .'

'Don't say, "but" Selda. Just ask. Ask someone you trust. Please.'

170

'All right. I'll ask my teacher. I'll ask Fräulein Altmann. She's very nice and she's been very kind to me. She'll know what to do.'

'She won't tell anyone, will she?' He sounded anxious again.

'No.' But would she? Surely not. Selda remembered how helpful Fräulein Altmann had been about Pembe's accident.

'Are you sure?'

'No, but . . .' She would have disentangled her arm, but the crowd pressed so close.

'It's seeing you that's made me feel different,' he said, 'suddenly, I've had enough. I get to thinking more and more about those older Turks, men who have never been back to see their families. I can't become like them. I thought one could take anything, you know, just harden oneself so that nothing matters any longer, but you can't, Selda. Or I can't. Do you know that your brother Ahmet always used to talk about you? I felt I knew you before I'd even seen you. He told us that the rest of his family were coming in the autumn, but he always talked about you, differently. He said that you were the one who would make a success here.'

'But I haven't. Pembe and Fatma get on much better than I do. They have lots of friends. They're happy here.'

'That's different. Anyway, it's more difficult for you. You have further to go, don't you? But you'll get there, Selda . . . I know you will.'

She did not know what to say to him and she did not quite know what he had been saying to her. She was almost scared of him. She could not see his face, only the darting movement of his eyes behind the mask.

'Look at me Selda. Look at *us*, my father and I, soon we'll be as dumb and helpless as the animals we look after. If I don't do something soon, I think I'll go mad, I . . .'

'I'm sorry . . .' She was, too, but also disconcerted. He seemed so much older than her now and she felt so confused.

'Don't be sorry, Selda.'

'Look! There's my sister.' She was relieved to see Pembe's fair curls suddenly reappear in front of her. 'I have to get my sisters!' she cried.

'All right. You'd better go then.' He pushed a way through the crowd for her so that she could rejoin them. A massive lady, padded all over with pillows, swooped down upon the three of them and tickled them with a brush made of bright pink feathers. Pembe laughed so much that she could hardly stand but clung helplessly to Fatma's shoulder. When Selda looked round, Ferhat had already gone.

When she turned back to watch the procession, she found that her attention was drawn not by the fantastic and beautiful costumes of the mountain trolls who now passed, but by a face in the crowd opposite. It was Adnan Hoca. He was watching them. He stood alone in the crowd, unsmiling and disapproving. He was watching the girls intently and coldly and he rubbed the palm of his hand gently over his close, black beard.

That evening, Selda wrote to her grandmother again. She wanted to describe *Fasnacht*, but it was difficult to do. She could not think of anything in her grandmother's experience that was like it: nobody dressed up and wore masks in Turkey. Still, she would try to recreate the scene for her as best she could. In fact she enjoyed it more in retrospect than she had while she was there. When she ran down to the post office the next morning, she was astonished to see that the street sweepers were already out, sweeping the streets clean. If a few chocolates had not stuck in the gutters you might never have known that *Fasnacht* had come and gone.

During the second week the town gradually filled up again. On Monday school reopened and the children who had been in the mountains came back with sunburnt faces, as though it were high summer. Giselle's fair skin was freckled and her nose was peeling.

'Have you seen him again?' she asked as soon as they were alone in the playground. Selda nodded and described the *Fasnacht* meeting.

'Do you think I should tell Fräulein Altmann?' she asked and Giselle replied that she thought that the teacher could be trusted.

An opportunity arose a few days later when Fräulein Altmann asked Selda to stay behind at the end of an afternoon.

'I have some good news and some not-so-good news,' she said, drawing a chair up to Selda's desk. 'You know that here, in this part of Switzerland, we still change classes in the spring? After Easter, this class, the fourth, will become the fifth. I shall still be the teacher and my pupils will go up with me. The children in the sixth class, where your sisters are, will go on to one of the secondary schools, or most of them will.'

'Yes?' Selda waited, her heart pounding and pounding.

'Now you, Selda, *will* go up to the fifth class with the others. I'm delighted for you and I have to say that we teachers are all very impressed by what you've done. I don't know your final mark exactly, but it's in the top half of the class. Anybody should be pleased with that, Selda. Well done . . . Now . . .'

'What is it, Fräulein Altmann?'

'It's about you sisters, Pembe and Fatma. I wanted to, well, warn you.'

'Warn me?' the pounding was even fiercer.

'Yes. I'm afraid that they won't be going to secondary school not yet. Frau Steinfeld feels that they are not ready.'

'But they are so happy in school!' Selda could not understand it.

'That's good,' said Fräulein Altmann.

'But their teacher always said that they mustn't worry, that she was pleased with them . . .'

'But she is, Selda. Why should they be unhappy and worry? They are doing their best. We know they are. We don't really expect our foreign children to catch up so quickly, it takes time. Foreign children need to work more slowly and that's not a crime. We understand. In a year's time, Pembe and Fatma may be ready, and if not, it doesn't matter.'

'But they can't do another year!'

'Why not?' Fräulein Altmann looked at her questioningly. 'This is Switzerland, now,' she said gently. 'This is the way we do things.'

Selda could not begin to explain, so she said nothing.

'I wanted you to know,' continued Fräulein Altmann, 'before the letter from the school authorities arrives home. Your parents and your sisters may be a little sad and disappointed, and I hoped that you could help them, if you understood. It really is for the best, Selda. And I'm sure you'll be a great help to your family at this time. We Swiss have a lot to learn from our visitors: your families are very close and help each other. I've often seen it.'

Selda nodded again. If Fräulein Altmann really knew, she'd probably find out that there wasn't much difference between families. Still . . .

'You look worried,' said the teacher. 'Tell me, is something else wrong?' She spoke so kindly. Surely this was the chance.

'It's not just my sisters . . .'

'What is it then? Do tell me.'

'It's a friend, this other friend . . .'

'Ah, you must mean Giselle, Giselle Hebel. Now Selda, you mustn't worry about her too much. I do know about Giselle. I know about all my pupils, or try to. That's our job. I've been delighted to see how well you and Giselle get on together. I hear that she's even spent time with your family. It must be a great help to her, and, of course, nice for you. But you mustn't worry about her too much.'

'It isn't Giselle.' Selda was surprised. Why should it be?

174

Giselle was one of the better students. Had she misunderstood Fräulein Altmann?

'Who is it then? I'll certainly help, if I can.'

'It's this other friend. This person I know. They, they . . .'

'You can trust me, Selda.'

Could she? Surely this *was* the person to tell, this open-faced, fair-haired woman, who had been so kind to her. Who tried to understand. So Selda took a deep breath and began to tell Ferhat's story. She explained how Ferhat and his father were trapped, working as illegal immigrants, for the lowest of wages. She explained how they were unable to do anything else but hide away, desperately working and working for their money, which they sent back to look after the rest of the family in Turkey. She explained how Ferhat had been ill after an accident and how they had not dared to go to a doctor, in case the doctor informed the police. Then she explained that now, he could not bear it any longer and that he wanted to escape from the prison by learning German, and trying to live like a human being in Switzerland. It did not seem too much to ask.

'He only wants a few books. Old ones, he said. And not as a present, just to borrow. He'll give them back. I mean, Fräulein Altmann, if he was in Turkey he would be in high school still.'

'But Selda, this is dreadful! I'm so glad you trusted me enough to tell me . . . but what can I say? A few books aren't going to solve his problem.' Fräulein Altmann looked very upset.

'It doesn't matter, then,' said Selda, dejectedly and got up. 'I shouldn't have mentioned it.'

'Wait, Selda! Of course you can have the books. That's not what I meant. I meant that this is *more* than a problem of borrowing books. It's wrong: nobody should have to live like that, and especially not anyone young. I wish you'd told me before.'

'But what could you do?'

'I don't know.'

'It doesn't matter, Fräulein Altmann. He didn't ask for any other help. He just asked me to help him with the German.'

'Of course you can have some books. We have boxes of old school books in the storeroom. You can take as many as you can carry. We'll go and look together, if you like.'

'Can we? Oh, thank you, Fräulein Altmann. I knew you'd understand. I told him you would. It's all he wants . . .'

'But Selda, this won't help. It's not enough.'

'It is. It will help, honestly. You can't imagine what it's like, Fräulein Altmann, being a foreigner. It's like being struck dumb, suddenly, and not being able to speak or understand. You stop being a person. It's like being an animal, perhaps, always waiting and watching and being fearful. It's –' suddenly, she couldn't go on. She buried her face in her hands and began to cry.

She, Selda, the girl who never cried, the girl who was as tough as a boy, people always said, now sobbed more loudly than poor Demet had ever done.

'Selda!' cried Fräulein Altmann. 'Whatever's the matter? I didn't know you felt like this?' She offered a packet of tissues. 'Look, I know it takes time to settle in and learn a new language. But you're not the only one in the class. Marco came from Italy two years ago and Susan's parents are English. They both had a hard time, at the beginning, but they've settled in. You're doing wonderfully. Nobody thinks you are dumb!'

She was right of course, but Selda was past caring. It did not help, knowing that there were other children in the same position as herself. Other people were different. It was she, Selda, who mattered, and nobody, not even Fräulein Altmann, seemed to understand that. Only Ferhat understood, because he lived it. She felt so shut off from everybody else, so useless and helpless. It was like being struck dumb and then being praised for croaking. She remembered a girl, along her grandmother's street in Izmir. This girl had been paralysed after a sudden, violent summer fever. Nobody quite knew what was wrong with her, but now she lay all day long on a sofa, twitching and jerking and making noises. Only the girl's mother understood the sounds. Selda had been scared of the girl and had never wanted to go to her house on visits, but her grandmother had made her. Once, when she was there, the girl had kept crying out about something, making the same noise, over and over again. She had finally jerked her arms about and knocked over the bottle of water that stood by the sofa. The sound of breaking glass had brought the grown-ups rushing in, and they had fussed over the invalid, bringing more water and holding the glass to her lips. Selda had watched, horrified. She had been convinced that the girl had not wanted a drink at all. She had been trying to say something quite different, only no one had understood. That was how Selda felt herself to be, in Switzerland: as dumb as that poor girl. And Ferhat too. Only he must be feeling far, far worse.

'Selda,' Fräulein Altmann tried again. 'It does get better, I promise you. And it isn't only you who has to change and learn. We do too. There is a great deal that we must learn from our foreigners. Good gracious, Selda, look how much you've taught us.' She smiled. 'Now, has anyone called you a "stupid cow" since you came top in maths?'

'No, not really.'

'There you are! And *everybody* gets called names, sometimes.'

Selda wiped her eyes and tried to listen. She thought of Kemal Amca. 'Go on, show them what you can do!': that was what he would have said.

'Look, Selda, you've taught me something. I'd heard about illegal immigrants. But until you talked to me, I never, ever understood what they must feel like.'

'But you won't tell anyone, will you?'

'No. I promise you. I won't tell anyone.' She shook her head slowly. 'I'm not sure that it's the right thing to do, but I still promise. Your secret is safe with me.'

Fräulein Altmann got up and held out her hand.

'Now, cheer up and let's go and look for those books. As you say, that's something that I can do to help, and we have to start somewhere.'

Selda ran home with the bag of books hanging at her side. It was a start. She could already imagine Ferhat's pleasure when he opened the bag. She would go and help him regularly. She and Giselle would help him together. Spring must come soon and the evenings would get lighter. They could meet him after he had finished his work on the farm. They could go up into the forest, the three of them, and talk and study and read the books. Why, they might even end up teaching Giselle some Turkish.

She was so busy planning what might happen that she actually forgot that she *had* passed her class. But she had. She'd passed. She had got her grip on the mountainside and had not slipped down and she was not going to, ever.

Then she thought of her grandmother. She knew that she could hardly rush straight in and boast about her success to her family when Pembe and Fatma had failed, but she could write to her grandmother. How pleased the old lady would be. She could just imagine it: her grandmother would go up and down the street telling anyone who would listen.

Or, would have, if she could have read the letter. Now, strangely, it mattered. If only the old woman could have read just this good news. Still, she would write, all the same ... then, she had a brilliant idea: she'd send a postcard. That's what she'd do. She'd print it in big letters on the back of the postcard. She'd only write a little:

Dear Grandmother,

    I have passed my class. I kiss your hand, your loving
Granddaughter,

    Selda.

That was all that would be needed. She knew what would happen: the postman would naturally read it as he walked up the steps. He would knock on the front door and say: 'Congratulations! Your granddaughter Selda has passed her class!' She could just see the old woman spluttering with anger and pleasure at the same time.

Selda pounded up the stairs. She would write that evening.

Ten

Selda's family did not react to the news about school as she had expected them to. She expected her father to go straight round to the teacher to find out why Pembe and Fatma had failed. He didn't. He grumbled a lot and said that it 'wasn't fair' and that 'foreign children weren't treated properly'. But he did not do anything. Then Adnan Hoca and his wife, Hanife Hanım, came round the next evening and persuaded him that it was all for the best.

'Consider, dear friend,' said Adnan Hoca, 'do you *really*, as a father, want your girls to *have* to work? I must say that I feel that women are happiest as wives and mothers.' He smiled at his wife and she smiled sweetly back at him from under her head scarf. Hanife Hanım was a very nice woman and did not express any opinions in mixed company.

'No, no,' said Adnan Hoca, 'education makes women discontended. Look at my daughter now.' Selda looked. Adnan Hoca's daughter was seventeen and worked in the local biscuit factory. Fatma had once unkindly remarked that the girl looked so like a biscuit, it was surprising nobody had put her in a packet. It was true, though. She was short and round and pasty faced, as though she never got out in the fresh air. Now she flashed an enormous engagement ring on her plump, left hand and she chinked with a great deal of new, gold jewellery. Last summer she had been engaged to a cousin, a business man, back in their home town. The wedding was to take place this summer, when the family were back for their annual leave. Now the girl blushed deeply and hid her confusion behind a large slab of chocolate cake.

'Now, there's a happy girl,' said her father. 'She's never caused me a moment's worry. Nor her mother. And why, Turgut Bey? Well, I'll tell you our little secret: we are careful parents! We've taken good care of her and in these modern times, a good parent can't be too careful!'

His wife nodded and looked suspiciously around the crowded little flat as though even there, dangers might lurk.

'Now, I, like you, am a modern man,' said Adnan Hoca, stroking his scruffy little beard. 'I'm not saying that we should lock up our daughters. Oh no. My daughter works in the factory and I'm proud of it! And I've put *all* her wages into a special bank account, for her trousseau. Now, that's what your girls can do, Turgut Bey. They can work until they marry. After all, we all know that the Devil finds work for idle hands. Let them work, Turgut Bey, but don't let them think about 'careers'. It's not suitable for girls.' He turned to Pembe and Fatma and smiled at them sympathetically. 'Now, cheer up, young ladies. Nobody needs a fancy education. Look at your father: he's provided you with this lovely home, all with no education at all, I'll be bound!' Adnan Hoca smoothed down the little ratty bits of his beard, to remind them that actually, he did have a superior education.

Turgut Bey had been obliged to smile. Selda opened her mouth to protest, but caught her mother's warning look and shut it again. And that had really been that: her parents were reconciled to the girls' failure.

Pembe had cried, but mainly because she would now be separated from Ramona. Fatma had laughed and said she wasn't going to bother any more about school, anyway. Selda was left with the uncomfortable feeling that she was the one who had done the 'wrong thing'. She was very glad she had never spoken about her ambition to go to the gymnasium at home. She could imagine what Adnan Hoca's views on that would have been. The only people she told were her grand-mother and Ferhat.

Now that the winter holiday and *Fasnacht* were both over, spring had arrived at last. Unbelievably and magically, in parks and in gardens, flowers bloomed above the frozen earth. Window boxes displayed little plants with faces, called 'pansies', which were brilliant with colour, even when the frost still darkened their leaves. Sevgi Hanım admired them so much that one day Ahmet bought her some as a surprise. As delighted as a child, she planted them out. She tended them with all the love and skill she had once used to work their small-holding in the village. She even began to make plans to grow tomatoes in a sunny corner of the balcony.

As the temperature slowly rose it began to rain torentially. It rained for days on end and once again you could hear the water rushing and roaring under the street. It was as if some underground beast had reawakened. Giselle and Selda heard it as they walked down to the library. They had established a routine now. Giselle always came to lunch on Wednesdays and Fridays, which were half days at school. Then they walked down to the library together and afterwards, by another route, they walked up to the farm. There, they played with Brownie until Ferhat had finished his work outside. He was making surprising progress with his German and Selda had to admit to herself that Giselle was a good teacher. She made him talk. She was endlessly curious, asking him again and again about himself and his family and about life back in Turkey. Ferhat, of course had to reply and Selda, of course, listened to all he said. Watching him learning to speak in German was a bit like watching someone come alive again.

Then Herr Hebel gave Giselle a brand new pink racing bike as a reward for passing her class. In a single wild afternoon, Giselle taught Selda to ride the old one. The days lengthened and the sun shone more and the two of them began to ride over to the farm more often. Ferhat, who was fully recovered, was back working very hard but he always seemed pleased to see them. Some of the sows had farrowed and once he took them to see the piglets. Selda watched in horror and fascination as the squealing, tumbling pink babies swarmed around their mothers who were closely penned in to stop them lying on their offspring. Several times when she looked up at the farmhouse, Selda thought she saw the face of old Bauer watching from the window, but nothing was ever said. She saw Ferhat's father, too, but he always turned his back on them. There he would be in the distance, working furiously, like a machine, repairing the fences or cleaning the ditches in readiness for the torrents of icy water that would soon flood down from the melting snows in the mountains.

One Wednesday afternoon Selda saw primroses on a sheltered bank on the farm. They were as pale and unexpected as moonlight amongst the damp mosses and newly shooting blades of grass.

'Look at these,' she cried, jumping off the bike and bending down to pick some for her mother.

'Don't!' warned Giselle. 'It's forbidden.'

Selda looked up at her in disbelief.

'Forbidden?' She could not see that they belonged to anyone.

'You're not allowed to pick the wild flowers here in Switzerland. They're protected by law. It's the way we look after our countryside. If everybody picked what they fancied, there wouldn't be any wild flowers left in a few years.'

Selda drew back her hand. It did make sense. She had read in the Izmir papers about whole mountains and valleys being stripped of bulbs and flowers in southern Turkey.

'Can't you pick *any* flowers?'

'Some you can, very common ones, dandelions and things, but not these. Weren't you listening in class when Fräulein Altmann was talking about it?'

'I don't think I understand what she was saying.' It was

true that she still sometimes entirely lost the track of a conversation.

'You must have. She was telling us about the trip.'

'What trip?'

'Selda! Don't you know anything? Our class trip, you idiot. Fräulein Altmann even sent letters by post to make sure nobody forgot them. Hey, what's the matter?'

'What letters? My family didn't get a letter. Honestly, Giselle, I never knew about this trip.'

'Well, ask your parents this evening, or better still, talk to Fräulein Altmann about it. Anyway, the letter said that on the trip we'll be going to an area where there are special mountain flowers and that none of them can be picked. We can take photos, if we like. That's what I'll do. I've got a super new camera and I never know what to take. Now I can take flowers . . .' She chattered on but Selda was not listening. She was thinking about the letter that had been posted home from school. They had never told her. Her parents did not want her to go, that must be it! No, she mustn't jump to conclusions, that was wrong. She must ask them about it as soon as she got home. Perhaps they had just forgotten.

Giselle was still chattering on about what they would do and see on the trip, so Selda, to join in, asked if they would see primroses up there.

'Primroses! Of course we won't, it's much too high,' said Giselle scornfully. 'It'll still be winter up there and the only flowers will be a few rare winter things, if they aren't covered in snow.'

'Why will it be winter up there when it's spring here?'

'Because of the altitude. Haven't you any mountains in Turkey?'

'Yes, but . . .'

'I bet they aren't like the mountains here. You should see St Moritz, where we have our chalet. Now that's really cold up there. And there are mountains all round. It's so cold that even the waterfalls freeze in winter.'

'They can't.'

'They can, I've seen them. Don't you believe me?'

'Yes, but . . . '

'Honestly, Selda, you're just like everybody else. They don't believe me. But I'm telling the truth. You can see great, frozen waterfalls up there: flowing streams stopped and frozen solid in the air, as they tip over the sides of the mountains.'

'They must look wonderful,' said Selda. It was difficult to imagine.

'Wonderful?' said Giselle, jumping back on her bike.' It's not particularly wonderful, it's just very, very cold, that's all.' She started to pedal away.

'I'd love to see it,' called Selda, struggling to keep up.

'Would you? Why?'

'It would be, well, I can't say, really.' And she couldn't. She had no words to describe what it must be like to see the impossible actually happen. Here, in this country of lakes and mists and rain and snow, where the water ran and ran, both under the ground and over it, and where everything was washed and cleaned and set in order, now suddenly it seemed that this relentless movement could be stopped. The tons of water which slid over the edge of the mountain could be held back. Who, in all the world, would have believed that waterfalls could freeze? One might as well have expected to hold back the water of the Bosphorous.

'Do you see many up there, in the mountains, where you're going?'

'Many what?'

'Frozen waterfalls?'

'Yes, I suppose so. What's so interesting about them? You are an odd person, Selda. Who cares, anyway? If you're so keen on them, you'd better come with us next time we go. Then you can see for yourself. Oh, do hurry up.' She pedalled away so swiftly on the new bike that Selda, on the little old bike, could barely catch up and had to shout.

'Did you mean that?'

'No!' Giselle yelled back, over her shoulder. 'Of course I didn't. I don't care whether you come or not. I mean, I never have liked the mountains. Still, if you insist, I don't mind if you come with us. Bye!'

This time she clicked the gears on the bike and sprinted off up the hill to her house, her long legs going like pistons. Selda did not try to catch up. She had seen the Hebel's house from the outside: a huge, modern building, set in perfect gardens. She could imagine that the large, bare windows had a wonderful view, directly down upon the vast, grey lake. It was an isolated house, with only one or two others near it. The forest behind seemed to press down on it very closely and was restless and dark. You could imagine that there were many shadows in the house.

Something made Selda turn round and there, walking briskly along the track which they had just left, was a policeman. She felt her heart begin the thump. She stood where she was, waiting for him to pass. He didn't. He came right over to her. She gripped the handlebars and felt as though her face were on fire.

'Gruezi,' he said, very pleasantly, 'you won't forget to get a new registration number for your bike, will you?' When she stared at him in bewilderment, he added: 'Ask your teacher. She knows all about it. And take care.' He smiled again and walked briskly away and she breathed a long sigh of relief.

As soon as she got home she asked her mother if any letters had recently come from school. Sevgi Hanım, who was tending her window-box, did not look up, but said that her father would know about anything like that. He always opened the letters. When Turgut Bey came home from the factory he said 'no', there had been no letter and Selda believed him.

Pembe, who was watching television and only half listening to them, shouted helpfully above the din: 'But there was that letter two days ago, Father. You put it in your other jacket. Shall I get it for you?'

There was an uncomfortable silence, Sevgi Hanım had come in from the balcony and stood there clutching a bunch of yellowed leaves in her hand.

'Was it about the school trip?' asked Selda.

'How dare you question me about my letters!' raged Turgut Bey. Then he turned on Pembe' 'And how dare you contradict me!'

'Well, Father.' Ahmet got up slowly and switched off the television. 'Was the letter about Selda's school trip?'

'No. No, it wasn't. Well, well that is to say, I haven't had time to read it yet. We've been very busy at the factory.'

'You can read it now.'

'I haven't got it with me.'

'Pembe says that it's in your jacket.'

'Pembe had no right to interfere,' said Sevgi Hanım, desperate to keep the peace. 'Nor have you, Ahmet. Have you no respect for your father? Now, let's forget it, it's nothing to do with the rest of you, anyway. I'm sure your father knows best.'

'Mother, don't you think that Selda deserves better than that?' asked Ahmet.

There was another long, long silence. Then Turgut Bey said angrily and bitterly: 'If you all think that you can run this family better than me, you can do it!' He strutted into the bedroom and returned with the letter. He flung it towards Ahmet and Selda so that if fell to the floor between them.

'There you are! Read it! And do what you like! Only, don't blame me, when it all goes wrong! Don't you remember what happened on the last of those trips? Have you all forgotten what happened to your sister, Pembe? Have you? Well, I haven't. I care about my daughters. And just you wait, you'll see that I was right to try and stop Selda going!' He settled himself down in front of the television and turned up the volume as though trying to drown out everyone else's voice.

Ahmet looked at his father and shook his head slowly. Then he picked up the letter and opened it and together he and Selda read it. It was much as Giselle had said: the fourth class was to go on an end-of-term trip up the mountain outside Zurich.

'You go, Selda,' said Ahmet, patting her shoulder. 'Go and enjoy yourself, you deserve it.'

Her father must have heard but he did not turn round or say a thing.

'I don't want to go now,' whispered Selda. It was true. Her father's disapproval had spoilt it.

'But you must. Don't give in, Selda. Your going to do all right here. I know it.' He nodded towards their father. 'He knows it too, but he's scared. He's proud of you, really.'

'Is he?' She so wished that it were true.

If Turgut Bey were proud of his third daughter he certainly did not show it. But somebody else did. When Selda came came from school the very next day a letter from Turkey was waiting for her.

'At last!' she cried happily to her mother. 'Do you know, I thought that poor Demet would never, ever write. I misjudged her.'

'I don't think you did,' said Sevgi Hanım, and she pointed to the address written on the back of the envelope. It was the address of her grandmother's house and, now she looked at the envelope more carefully, this was not Demet's writing, either.

'You don't think something has happened, something bad?' said Selda nervously but her mother shook her head.

Selda tore open the envelope and a picture postcard of the bay of Izmir fell out. She turned it over. The writing was in pencil and big and childish:

My dear Granddaughter Selda,

Congratulations on passing your class. I am very proud of you.

Your loving Grandmother, Eda.

And then, underneath, in a proper grown-up hand: 'Your grandmother is going to my reading course' and there was the signature of a teacher.

Neither of them could speak for a moment. Then they both began laughing and crying at once and they shouted to Pembe and Fatma to 'come and look'.

'I don't believe it,' gasped Fatma. 'Grandmother, learning to read! And at her age!'

'I think it's a good idea,' said Pembe coolly. 'Now she won't pester us to read the newspaper to her all the time when we visit.'

It was incredible. They could not wait for the boys and Turgut Bey to come home. Selda hoped that their good news would heal some of the previous day's hurt. They kept taking the card down and marvelling at what the old woman had done. They knew of course that there were reading and writing courses held in the neighbourhood and that it was usually women whose families had not sent them to school who now went to learn. Their own grandmother, however, that was something quite different. In the quietness of the bedroom Selda looked at herself in the mirror and remembered that her grandmother, whom everyone said had been a handsome woman in her youth, resembled her. They shared the same dark, determined brows, the same strong, bony face. So this grandmother had actually dared to go to school . . .

Then she remembered the letters, all those letters which she had thought that no one, except herself, would ever read. She imagined the old woman on the balcony, holding the letters up to catch the full light, moving her rough finger along from word to word, saying them aloud as one did while one was still learning, and she was glad. She was so glad that she had written them. Now it seemed as though all along that obstinate old woman had been at her side, worrying about her, caring about her, watching her from afar and hoping that everything would turn out well. She put the postcard back into the envelope and into her pocket. Later she copied her grandmother's letter and address in tiny writing on to a piece of white paper. Then she rolled it up just like the fortune and kept the two of them together, like talismans.

Over the next few days the weather was particularly fine, and with less homework as the end of term approached Selda and Giselle went over to see Ferhat even more often than before. Sometimes Selda wondered if she were helping him at all, for it was Giselle who did all the talking. She chattered non-stop and followed him about like a little dog. She got in his way and didn't seem to notice but just kept on with her endless questions. He answered her and sometimes looked irritated, then, recovered himself and tried again to give a correct answer. It was Giselle who sat beside him in the barn and turned over the pages of the school books and corrected his pronunciation. It was Giselle who told him instantly when he had made a mistake.

As the evenings were lighter they began to walk up into the forest and it was always Giselle who walked beside him and talked and Selda who followed silently behind. She would have like to talk to him more, longed to, in fact, but Giselle hated it when they spoke in Turkish. She interrupted constantly, demanding that they both pay attention to her. She protested that it was unfair of them to speak in Turkish when they knew that she couldn't understand.

So Selda often kept quiet and just listened and watched. She liked watching. She liked being there with him. She even liked watching him work. Restless by nature, he seemed more at ease when occupied so Selda sat and watched him as he stacked the wood or forked the straw up into the trailer. Sometimes he had to clean out the goat's stall. One afternoon he was shifting sacks of grain. She watched him hoist them up on to his shoulder and then, bent under the weight, walk with then across the yard. Giselle, thinking that it was not hard work and that she too, could do it, seized a sack and almost overturned it. The grain started to gush from one corner and would have run out all over her if Selda hadn't jumped up and held the edges of the sack together. Ferhat shook his head mildly and called Giselle a 'naughty child' in Turkish.

'What did he say? Go on, tell me, I know he said something about me!'

She asked over and over again as if she half wanted to be punished for what she had done. Selda twisted up the corner and held it firm until Ferhat could bind it around with twine. He moved so quickly that he scraped her hand, but did not say he was sorry. Giselle noticed. She, scowled and walked away and went and swung on the old barn door, making it crack, until Ferhat shouted at her. Then she stopped instantly.

Sometimes Selda wondered if Giselle and Ferhat were playing some silent game, of which she did not know the rules but was still expected to umpire. She felt left out and forgotten, but she still wanted to be there and see him. She wanted to make sure that he was all right. She was thinking about him when she walked into the flat one afternoon, red faced and untidy, from the bike ride home. She was surprised to find Adnan Hoca's wife in the salon, taking tea with her mother. There was something odd about the way the visitor looked up and greeted her and about the way Sevgi Hanım was suddenly busy with the tea things and so avoided saying 'hello'.

Hanife Hanım was a thin little woman, or, to be more accurate, a woman with a thin little face. The rest of her had disappeared beneath a vast shapeless coat that was buttoned up to the chin and swept the ground like a tent. It was no proper colour at all, but like the dust that settles in abandoned corners. She, like her daughter, was as pale as a prisoner and the grey wool scarf, which hid her hair, was pulled as tight and close over her forehead as a second skin. Not a wisp of hair showed. Only her eyes moved. They darted between Selda and her mother, and Selda sensed that she had interrupted some difficult conversation. She kissed the visitor's hand and, when she touched it to her forehead, she felt its damp, limp heat and she wondered why Hanife Hanım had not taken off her coat on this lovely spring afternoon. As if to answer this unspoken question, the visitor patted the sofa beside her, so that Selda must sit there, then she leaned too close and said: 'I'm not staying, you see. It's not, I'm afraid, a social call today, dear. I've been waiting for you to come in, haven't I? Sevgi Hanım?'

Sevgi Hanım looked miserable and straightened an untouched biscuit on her plate.

'You see, dear, your mother didn't know about it. She's very upset, naturally.'

'Mother! What are you upset about?' Selda felt her heart begin to beat differently, flutter almost.

'She's upset about the Turkish boy!' said Hanife Hanım and cleaned her lips with a handkerchief.

'Yes,' moaned Sevgi Hanım.'' Oh, Selda! Everybody else knows! I can't think what your father is going to say! Of course, Adnan Bey hasn't mentioned it yet. But Selda, why didn't you tell me?'

'Yes Selda. Why didn't you tell your mother? Just look at the state she's in.'

'*Why* didn't you?' repeated Sevgi Hanım pathetically, and Selda saw that her mother was actually crying.

She looked from one to the other of the women. Why hadn't she told her mother? She looked back at her mother, sitting there with bowed head, listening to this dreadful visitor gossiping on and on, and accepting it all without question, and she realized that that was the exact reason why she had not spoken of Ferhat. Her family would have just turned her friendship into ugly, cruel gossip. and there was nothing to tell: all that she could have told, would not have been what they expected to hear.

> Bury secrets in your heart,
> To keep them safe for evermore.

'I've nothing to tell,' said Selda, in her most obstinate voice.

'Well!' Hanife Hanım looked like a disappointed child who has had a sweet snatched from its hand.

'Selda, how can you, when Hanife Hanım has come all this way to warn me?'

'Warn you of *what*?' insisted Selda, even though she had already decided not to tell. She had betrayed the secret twice, but would not now, not again. And never to this woman who peered so from the prison of her clothes.

'Selda!' begged Sevgi Hanım, 'please don't be so difficult. You must have known. You must have heard them talking. You've heard them, haven't you dear? And seen them together, oh, dear, I don't know what your father is going to say. He's always tried to be so careful with the girls, Hanife Hanım. I, too, as their mother . . . but since I don't go out myself, how was I to know? I didn't even know that there was a cinema in the town!'

Selda looked at her mother in astonishment.

'Whatever are you talking about?' she asked.

'Oh Selda! They've been to the cinema together! Hanife Hanım saw them! She says that everybody is talking about them. Everybody knew but us. Just think of it! All those times when Pembe and Fatma went in to see that girl, that awful Italian, Ramona, isn't it? Well, they said they were going to do their homework, but really, Pembe was meeting this boy there!'

193

If Selda had not hated Hanife Hanım so intensely at that moment, she could have leant back on the sofa and laughed with relief. But her scorn for this wretched woman with her malicious gossip, and her realization of what trouble such gossip might mean for Pembe, prevailed. She looked at her mother and regretted the weakness that had made Sevgi Hanım believe it straight away. She knew that she must speak with care. If ever there was a time for 'watching her step', it was now.

'What *are* you saying, Hanife Hanım?' she asked coolly. 'What *have* you been telling my mother?'

'Now, my dear, I haven't been saying anything. I've been explaining to your mother, for her own good, and for your sister's, of course, that Pembe has ... well, I don't quite know how to say it, not ever having had a problem like this with my own daughter, but, dear, it does have to be said.' She took a little gulp of air. 'Your elder sister, Pembe has, well, a "special friend", a young man . . . '

Sevgi Hanım made a helpless noise, like a creature, caught.

'Rubbish!' cried Selda as loudly and violently as she could and she heard herself sounding exactly like her grand-mother. 'What makes you come here and say things like that to my mother? It's just gossip, Hanife Hanım, idle factory gossip!' She had not known that she could be so angry. 'Why shouldn't Pembe have friends? Of course she has friends. She's a very popular girl in her class. She deserves friends. Everybody does. And what's so terrible if some of her friends are boys. What do you really mean, Hanife Hanım?'

'Selda, I didn't mean anything. I . . . ' Hanife Hanım felt around the edges of her scarf to make sure that no hair was escaping. 'I don't gossip. I'm just repeating what people have told me. After all, dear, I did see them coming out of the cinema. Adnan Bey has seen them too. He saw them at the

Fasnacht procession. He saw your sister talking to that boy, that Zeki. I'm not saying more than that.'

'But you are!'

'Selda!' Her mother tried to calm them, to restore peace.

'It's quite all right, Sevgi Hanım,' said Hanife Hanım, getting up. She smoothed down her coat and put her head on one side and said, in a voice as sweet as syrup: 'I shan't tell anyone else. You can trust me. I'm no gossip. But I do advise you, as one mother to another, that we should all be very, very careful. Nobody wants spoiled goods, do they?' And she drew the horrid grey scarf so far down her face that Selda was reminded of a lizard blinking against the sun. Then Hanife Hanım simpered at her reflection in the hall mirror and checked her buttons one by one as though she even distrusted the blustering spring winds outside.

'Well now, Adnan Bey will be waiting for me and we all know how impatient men are!' She stepped into her high-heeled shoes. 'If you'll forgive me for saying so, she added, 'I think your Pembe, lovely girl that she is, would do much better under a little more control. You really should think about the biscuit factory, Sevgi Hanım. It's such a nice clean place and all the workers are women, or very old men, if you know what I mean.'

She kissed Sevgi Hanım on both cheeks, as though nothing at all had happened and then she held out her hand for Selda to kiss, but Selda did not move. She wouldn't. She only said an indifferent 'goodbye' and Hanife Hanım had to pretend that she hadn't noticed and had only been going to put on her gloves.

They heard her going down the steps, tap, tap, tap and then again, tap, tap, tap, right down to the very bottom. At the last moment Selda ran out and lent over the balcony and spat vigorously in the direction of Adnan Bey's waiting car. Indoors her mother slumped in a chair.

'Look, Selda dear, let's not mention it to your father? I

mean, it's not necessary. If Adnan Hoca, an educated man, hasn't said anything, why should we? It'll only make trouble. What do you think? I'll talk to Pembe. It'll only worry your father to know . . . '

'Mother? Know what? Surely you don't believe that woman? How could you believe somebody like that?'

'But Selda, she said . . . '

'Yes? What did she say?'

'Well, nothing, really.'

'Mother, what *did* she say, before I came in?'

'It doesn't matter Selda. Let's forget it. I don't want to talk about it. Not now. Later, maybe.'

'With father?'

'No! With Pembe, of course.'

'Mother, you must tell me what she said.'

'Selda, you're just like your grandmother.'

'Am I?'

'Yes. I'm afraid so. She was always obstinate like that, keeping on and on about things that are better forgotten.'

'I'm glad I'm like her then. She'd never have believed such gossip. How could you, Mother? Hadn't you better tell me what she said then?'

'She said,' whispered Sevgi Hanım in a sad little voice, 'that the whole Turkish community in the town says that my Pembe has been seen talking to this dreadful boy, this Zeki. She said that she saw Pembe and Fatma coming out of the cinema with . . . with boys.'

'And?'

'Isn't that enough?'

'It's nothing!'

'Nothing? Selda, your sisters have, have . . . '

'Been to the cinema! Why shouldn't they? We went in Izmir. I expect they went with Ramona and her sister's friends. Ramona's very nice. You used to say so yourself. She was the first person to speak to Pembe and Fatma when they started school. She's got these older brothers and sisters, I don't know who, exactly, but some of them are in the secondary school. Fatma used to go sledging with them. You knew she did.'

'No, I didn't. You went with her, I thought. Anyway, it doesn't matter now. What matters is . . .' and she sighed and began to fiddle with the tea things. Then she turned to Selda. 'Now dear, do tell me what you know about this Zeki.'

'I don't know anything about him. Shouldn't you ask Pembe?'

Sevgi Hanım sighed again and went on to the balcony to look at her pansies. She stood there for some time, picking off the dead leaves and scraping at the soil with an old fork. When she spoke again her voice was so quiet that Selda had to come over to her.

'I didn't think it would be like this here. Switzerland is too different for me. Your father never said that it would be like this. If he had, I would never have come. I shouldn't have brought you girls. Then, in the end, he would have had to come back.' She dropped the leaves over the edge of the balcony and they went fluttering down to the next floor. Below them Selda heard a Swiss voice, sharp with irritation, mutter: 'Did you see that? Tossing their rubbish off their balcony, just as if they were still in their village!'

Her mother did not understand, but dusted the earth from her fingers and said: 'It wasn't like this, not when I came on that visit.'

'I know,' said Selda, trying to sound patient and she took her mother's arm and they went back inside and made fresh tea.

They were drinking it together when the girls came home. Pembe was a poor liar. When Sevgi Hanım asked them where they had been, Fatma replied instantly and cheerfully that they had been out with friends. Pembe giggled and bit her lip

197

and inspected her nails and finally admitted that they had been to the cinema. She went on in complete innocence to tell them that this week's film had been better. Last week's had been so boring they had left early. It had been a waste of money.

'Why are you asking?' Fatma inquired cautiously.

'I just wondered.' Sevgi Hanım was evasive, as if she did not really want to know. It seemed as though she were about to leave it at that, merely giving the girls a warning look. It was Selda who had to know more.

'Hanife Hanım was here,' she said roughly, 'gossiping about Pembe and some boy, Zeki.'

'Selda!' It was not her sisters but her mother who protested. The girls just pulled faces.

'Hanife Hanım? Oh, she would!' And Fatma laughed. She actually gurgled with laughter. Nor did Pembe seem particularly upset. She picked up one of the biscuits and began to nibble around its jam centre in a satisfied sort of way. Then she spoke quietly and to her mother: 'He's very nice, you know. You'd like him. His family are from outside Izmir. Bornova, I think. And his father doesn't work in a factory here but in an office. And do you know what Zeki plans to do when he leaves school? You'll never guess: work in a bank, a Swiss bank! Isn't that wonderful? He's *very* clever.'

'Is he?' asked Sevgi Hanım and took care not to look at Selda.

'Oh yes. I wouldn't be able to do any of my homework if he didn't help. Do you know, he's the only Turk in his class in secondary school even if it did take him two extra years to get there . . .'

'He must be very hard working,' said Sevgi Hanım, awkwardly. 'All the same, you should have told me.'

'I was going to, naturally . . .' Pembe said softly, and Selda saw them exchange a cautious glance of new understanding.

'It's just that people talk so,' said Sevgi Hanım,' and in a

198

little place like this, when all the Turks know one another, well, people will . . . '

'Mother!' said Fatma robustly. 'Now don't start imagining things. It's different here. They're school friends: we go around in a group. We need to anyway, we are all foreigners, the Italians and us. We get on well together. Lots of people go to the cinema on Wednesdays and Fridays and they asked us to go too. Don't you want us to go?'

'Yes. Yes of course I do. But I worry so. And Hanife Hanım frightened me. There's no need to be frightened, is there, Pembe?'

'No-o.' Pembe looked up from her lashes and she and her mother exchanged another glance. 'No-o, not really.'

'I see,' said Sevgi Hanım. 'I never wanted to bother your father with such nonsense anyway, and now I won't have to. He's had enough to worry about this week, hasn't he?' She smiled at all three girls but her brightest smile was for Pembe.

Then, unusually, Pembe and Fatma began to help their mother gather up the tea things and went with her into the kitchen to help prepare the supper. A moment later Pembe came back and closed the sitting-room door, saying that she did not want the smell of fried onions to go all over the flat. Selda sat on. She had intended to write to her grandmother, but didn't. She took a piece of paper from her school bag and wrote the address and the date, then leant back with pen poised. She found herself thinking of Giselle's casual invitation to go with the Hebel family to their holiday home in the mountains. Two hours ago, before Pembe and Fatma returned, she had not been sure if she wanted to go. Now, something in the house had changed and she wanted to go. She could hear the tap water running into saucepans and the scrape of spoons and the busy thud of the knife on the chopping board. She could hear the murmur of Pembe's and Fatma's excited voices, telling and telling whatever it was they wanted their mother to know.

Selda knew that she had been left out of some understanding between her mother and her elder sisters. It hurt a little, but she also knew that she did not want to go into the kitchen and be part of the plotting and planning that would be taking place there. For the first time in her life she wondered what it must be like to be part of another family, Giselle's maybe. Then she thought of Ramona. Did she have to hide from her family where she went on the free afternoons? And what about Giselle? What did she say to her mother? Could she look up from the breakfast table and say to Frau Hebel: 'Yes, I'll be having lunch with Selda and in the afternoon I expect we'll go and see that Turkish friend of hers'. Was it like that in the Hebel household?

She could not imagine the Hebels exchanging secrets in some hot, steamy kitchen. She imagined them rather as the model figures that you saw in the doll's houses in toy shop windows: each perfectly moulded and dressed, but rigid and alone and fixed, there, in the still, unlit rooms of the house. Up to now Selda had only stood at the Hebels' gate and waited for Giselle. She had not wanted to walk up the drive and ring the bell. Suddenly she was curious. She wanted to go inside that house. She wanted to see the view of the mountains and lake which those huge, bare windows must give. She wanted to saunter through those large, perfect rooms. She wondered what it was like to have a front-door key and to come and go unremarked. Even Giselle's small brother Anton had a key. It swung from his belt at the end of a large coil of luminous green plastic and she knew that he often let himself into the empty house just like a grown-up. Up until today, the silent house had always seemed rather threatening. Now Selda was not so sure. Maybe it was a life of more freedom. Maybe, she day-dreamed, maybe she could go to the mountains with the Hebels.

Maybe, if she went with them, she could see how the green grass of spring gave way to the icy heights above. Then she could also see if the waterfalls really did freeze as they tumbled over the rock edges. And up there, she could be independent. She could become a new person, a different person. She would no longer be just this Turkish girl, somebody's clever daughter and somebody's younger sister, the odd one in the family, who was difficult and obstinate. No, up there, in that different, frozen land, she could start again. She decided that if Giselle asked again, this time she would accept the invitation. She would set out into this new territory more courageously than she had set out from her grandmother's walled garden. This time she would not even want to look back.

The front-doorbell rang. The kitchen door opened instantly. Somebody ran lightly down the hall. Somebody was hurrying to let Turgut Bey in, for he never carried a key. She heard her father ask: 'What smells so good?'

'Eggs with onions.'

'What a surprise! My favourite supper! And I thought you women had forgotten how to cook a simple Turkish meal like that.'

'As if we would,' said Sevgi Hanım, and behind her Pembe laughed softly.

Eleven

In the lakeside villages the snow had finally melted away and in the town several trees had burst into bright pink blossom. It was as though a strong hand had released its grip and the countryside had sprung alive.

'Well!' exclaimed Sevgi Hanım, leaning over the fence to take a closer look at one of these trees. She would have liked to have broken off a spray of flowers, but was afraid that somebody might see her.

'Do you see that, Selda? Do you see that the flowers are full out before the leaves? It doesn't seem natural, does it?' They were on their way back from school, walking slowly and enjoying the sunshine. They had been talking to Fräulein Altmann about the fourth class trip. It had been difficult to persuade Sevgi Hanım to come to the school to meet the teacher but in the end Ahmet had succeeded.

'The Black Sea must be a bit like this, or that's what your Kemal Amca always said. He said it was cool and green and wet, with everything growing at such a rate.'

'Have you been there?' Selda asked.

'No. I never wanted to, either. I wasn't like my brother. Kemal was always a wanderer. Even as a boy he used to sit out on the main road, watching for cars going past. Not that there were many cars in those days, only a handful of families had them in Izmir, but he still watched.'

'Didn't you want to go anywhere, when you were young?'

'Me? No, why should I? I was quite content. Even when your father took me back to his village as a bride, I was happy. When business got so bad and your father decided to

go and work abroad, I didn't want to go with him. I thought
he'd only stay a couple of years. I thought he'd save a bit
and then come back. I didn't want to go and leave my
country. I'm not like Kemal and your father, wanting to see
new places. I don't think women do . . . '.

'But *I* do!'

'Well, you may think you do, because you're a child,
Selda. Children can't know what they want. But you will,
later. You'll want to have your own home in your own
country. That's normal.'

'But I don't want that.'

'Selda, why must you always be so difficult?' Sevgi
Hanım's slow step had quickened and her cheerful tone had
changed to one of irritation. 'Why must you be so obstinate?
You make things very difficult for yourself and for other
people.'

Selda knew that Sevgi Hanım had not wanted her to go on
the trip and she was grateful to her for having agreed. Now
she put her arm through her mother's and as they both
paused to look at an early, unexpected brilliance of red bulbs
they heard raised voices burst out into the silent street. A
dispute seemed to have broken out at the door of the Co-op
over the road. A woman in a black fur jacket had run from
the entrance and now stood in front of the plate-glass window, shouting and holding at bay, it seemed, a small group
of shop assistants and customers. She shouted dreadfully
and her voice rang unchallenged in the stillness. She was
swearing, too, and staggered on black high heels as arched
and sharp as talons.

Selda gripped her mother's arm. One of the shop assistants, smiling nervously, stepped forward. She held something out on the palm of her hand. It was something small,
wrapped in silver paper. You could tell that she was coaxing
the other to take it, that she was offering to make peace in
some unexpected battle. The woman in black stumbled away

203

as though threatened, but instead of going away up the street, she moved sideways and came up against the dusty glass window. The assistant took a step closer. The other, trapped by the gleaming wall of glass, rubbed her head back and forth against it as though seeking some escape. Selda and her mother, clinging tightly to each other, came up the street in horrible fascination. They moved with no sound at all. Selda recognized Giselle's mother and felt suddenly sick.

Frau Hebel sprang at the assistant and knocked from her hand what was being offered and then she kicked at it. Once, twice, she kicked it along the street and into the gutter. In the confusion the shop assistant tripped and fell down. The small crowd instantly gathered around the figure on the ground, helping her to her feet and putting their arms around her. Frau Hebel stood alone swaying and smoothing down the sleek, black fur of the jacket as though she were the one who had sprawled on the stones. She looked around her in a confused but mechanical way, as though she had forgotten something. Then she called shrilly: 'Anton? Anton?'

Selda saw him then: a little boy, standing on his own in the doorway of the shop, intently peeling the silver paper back from a bar of chocolate. He was not looking at anyone.

'Anton? Come here at once!'

He did not seem to hear her, but picked at the wrapping, bit by bit.

'Come *here*!' Her voice was a scream.

He bit off the end of the chocolate and Selda could see him struggling to swallow a large chunk.

'An-ton.' Now her voice was low, but full of menace. His mother stepped towards him and Anton fled. He ran in a wide circle, avoiding both his mother and the crowd, and when he was clear of them all, he stopped. He looked back and shrieked over his shoulder: '*Blöde Kuh!*' and then ran on up the street all alone,

'Well!' exclaimed Sevgi Hanım. 'Whatever was all that

about?' She shook her head. 'And I always thought the Swiss were such well-behaved people.'

'I don't know what it was about,' whispered Selda miserably and they walked the rest of the way home arm in arm.

It seemed that scandal travelled just as quickly in the clean-swept streets of the little Swiss town as it did in the thronging byways of Izmir. Ali, coming straight in after work, already knew all about the incident. The factory was alive with the gossip that Frau Hebel, the crazy wife of the town's leading citizen, had been caught shoplifting!

'People say that she had her pockets stuffed with chocolate, packets of it, can you imagine?' He laughed. 'The Hebels are rich enough to bathe in the stuff if they want to!'

'They say that she's been arrested,' added Turgut Bey, with some satisfaction.

'It wasn't like that at all,' said Selda furiously and then stopped. She had not intended to talk about it.

'How do you know?' asked Ali curiously.

'You don't mean . . .' began Sevgi Hanım, looking at Selda. 'You don't mean to tell me that that woman, that wicked tramp of a woman on the street, was Frau Hebel, was your Giselle's mother?'

Selda nodded. There was no escaping it.

'I . . .'

'What? Did you see it, then?' asked Turgut Bey eagerly.

'Oh yes. I did,' said Sevgi Hanım. 'I saw everything and so did Selda. But she never told me that that woman was Giselle's mother! To think I've made that girl tea and cakes and treated her like a daughter, better than a daughter, really, making all those special lunches, and all the time she was just the daughter of a criminal, a common thief!'

'That's not true!' cried Selda.

'Yes it is. Your father has just told us that the woman has been arrested. Selda, you're never to speak to that girl again, not after what we've seen today.'

'What did you see?' Ali had settled down in front of the television. 'Come on Selda, but tell us quickly before the match starts.'

Selda looked from one to the other of her family. What had she actually seen out there on the street? Not much, really, when she thought about it. Watching Frau Hebel had been like watching some frail, scuttling black beetle, caught unexpectedly in the bright sunlight, before it could get back to the safety of the shadows. She'd only seen that and then Anton running away up the street, escaping as fast as he could. She was certain that what she had seen had been some other tragedy and not at all what they were gossiping about in the factory.

'Well?' insisted Turgut Bey.

'There isn't anything to tell. Frau Hebel was shouting and the people from the shop were trying to make her take something and . . . and . . . '

'And she attacked that shop assistant! Tell them Selda. You must have seen it,' urged Sevgi Hanım.

'But I didn't see that.'

'Yes you did. You must have. I did. I'll tell them then. I'll tell them what you saw,' declared Sevgi Hanım.

When she had finished Fatma remarked coolly: 'I can't see what everybody is making such a fuss about. Everybody in the town knows that Frau Hebel is crazy. She drinks, they say.'

'Fatma, don't talk about things like that,' said Turgut Bey crossly.

'But father, it's true,' interrupted Pembe softly, not raising her eyes from the television screen. 'Ramona told me ages ago. Everybody at school knows. That's why Frau Hebel is so odd. Everybody laughs at her behind her back and at Giselle. That's why nobody is friendly with her, except Selda.'

'I didn't know that,' said Selda.

'Well I never,' said Pembe in a tone of exaggerated surprise.' I thought you were the clever one who always knows everything.'

The next day was Wednesday and in the morning Giselle was not in school. Nothing had been mentioned at home, but when Selda returned at lunch-time, she noticed that the best china, which Sevgi Hanım always used when Giselle came, was not set out on the table. It was a dreary meal and Selda was glad to get out of the house when it was over.

She was worried about Giselle and so, when she went to get the bike out of the cellar, she decided to go up to the Hebels' house to see if she was all right. She pedalled slowly up the hill towards the forest. Then she propped the bike up against the wall and began to tread the crunching gravel path. The gardens were very beautiful. Somebody had recently mown the lawns in perfectly straight lines. It seemed colder up there, for the forest towered so steeply above the house that almost all was in shade. There were hardly any flowers and all was green and brown and grey – and perfect. Yes, it was as she had anticipated: from this vantage point you could see almost the whole sweep of the lake. She rang the bell but it appeared that nobody was at home. She had rang it several times and was just leaving when something made her step back and look up.

She saw Anton. He was standing by an upstairs window still dressed in pyjamas, watching her and sucking his thumb.

'Where's Giselle?' She shouted and pointed to the front door, but he did not move. He just stood there watching her.

'Is she at home?'

He shook his head, then he said something that might have been 'at school', but she couldn't hear clearly. Then his pale face was gone. She rang again and again and waited. When it was clear that he was not coming down, she left. She walked back down the shifting, growling gravel and wondered where she should go.

She would start by looking in the library. Perhaps Giselle had gone there. On the short bike ride Giselle had always sailed ahead and Selda had followed, usually having to go faster than she wanted to, to keep up. Now, setting out alone, she went very slowly at first, with the wheel slithering against the restraint of the tightly clamped brake. She passed the co-op and then the corner garden with the spring flowers. They were even more vivid in the midday sun. The breeze that blew against her face was warm and full of the scent of freshly opening blossoms. The bushes and hedges were alive with twittering birds. They swooped low over the gardens and some had moustaches of dried grasses trailing from their beaks.

Selda released the brake a little and felt the wind ruffle her hair back from her forehead and press against her eyelids. The bike gathered speed and though she put her feet out, just in case, she let it freewheel down the rest of the hill. It felt wonderful.

Giselle's bike was not outside the library. Disappointed Selda went in and handed back her books, then picked out four more almost at random. She tried to think where Giselle might be. Of course. She would be at Bauer's farm. That's where she would go. She would go to the safety of its warm, dusty barn where nobody knew about the Hebel family.

Only Ferhat. Suddenly Selda had to see him. That was where she must go. She ran back to the bike and started to race up the hill, pedalling so fast that she thought her lungs would burst. She had a frightening sense of something being wrong. Something was going to happen to Ferhat. Why had that policeman been walking back from Bauer's farm the other afternoon? They had never seen one there before. Why had he spoken to her? She had been riding the bike for ages and nobody had ever mentioned that you had to register bikes. The policeman must have been suspicious. He must have been watching her, or how did he know that her teacher was a woman? Perhaps they were watching her and Ferhat and his father. And Giselle too? Suppose Giselle had spent the whole morning up there on the farm, following Ferhat around, talking to him, getting in his way and so drawing the attention of the police to him? They would be even more suspicious then. Or, and this was the worse thought of all, suppose Giselle *had* spoken about Ferhat at home? Perhaps she had told Frau Hebel about him, and now Frau Hebel was arrested, and had told the police, and . . .

She pounded at the pedals. She knew that she was thinking more and more wildly, but she could not stop. Suppose the factory gossip about Frau Hebel was true: perhaps she did 'drink'. Drink did make people act in an odd, ugly way; Selda had seen it. Drunkards talked too much. Everybody knew that. Her grandmother had always said that drink pickled people's brains and made them as sour and shrivelled as vegetables left too long in vinegar. Selda remembered the fisherman's bar in Izmir where all the local drunkards went. There they would be, sprawled at the tables drinking cheap wine long before breakfast, calling and shouting to each other and anyone else who would listen. The girls had always been warned to cross the street and 'not to look', but Selda, being curious, had looked. She remembered it now and wondered if Frau Hebel might also be like that, talking to whoever would listen. It somehow seemed worse, that she was a woman, and somebody's mother. Did people's mothers really drink?

Maybe it was all just gossip. Maybe she was just frightening herself. She must stop it. But all the same, she must make sure that Ferhat was still safely there on the farm. Until this moment she had not admitted to herself how much she cared about him, about this stranger, whom she hardly knew, and who had entrusted his secret to her.

'Please, please let him be safe,' she gasped as she turned off on to the track.

She had a stitch in her side and her legs ached and she wished that she had never, ever told Giselle. She should not have taken that risk. It would be her fault if anything happened to him now.

The farm looked as it always did. She slowed down trying to regain her breath. There were the piglets, grown now and scampering out in the field, enjoying the sun. And there, hanging on the apple tree, was a jacket. It was Ferhat's father's jacket. She knew for sure because the yellow scarf, half tucked into the pocket, trailed out in the breeze. They must still be on the farm! She was so relieved that she slowed right down. He might be working somewhere near after all. She looked about her, but could not see him and her heart began to thump again. She could not see anybody. She scanned the fields. Somebody had been ploughing, but the tractor had been left halfway down a furrow. Where was everybody? It was very quiet: there was no sound of anyone working, no sound of axe on wood, no clank of machinery, no hasty, greedy noise of animals being fed.

Had she come too late? She felt suddenly and desperately sick. They must be in the farmhouse. That was it. Perhaps they were having lunch in there; after all, she'd never been there at this time before. She decided to walk around and have a look, even if the old man shouted at her. She had to know. Selda leant the bike against the side of the barn and walked quickly round the corner of the farmhouse. She walked straight into two policemen.

There they were in the brilliant sun, leaning against their black-and-white police car and talking to old Paul Bauer, the farmer. He was seated on a weather-beaten, wooden bench in a warm, sheltered spot by the kitchen door. A couple of farm cats lay near and as Selda approached an old dog got up stiffly and walked to the end of his chain and looked at her but did not bark. The policemen turned towards her in surprise and Paul Bauer, who seemed to be eating a lunch of bread and cheese, stopped in mid-bite and stared at her over a huge hunk of crusty bread. And recognized her. She knew it.

For one second, she thought of running: they could not have followed her back along the track in that police car. Then, ridiculously, she remembered the fortune teller's riddle which Fatma had got:

> 'Dogs are fast,
> And men may be faster,
> But watch where you run,
> Or you'll run to disaster.'

No, she was not going to run away like a coward. And why should she? She had not done anything wrong.

'*Grüezi*,' said the policeman, and it was the same one. She remembered his reddish hair. 'So we meet again.' He spoke kindly but he was watching her very closely.

'Hello,' said Selda and made herself smile. That was what Kemal Amca would have done. And more. She opened her arms and looked the policeman full in the face and said, with a little laugh: 'I haven't registered the bike yet, I'm sorry. I don't really know how to do it.' She smiled again and wondered if she was going to be sick.

'Like I said,' smiled the policeman, 'you need to ask your teacher. You're in Fräulein Altmann's class, aren't you?'

'Yes.' He had startled her though, knowing that.

'My boy is in your class. Christian. He knows you.'

'I see.' Selda knew Christian. He was the red-haired boy, the best football player.

'Settling in, are you? In Switzerland, I mean?'

'Yes thank you. It's . . .' She knew she must be careful. 'It's very, very beautiful here.' 'Do you think so?' He looked pleased, but they were still watching her. And they were going to ask her about Ferhat. She knew it. And she was ready for them.

Old Paul Bauer had been watching her too. Now he laid aside his meal and brushed the crumb's from his front.

'Oh? You like the countryside, do you?' asked the younger policeman in a mocking tone.

'Yes. Yes I do.'

'Well, well! I thought you foreigners only came for our Swiss francs!' He grinned at his colleague, but the red-haired man did not seem to think it funny and old Paul Bauer got up very, very slowly, with the help of a stick. He straightened himself stiffly and painfully. The dog came over to him and touched his nose into his master's hand. The old man fondled him gently then turned to the younger policeman, and said: 'Well, you're wrong again, aren't you officer?' His voice was shaky at first, but now got stronger. 'This little girl has been coming here all through the winter, to feed my rabbits. All through that bitter snow, she came when the other youngsters were up there sledging. I watched her. I saw her, feeding those rabbits, bringing bread, knocking the snow from the grass to give them something fresh. Now only a nature lover does that. She's a good girl, even though she's a foreigner.'

He turned back to look at Selda. 'She's a real animal lover, this one. I can always tell. And what's more, people who love animals love the countryside too and respect it. And they respect people!'

'Well, well, Herr Bauer, what a fine speech!' The younger policeman pulled a face of mock surprise. 'Now, perhaps you'd like to tell us why, if you are so keen on respecting people, you keep illegal immigrants on your farm!'

'Who says I do?' He answered sharply for such a sick old man.

'Look here, Herr Bauer, you know and we know it. Everybody knows about your workers, why don't you just come down to the station with us, so that we can talk about it there?' The red-haired policeman looked quite upset.

'I've said all I've got to say,' said Herr Bauer, roughly. 'Now, go and search my farm. Go on. Go and search my house. Go on. Turn an old man's house upside down. Go and "find" my illegal immigrants, and much good may it do you!'

'You know very well that they've already flown! Somebody has warned them off!' The younger man was already getting back into the car. The other looked at Paul Bauer and shook his head, sadly. Then he turned to Selda and smiled.

'Now.' He tapped the handle bars. 'Don't you forget about that bike any longer and take care.' Then he too got into the car and slammed the door and they drove off, bumping up the bank in front of the barn.

Paul Bauer slowly sat down on the bench again and the dog crept over and lay across his feet. He took another bite at the bread and chewed delicately. Selda thought that they had forgotten her, so she turned to go. Then he spoke gruffly.

'I frightened you, didn't I, that day?'

She looked at him, not understanding.

'That day, way back, when I banged on the window.'

She nodded, remembering now.

'I only wanted to tell you not to give the rabbits food with snow on it. It upsets them. It makes them ill, you know. They're delicate things, rabbits.'

'I thought you were angry with us,' said Selda.

'Me? No. Why should I be? I don't interfere with anyone. I just wish that they would leave me alone. Look at the trouble people cause, always interfering, telling me how to run my farm. Wanting to buy my land. That's why they do it, you know.'

'Do what?'

'Spy on me. Tell the police about my workers. They think they can force me to sell up if I can't run the farm. Then they can buy my land cheaply.' He shook his head sadly. 'Now I've lost those two. Best workers I've had for years. Hard workers too.' He looked at her closely and half smiled. 'Honest workers, especially the younger one, always ready to do what I told him. He worked so hard . . . when his friends let him . . . nice-looking lad too . . .' He had half closed his eyes against the midday sun and there was an old, knowing smile on his face.

She knew that he wanted her to say something, but she couldn't. So it *was* true. Ferhat was gone. Not with the police. But gone, all the same, and without saying goodbye. Gone, just when she realized how much his friendship meant to her.

'Herr Bauer,' she began, 'you . . .' but she couldn't finish, because the words dissolved.

'You wanted to ask me if I knew where they'd gone. Didn't you?'

She nodded.

'I can't tell you. I don't know where they've gone. I wish I did. Don't think so badly of me, young lady. He was a nice boy, that young one. Do you know, he'd started to come in of an evening, these last few weeks. He'd have a chat. Not much, but it was a beginning. He talked about his home.' He bit into the rest of the bread and chewed slowly. 'And you. Oh yes, he was a nice boy, that one. They needed work and I needed workers.' He shook his head again and irritably banged the crumbs off the bench. 'So now I'll have to find somebody else, and at my busiest time of the year! Why can't people mind their own business?'

'You've no idea at all?' She had to try, just once more.

'No idea. One minute they were here and a couple of hours later, I see the tractor left in the field and they're gone. Just like that. The father even left his jacket hanging, I saw it from the window. So they can't have got that far. But don't you worry too much, they'll be all right. Now, I've got to go in. I get stiff when I sit too long, these days. Don't look so sad. Run along and have a look at my rabbits for me. Eh? There's no evil in a rabbit, and they're good company, not stupid, like people think.' And he laughed again, and went in . . .

In a way, it was all she could do. So he was gone now, and there was no one else to talk to. Only Giselle, who had disappeared. Only Brownie. She went into the barn and her eyes were dim with tears. With Ferhat gone, who then would feed the little rabbit? He was still separated from the others and so would starve down there, all alone. She crouched by the cage, but could not see him. She undid the latch but he still did not come out. He had always come before, standing up against the wires, recognizing her, she was sure. She lifted up the cage door and felt inside behind the pile of sacks, towards the sleeping box. Something had been pushed in front of the entrance. She pulled it away and dropped it on the floor as Brownie made a sudden mad dash for his freedom.

'Ferhat!' she called as though he were there and could have helped her. Once again she only just managed to grab one of the rabbit's back legs and she held on, though it squealed. When it finally lay still in her arms, she felt its heart beating wildly against hers.

Then she looked at what had fallen to the floor. It was a thick, brown envelope and there, on the outside, was her name, 'Selda'. It could only have been left by Ferhat. Who else would be certain that she would go and look at Brownie? She began to walk towards the door. Now the rabbit struggled wildly, scratching her. Had it scented the spring air and heard the flight of sparrows which swooped past and settled, twittering and busy in the hedgerow? She could not open the envelope with the rabbit struggling in her arms so she turned back towards the cages and, as she did so, Brownie, as if aware that she would shut him up again, began a more desperate fight to escape.

And why shouldn't he be free? Why should anything be so

caged up and imprisoned? She knew that she wanted no part of it, ever, and so she turned back from the barn. She bent down on the spring grass and opened her arms wide and let Brownie leap free. For a moment the little animal crouched still. Then it scampered merrily to the primrose bank and browsed there among the flowers as though it had been doing that all its life. It sat up and licked its paws and went daintily up the bank. It paused again at the top, disappearing into the thousand different greens and browns of the waving grasses. Finally it made off, streaking across the field, leaping from tussock to tussock and once, as though to celebrate its freedom, it kicked its heels up in the air in a wild, turning leap, and was gone.

She was alone on the path. Slowly, she opened the envelope half guessing what would be inside. It was their money. She counted it. There were 5,000 Swiss francs, and they were still rolled up with the rubber band around them. It was a lot of money, especially when one changed it into Turkish lira. And they had trusted it all to her. And there was a letter, written on the back of a torn-up paper sack.

Dear Selda,
    We have just been warned that the police will come and pick us up this morning, so we must leave at once. My Father and I would like you to give this money to Ahmet. It is for my Mother. Ahmet knows what to do. Please tell him what has happened as soon as you can. Thank you for everything: I could never wish for a better friend than you, and I hope that one day, all your dearest dreams will come true.
    Yours, Ferhat.
Please do what you think is best for Brownie.

So he had cared for her. He really truly had. And he had trusted her. Those 5,000 francs must represent nearly all the money they had in the world. He had trusted her with the whole being and safety of his family. Now she knew what to do: she must forget about Giselle and find Ahmet as soon as possible. She got on the bike and began to cycle home. Half-way along the track she stopped to blow her nose and to look back just once more, in case she could still see Brownie. She couldn't of course, but something else caught her eye. Something moved up in the forest. Something bright flashed through the trees, and somebody, surely, was calling her name.

'Sel-da! Sel-da!' It was Giselle, swooping down on her pink bike and shouting: 'Selda! Wait for me!'

Twelve

Selda waited until Giselle had skidded to a halt beside her.

'He's gone,' she said, 'he's gone without even saying goodbye.'

'I should hope so,' snapped Giselle, unsympathetically. 'Did you want him to hang around until the police got him, just so that you two could say a dramatic goodbye?' She did not seem at all surprised that Ferhat gone.

'Well, no, but . . . Selda had not actually thought of it like that. Giselle was right, of course.

'But, but how did *you* know that the police were coming for him?' An awful, ugly suspicion began to form in a dark corner of Selda's mind. She looked at her friend and Giselle looked at her and understood what she was thinking. Her pale eyes were colder than any ice and her voice was razor sharp.

'I didn't!' Giselle hissed. 'I did not tell anyone, whatever you think! And anyway, I don't care what you think. Do you know something Selda? You're as suspicious as everyone else. Just because we have problems in my family, just because my mother's ill, and . . . and things like that, just because she's different, nobody trusts me. Everybody acts like I'm, well, "different" too. And you're just as bad!'

'I'm sorry,' whispered Selda, aware that once again, Giselle was right.

'Well, I didn't tell, I'd rather have died! Why should I, anyway? You and Ferhat are the only two friends I have. Or were . . . great friend you turned out to be, thinking such dreadful things about me.' But she did not cycle off. She stayed there, scuffing her shoes in the mud.

218

'I'm sorry.' Selda was, too.

'I didn't tell your secret, Selda, honestly.' Giselle spoke more quietly now.

'I know you didn't.' Selda also wanted to make peace. 'It's just so . . . so awful . . .'

'Well, it could have been worse,' said Giselle, robustly.

'How?'

'If the police had caught him, you idiot!'

'I suppose so . . .'

'Aren't you pleased? You're an odd person too, Selda. I thought you'd be delighted. If I thought you'd feel like this. I wouldn't have bothered.'

'Bothered?'

'Yes, "bothered". Who do you think warned him, Selda? A bird? Selda, it was *me*. I warned him.' She looked pleased, all the same.

'You warned Ferhat, but how?'

As they began to walk slowly back pushing the bikes, Giselle explained that on the evening before, the police had come round to their house to talk to Herr Hebel.

'You know what happened at the Co-op yesterday, don't you?' she said quietly. 'Anton told me that he had seen you there, so I knew you'd seen . . . seen my mother, and things . . .'

'I didn't see anything much, Giselle, honestly. It all looked like a mistake. She . . . your mother, I mean, she didn't *do* anything . . .'

'Didn't she?'

'No. Really. It looked like an accident, that the other woman fell down.'

'I'm glad,' said Giselle, looking happier. 'Anyway, the police came to our house to talk to my father about what had happened, and, well, I listened at the door. I know that you're not supposed to and all that, but I was so worried. I mean, my mother's ill, Selda. She doesn't mean anything

219

bad, and I wanted to hear what the police were going to do.'

'I'd have listened too,' said Selda.

'Would you? Well, after a bit, they were just chatting. My father told them that he would take my mother to this place tomorrow and they said "fine" and then they chatted and one of them mentioned Bauer's farm. My father had asked them if they were having a busy time in town and they said "a bit of this and that, just the usual, a bit of illegal parking, illegal speeding and illegal immigrants". One of them said that it was a nuisance, they'd had another complaint about Paul Bauer, that he's got illegal immigrants working on his farm again. That's how I knew.'

'So what did you do?'

'I wanted to go and let them know that evening, but I couldn't. Dad was going to take Mum back to this, this place; it's a sort of hospital, a clinic she goes to sometimes. They went that evening, as soon as the police had gone and that meant that I couldn't leave the house because of Anton. He doesn't mind being alone in the daytime, but he won't be left alone at night. He's scared of the dark. I thought about phoning you, but I knew your parents would never let you out at night. So I decided to get up early and go to the farm alone. I didn't want to go to school anyway. I knew that everybody would stare at me and ask questions about my mother, and I hate that.'

'Then you went to the farm this morning?'

'Yes. I saw Ferhat first. He was driving the tractor and at first he wouldn't stop. He thought that I was just fooling around. In the end I stood in front of it and he *had* to stop!'

In spite of herself Selda smiled. She could imagine the scene, with Giselle hair flying and arms held out, stopping the great tractor in the middle of the ploughed field.

'I told him what I had overheard. It was difficult to get him to understand. I had to say it over and over again, but finally he seemed to get it and he went over to his father who was with the pigs. They talked for quite a long time, argued, actually, you know, waving their hands about, then they went back into the pig sheds and brought out these two bags. It was as though they'd had them there packed and ready, waiting to leave. But then they argued again. Ferhat told me in German that he had to go back to the barn. His father gave him something small and rolled up, but he put it straight in his pocket and I couldn't see what it was. Then I just waited on with his father. It was awful, that, just waiting. It seemed like hours, but I don't think it was more than ten minutes. Then they went. They shook hands with me and said something, something beginning "*allah*" . . .'

'That's "goodbye" in Turkish.'

'Well, they said that and then they walked away, along the edge of the ploughed field and up into the forest.'

'Didn't he, they, say anything else?'

'Yes.' Giselle picked at the rubber grips on the handlebars of the bike. 'Yes, he kept saying, "Tell Selda, tell Selda what has happened."' She took a deep breath and added: 'He was really glad that I had warned them, I mean, he said thank you and that, but it was you he wanted to see. I could tell.'

They were silent for several minutes.

'He left a letter for me,' said Selda eventually. She pulled it out and translated it as best she could.

'Goodness,' said Giselle. 'Nobody has ever written anything like that to me. Not even my family.'

'I'm sure that he would have written to you too, if his German had been good enough,' said Selda.

'Do you really think so?'

'Yes.'

'Maybe you're right.' Giselle looked unconvinced but still smiled.

They continued in silence, both wondering what would happen now. Selda knew that she ought to tell Ahmet quickly, but she was not sure where he would be. In front of the block of

221

flats Giselle turned her bike in the direction of her home.

'Wait!' said Selda. 'Let's go in and have tea.'

'I don't know,' mumbled Giselle, uncomfortably, 'what about your mother? She saw what happened yesterday, didn't she? Are you sure she won't mind?'

'I don't know,' said Selda, trying to be honest. Then she remembered her grandmother, who never turned anyone away. No filthy, stinking beggar, no gibbering madman, no clever rogue, was ever turned away from her door.

'I'd better go,' insisted Giselle, reluctantly.

'No!' cried Selda. 'Of course you mustn't. You're *my* friend and *my* guest. Giselle, I'm sorry about your mother. I didn't know that she was ill. Come on now, I'm dying for my tea.' She led the way, determinedly running up the steps and ringing the bell.

Sevgi Hanım did not slam the door in Giselle's face as she had threatened but her greeting was cool and instead of rushing off to prepare some delicious meal for the visitor, she only remarked that there was still some tea left in the pot. Then she went into the sitting room and busied herself with her knitting. Selda and Giselle exchanged glances, but said nothing and, for the first time, Selda actually enjoyed having her friend in the house. They made fresh tea for themselves and sat in the kitchen drinking from the everyday glasses and nibbling biscuits straight out of the packet. For the first time too, Giselle talked about her home. She had eaten ten or twelve biscuits before Selda had eaten two. Selda joked that it looked as though Giselle were starving.

'I am,' said Giselle bluntly, 'well, sort of. There's never anything to eat at home.'

'What?'

'It's because of my mother's illness. She doesn't cook anything.'

'I suppose she doesn't feel well enough to cook, if she's ill,' said Selda carefully.

'It's not ill like that,' said Giselle, stirring her tea. 'People think that she drinks. Everybody says that, I know they do. I've heard them. "Your mother's an alcoholic," that's what they say at school. And in the factory. It isn't true, Selda, really it isn't. It's not drink she takes, its pills.'

'Pills?' Selda did not understand.

'Yes. She takes these special pills. They help you to lose weight. She started taking them after Anton was born. She wanted to get slim again and these pills stop you feeling hungry and eating too much. She stopped eating and so she felt very tired and then she started taking pills to make her feel energetic. Then she needed pills to help her sleep at night. Then she needed something different to make her wake up in the morning. It's awful, Selda. She always says that she's stopped, but she hasn't. She's got drawers full of pills. Boxes of them, hidden at the back of her wardrobe and in the pockets of her clothes. I've seen bottles of them stuffed away behind the saucepans in the kitchen.'

'But why? I mean, why did she want to be thin?'

'I don't know, really. She was an actress before she married. An actress and dancer, here in Zurich. She stopped working in theatres when she married my father. He's a lot older than her. I think she really missed the theatre, you know; now there's nothing to do all day and Father's always away, looking at one of his factories, or on a business trip. Anton and I were here, but we always seemed to be in her way, making a mess of the house and things. So, after Anton was about a year old, she decided she wanted to go back to acting, and that's when she started taking the pills. She said that she needed to get her figure back, after the baby. "I need to get my dancer's figure back," that's what she always says.'

'But she's got it, hasn't she?'

'Oh yes. But look at the cost.'

'The cost?' Selda remembered the fortune teller. He had told her that there was a cost to everything.

'Yes. The cost to her. She can't live without those pills now. They've ruined her life. They make her so odd, so bad-tempered, so impossible. It's like she's always waiting, ready to explode. You know that she's like, you've seen it.'

'Yes.'

'It's awful, Selda, it really is, and we pay the cost too. Ours isn't like a home at all. She never cooks anything because she can't bear to eat and she doesn't want to see other people eating. Do you know, when they have business friends round, a cook comes in and does all the work. So you were right, Selda. Some of the time I really do feel starving. It was always so good coming here to your family. There was your mother, always at home, always welcoming me and always pleased to see me. And she was always pleased to cook something special, just because I liked it.'

'But not today!'

'Oh, it doesn't matter. She means well, your mother, I can tell.'

Selda nodded. Giselle was right, once again. Sevgi Hanım did mean well. Selda saw it more clearly now.

'What about your little brother Anton?' asked Selda, suddenly remembering the pale face at the window.

'He manages, I suppose . . . In a way, it's easier for him. He's still little and people feel sorry for him. He's nearly always at other children's houses. He gets fed there. He asks Father for money and then he buys chocolate with it. That's what happened at the Co-op, yesterday. Anton took four bars of chocolate and my mother didn't realize and only paid for two. When they asked her to pay for the other two bars, she thought they were accusing her of being a thief. Her, Frau Hebel! I can see how she felt, but she didn't have to lose her temper like that, did she? I mean, they tried to give her the chocolates and say that it didn't matter, but that made her feel even more angry. Then when she got home, she said that it was Anton's fault. She blamed him and he was really upset that night; he cried and cried. Still, at least he's got friends at school. I suppose he's a nicer person than I am because people like him. Nobody likes me. I just make enemies, except for you and Ferhat.'

They were silent then, sipping their tea and thinking about him. Selda glanced at the clock. She had been aware of time slipping by, but had been so held by Giselle's strange story of life in the Hebel household, that she had not said anything. She knew that she must find Ahmet quickly and tell him that Ferhat had left the farm. She still did not know where her brother worked, only that the restaurant was in "the next village" as he had said one evening. The next village could have been in any direction.

Then she had an idea. Zeki might know. The wonderful and quite exceptional boy from Bornova, the famous 'Zeki', knew, according to Pembe, all there was to know about Switzerland and about the Turkish community around the lake. It was Wednesday afternoon; with any luck Zeki would be at Ramona's.

Together they knocked on Ramona's door and asked if Zeki were there. Ramona said 'yes' but, it was Pembe who came to the door, looking suspicious.

'I only want to ask him something,' said Selda. So, reluctantly, Pembe allowed her sister to see the young man of whom she had heard so much.

Zeki was rather a disappointment. He was a short, plump young man with his name in fat gold letters on a chain round his neck. He had the shiny, tidy look of a young man whose mother devotedly presses his trousers and polished his shoes before he leaves the house.

'So you're Pembe's little sister,' he said in a patronizing way.

Selda smiled brightly. She was not going to be provoked, not by anything today. Standing in the hallway, she could hear the beat of loud music coming from the other room. Zeki tapped his smart new shoe in time to it as he waited impatiently for her question. She had worked out exactly how she would ask it.

'Zeki Abi, you know the restaurant where my brother Ahmet works . . .'

'Of course. It's the Sternberg, everybody knows that. What of it?'

'Well, my friend here doesn't believe that Turks can run a decent restaurant. She says that only the Swiss can . . .'

'Does she? What a stuck-up know-all! Well you can inform your grand friend that the Sternberg is run by a friend of mine, well, of my family, actually. He's called Adam Taner and he runs the best restaurant in Walder.'

'Oh, thank you,' said Selda, in a polite little voice. 'Can you tell her in German? She doesn't understand Turkish.'

So Zeki said it all again in very fierce clear German. The two girls thanked him and hurried off.

If Zeki's appearance had disappointed Selda, his information had not. Now they knew exactly which village to go to. Giselle was sure that they could cycle over to Walder in fifteen minutes and that was what they decided to do. Selda, who had not cycled on a main road before, was terrified. The cars and lorries rushed past in a cloud of dust and foul-smelling fumes and she was afraid that Giselle, on the faster bike, would get too far ahead and turn off, when she wasn't looking. She was relieved when Giselle slowed down outside a small restaurant on the main street. It was the Sternberg.

Although it appeared to be quite empty, it took some courage for Selda to push open the door. She had never been into a café or a restaurant in Switzerland. Giselle, however, was quite at home and knew exactly what to do. She went straight to one of the check-clothed tables and sat down. It did seem very small and quiet for a 'best' restaurant. A man came over and asked what they wanted and Selda opened her mouth to ask for her brother, but Giselle kicked her under the table and said that they wanted two large ice-creams.

When he had gone away to bring their order she whispered: 'See. There are the kitchens, go and look quickly.'

So Selda did. Ahmet was there, in an apron and rubber gloves, cleaning out an oven. They stared at each other, both unable to say anything.

'What's happened?' he said at last.

'Ferhat's gone!'

'Selda!' He came with her and sat down at their table.

'Selda, you shouldn't have got involved in this,' he said, after she had explained a little. 'You should never have been meeting Ferhat like that, and in secret too.'

'Don't make it sound so wicked,' said Selda. 'It wasn't "like that" at all. He was a friend . . . *is* a friend. I like him, Ahmet. Why shouldn't I? I liked him and I wanted to help him. Just like you. Aren't you his friend? Don't you want to help them?'

'Ye-es.' He looked at her carefully, at this little sister whom he used to swing up in the air and twirl around.

'Then, what's so different about you and me?'

He didn't answer her but bowed his head and listened while they told him what they knew.

'Have you got the money?' he asked at last.

'No. It's at home. Why should I have brought it? It's for his mother, isn't it?'

'Yes. Well, that is, not *all* of it.'

'What do you mean?' She looked at him curiously. 'Tell me, Ahmet.'

'It's better that you don't now.'

'Ahmet, you must tell me. I'm not a little girl any more.'

'All right. If you must know. But I'm warning you, you won't like it. Some of that money is owed to me. I keep it as payment for my help to them. I and some friends arrange work for these illegal immigrants. We help them move from job to job, and they pay us. It's a risk we take, Selda. We'd be in trouble if the police knew we were doing it. So they pay us, naturally.'

'But that's wrong! Ahmet, how could you? It's stealing!'

'It's not. They want me to help. They need me. Look Selda, he didn't just run off did he? The first thing he did was try to get in contact with me. He's no fool, he knows that he needs me. How else do you think the rest of his money will ever get back to his family in Alanya? By carrier pigeon? Do you think they can trust the post? Suppose the letter got lost, or stolen. They can't go to a bank because they don't have an official address here in Switzerland. They are not even supposed to be here, are they? So, what do they do? They give the money to me and I give it to someone I trust who is travelling back to Turkey. And that person takes it right to his mother's house in Alanya and puts the money into her hand. And of course he has to get paid too. It's only fair, Selda.' He looked at her more gently. 'I'm sorry,' he added. 'I knew you wouldn't like it.'

'But it's wrong,' she cried. 'They've got so little and even that is taken away from them. How can you do it Ahmet?' It made her feel so angry.

'It may be wrong,' he said. 'But it's life.'

'Well, it shouldn't be! And you shouldn't do it! You never used to be like this, Ahmet. You used to help everyone, just out of kindness.

'Like you,' he said, but it was spoken sadly, and he was not mocking her.

'That's what you were doing that night, wasn't it?' she asked suddenly. She remembered the night Ahmet had come running in with his face and hands hurt and muddy.

'Yes.' He remembered it too. 'But it was a false alarm, that night. We thought that there would be a police raid on the farm, so they went up into the forest and hid. I went up to get them later, after I had heard that the raid had taken place in another town. We were hurrying back when I tripped in the dark and rolled down a steep bank up there in the forest. It was just an accident. Nothing happened that night, but we had to use the safe hiding place up in the forest. That's where they'll be now.'

'Waiting for you?'

'Yes. Actually, no. It's another man's turn to go tonight, if anything happens. That's how we work it. I'm always working here on Wednesdays. I couldn't just walk out like that. The owner would be suspicious'.

'So this man, this "friend", will go up into the forest tonight, and, for a price, tell them where it is safe to go next.'

'Yes. Only he won't be going now, will he? He won't go unless he's paid and you haven't brought the money.'

'Do you know where they are to go?'

'Of course I do.'

'So anybody could go up and tell them?'

'I suppose so, but who would want to?'

'I would. I could go.'

'Don't be stupid, Selda.'

'I'm not being stupid. I could easily go.'

'You couldn't.'

'Why not?'

'Well . . .'

'And don't tell me that I'm a little girl!'

'I wasn't going to.' He scowled at her in exasperation. She was so obstinate, this one. But he admired her for it.

Giselle had been listened to them speaking in Turkish and had been unable to understand a word.

'What about me?' she asked, reminding them of her presence.

'You?' said Ahmet, speaking German now and misunderstanding her. 'You mean that you would help?' He shook his head. 'What could *you* do? You don't know any Turkish. Anyway, it's altogether a crazy idea. Let's forget it. You should never ever have even talked to him, Selda. In fact, it sounds to me as if the two of you pestered the boy so much, you caused all this trouble with the police. Somebody must have seen you and reported it. I bet you didn't think of that when you were pretending to be his guardian angel.'

'Yes I did and it makes me more determined to help. Please Ahmet. If you can't go and this other man won't, then I must go.' She turned to Giselle and said in German: 'We can go together, can't we?'

'Of course we can,' cried Giselle eagerly.

'Ahmet, listen to me. I *have* to do this for him. I owe it to him. Don't you remember that first Saturday in Switzerland? You weren't there, but we told you about it, when I ran in front of that car. If he hadn't shouted out "stop" I'd have been run over. I know it. And think what a risk he took, drawing attention to himself like that. He took that risk for me, a stranger, and he let everybody know that he was a Turk.'

'Mother and Father will never forgive me,' said Ahmet grimly, taking a piece of paper from his pocket.

'Well that won't make much difference, they don't anyway,' replied Selda.

'That's true. Look, this is it.' He spread a piece of paper out on the table. 'They have to go to this address and ask for a Herr Stamm. He has a house-decorating business.'

'All right. Now, where shall we find them?'

He looked around again as if to reassure himself that nobody was listening and then he turned to Giselle.

'You know the woods above your house?'

She nodded.

'You know the track up from the sledge run? Yes? Well, you follow that up for about twenty minutes, perhaps longer in the dark, then, there's a clearing with that hut in it.'

'The bird watcher's hut?'

'Yes, that's it, that's where they'll be. Not in the hut, but about fifty metres further up. There's a sort of drainage ditch dug to take extra flood water in spring. It should be dry now. Anyway, that's where they'll be. Now, listen carefully: as you approach, you have to call . . . '

'Call?'

'Yes, like you'd lost a dog or something. You know, just in case anybody is around and watching. One of you calls, to warn them that you're there and then you go towards the ditch, as though you're really looking for something. Then, when you're sure that it's safe, you say *"das ist es!"* Now, do you think you can do it?'

'They both nodded.

'All right. But you must take care. Both of you.'

Selda jumped up, longing to be off, but Giselle asked: 'What about paying for the ice-cream?'

'I don't know,' he said, shaking his head. 'Whatever am I doing sending you off like this? The least I can do is pay for your ice-cream.'

'You're not sending us,' said Selda. 'We want to go.'

They got on their bikes and began to cycle back in single file with the rush-hour traffic thundering past them. Selda realized too late that the road was taking them right past the Hebels' factory at the precise time when her father and Ali would be leaving work.

Thirteen

'Selda! Selda!' It was her father and brother who were shouting at her. Selda recognized their voices but pretended not to have heard. Then she saw them amongst the crowd, and still hoped to cycle by, but they'd already noticed!

'Selda! Wait girl! Selda!' Now she could not ignore them for she had heard their heavy running footsteps and anyway Giselle had already braked and looked back. She was furious with herself for not having thought about this and used another street. Suppose her father held on to the bike and insisted that she walk home with him? She couldn't very well run off could she? Once home, she could not leave: their shouting barred her path and held her back.

Giselle Hebel, as cool as ice, looked from father to daughter and knew exactly what to do. She got off her bike and parked it at the kerb with great, slow, calm deliberation, like the daughter of a true actress. Then she smiled graciously at everybody in general, for they were all her father's employees who thronged out of the factory gates. She said 'good evening' to several people who knew her by sight, but she saved her most brilliant smile for Turgut Bey. She smoothed down her blown hair and, smiling widely, walked straight up to him, holding out her hand. He looked from side to side a couple of times, but there, in front of everybody, he had to acknowledge her. When Giselle was sure that people were hanging back, watching them, she spoke loudly in her clear, brittle voice: 'Thank you so much for allowing your daughter, Selda, to spend the evening with me. My father, Herr Hebel, will be delighted to see her, and we'll bring her back by car, after dinner. That is all right, isn't it?'

'Yes. Oh yes.' Turgut Bey was mesmerized by his boss's daughter. He held on to her hand, shaking it a moment longer than was necessary and repeating 'yes yes', and watching her as helplessly as the swaying snake which moves to the controlling rhythms of the charmer's pipe.

'Don't . . .' he began, once.

'Don't worry! Giselle interrupted authoritatively. 'She won't be late. Our chauffeur will bring her right to the door, so you needn't worry.'

'I see.' What else could he say?

'And thank you, so much.' Giselle withdrew her hand now and walked back to her bike.

Turgut Bey stared after her. The cheek of it, the audacity of it! And her, just a slip of a girl, talking to him, a grown man, approaching him like that, on the street, as though she were his equal, or more. How dare she take his daughter away from him like that! Why, after all those years apart, he wanted those girls waiting at home for him in the evening. They should be there, waiting for him, the father. They shouldn't be running off to other people's houses. Once again he bitterly regretted bringing those girls to Europe. Adnan Hoca was right. 'Did you see that, Ali?' He turned to his son, speechless with anger now, but Ali was neither listening to him nor looking at him. He was waving to the girls and turning aside to a workmate.

'Yes,' he remarked cheerfully, 'the little dark one is my baby sister. Yes, she's settling in fine thanks, as you see. I'm really proud of her and the effort she's made.' Turgut Bey listened to his son in disbelief.

'It makes you think,' continued Ali, 'I wish I'd stuck in school a bit longer. I might have done better than this, then.'

'Ali!' protested his father.

But Ali was still not listening. He cupped his hands

233

around his mouth and yelled down the street: 'Hey Selda! You just take care on that bike!' as though that were all that mattered!

When they were well out of sight, the two girls slowed down.

'I hope you didn't mind my saying that,' said Giselle. 'It was all I could think of at the time.'

'It was perfect. Thanks.'

'And the chauffeur can drive you home, afterwards.'

'But what will your father say?'

'Nothing much. Why?' Now Giselle was surprised. 'My father may not even be at home. He was going to see Mother at the clinic and then on to visit one of our factories near by. He probably won't be back until late.'

'What about Anton, then?'

'Oh Selda! I forgot all about him! We'd better hurry, you know he's afraid of the dark.'

'Do you think he's been alone there all day?'

'No. He always goes to friends. It's just at night that he won't stay alone.'

'Then what will happen when we go to find Ferhat?' cried Selda.

They stared at each other, both slowing the bikes in their confusion.

'Couldn't we take him with us?' asked Selda eventually.

'Oh no!' cried Giselle. 'Not Anton! He's a pest. He'd spoil everything. No, I don't want to take him.' She spoke with real passion.

'Couldn't we make it sound like a game? You know, like hide and seek.' Selda remembered the wonderful games that she had played along the dark summer streets in Izmir.

'You don't know Anton,' said Giselle, bitterly. 'I know he seems so sweet, but he's a trouble maker. He's been trouble since the day he was born! He's always being "nice" to people.' Sucking up to them!' Giselle's anger surprised them both.

234

'If that's how you feel,' said Selda, after a minute or two, 'I'll go on my own.'

'You can't.'

'I can.'

'You wouldn't dare.'

'I would. I'm not afraid of the dark. I like the dark and the night. You wouldn't know, but back in Turkey, that was my favourite game as a kid, playing hide and seek in the dark. The whole street played, except Pembe. They were terrific games. I'd go anywhere in the dark, now.'

'Couldn't we just "forget" Anton?' asked Giselle in a small voice.

'No.'

'Well, what can we do?'

'I don't know!' But suddenly she did. 'Look Giselle, we *can* take him. If you could manage my father so well, you can manage Anton too. I know you can. You were brilliant back there, now go on, do the same with Anton. He's only a little boy. And he's your brother.'

'I wish he wasn't. If he hadn't been born, my mother wouldn't . . . you know . . .'

'It's not *his* fault. But I know what you mean. Sometimes I feel like that about my brothers and sisters, especially Pembe and Fatma.'

'Do you? I thought that you, well, you foreigners always got on better in your families than we do.

'I think we're all the same,' said Selda, slowly. 'Anyway, about tonight, we *can* take him, Giselle. He'll be as good as gold, you'll see. Anyway,' and she laughed, 'he's frightened of me. Don't forget, I pushed him over in the playground.'

They had passed Selda's block of flats now and were cycling up the steep hill to Giselle's house.

'What shall we tell him?' asked Giselle as they got off their bikes at the gate and began to push them over the deep gravel.

'I know,' said Selda excitedly. 'We'll tell him that we have to look for Brownie!' As she spoke the plan took shape in her mind.

She explained how she had set the little rabbit free that morning. Now they could pretend that they were going up into the forest to see if it was all right. Since Anton was such a little boy, he would not think it a strange thing to do. They could even take up some food and while Selda was talking to Ferhat, Giselle and Anton could be scattering crumbs for the rabbit. It seemed like a reasonable plan and, in the end, Giselle agreed.

When she finally entered the Hebels' house, Selda found herself staring around in astonishment. If Frau Hebel had always looked like a picture from a smart magazine, so did her house. It was quite perfect. Even the flowers in a vase in the sitting room matched the pale pink carpet on the floor. There was nothing out of place: no half-read newspaper had been tossed to one side, no knitting stuck from the corner of a chair and no forgotten mug or cup stood on a table. It was beautiful and luxurious and very, very still. Anton was sitting on a stool in an immaculate white kitchen. He was watching a small television and eating crisps from a packet. He looked pleased to see them and held out the crisp packet.

'I thought you were never going to come back,' he said. 'I'm sick of being on my own.' He glanced towards the window sulkily. 'You *always* leave me alone –'

'You always . . .' began Giselle crossly, but Selda interrupted loudly.

'Go on, tell him!'

'All right. I was going to. Anton, we've come back especially for you: we want you to come with us, and help, if you're not too busy . . .' Her smile was very winning.

He looked up at her then, interested, and listened as they explained why they wanted to go up into the forest.

'It's Brownie's first night up there alone,' said Selda.

'Poor thing.' Anton was sympathetic.

'We thought we'd take him something special to eat.'

'Do you think he'd like crisps?' asked Anton.

'Not really.'

'Well, there isn't anything else. I looked.'

He was right too. The cupboards and fridge were almost bare of food. There were a few tins and packets, some milk, half a loaf of bread and a bowl of fruit. They decided to take some apples and some of the bread. Selda secretly wished that there had been something which she could have taken up to Ferhat and his father, but there wasn't.

It was nearly seven when they left the house and Anton hesitated on the door step, looking nervously towards the darkening forest. Selda held out her hand and after a moment he caught hold of it and clung on tightly. Giselle said that she knew a short cut that ran from their garden along the edge of the woods and came out just above the sledge run. They saw nobody else out in the darkening wood, except for somebody with a dog; a woman, Selda guessed, from her quick, light step, but they passed by each other without speaking. Selda gripped Anton's hand more tightly and the three of them walked so close together that they kicked each other in the dark. These winding, indefinite paths were not like those distant Izmir streets where she and the other children had run and shouted and hidden, but never got lost. Those streets had always been enveloped by the lingering warmth of the day's hot sun.

Now the pine needles shifted and sounded with each hurried step and the sharpening evening breeze smelt of the resin which oozed unseen from the hidden, red-barked trunks. That too reminded Selda of something. She paused; she had a stitch in her side from walking too fast and her lips were dry. She licked them and she remembered: it was the ice-cream she had eaten in Istanbul. That had been made with the gum from pine trees. Oh, how long ago and far

237

away that summer evening in Istanbul seemed. And that girl who had licked the cool, sweet ice-cream and then fallen asleep on the cushions in the back of Kemal Amca's lorry, that little girl seemed to be almost someone else, and not her at all. The real Selda was here, now, hurrying through these unmarked tracks and paths, in order to –

'Giselle!' she cried, hanging back, stopping them all.

'What?'

'Giselle – ' Fear closed around her throat like a noose.

'What's the matter now?' Giselle tried to move on and Anton was dragged between them.

'Suppose he isn't there?' whispered Selda. She hadn't thought of it before. Maybe they were too late. Maybe Ferhat and his father had already gone. Maybe they had waited for a bit, but had left, in the end. All afternoon she had been so excited, so sure that she could help. It had been like some adventure in a film and she had been so certain that she would see him again. Now doubt tormented her. What would she do if he wasn't there?

And if he was there, what then? What was she going to say? She hadn't thought about that either. Would she just wish him "good luck" and "a good journey" and then wave goodbye? And never, ever hear of him again? For that was what would happen, wasn't it? And she had thought that she was being so clever! Some cleverness this was, to help him disappear.

'Please, please let him be there.' She hadn't meant to speak out loud.

'What?'

'I meant, suppose he's not there,' she said, trying to sound calm in the dark.

'Well,' said Anton sensibly, 'if he's gone, then that'll mean he has found somewhere to go, won't it?'

'Ye-es.'

'After all,' his shrill voice rang loud and clear,' you

238

wouldn't want him to be out there all alone, with nowhere to go. And in the dark, would you?'

'No.'

'You wouldn't have let him free, otherwise, would you, Selda? Selda, would you?' Anton renewed his grip on both their hands and the two girls exchanged a look over his small, fair head.

The last light had faded quickly and the spring night was alive with things that moved and stretched and swayed with quiet stealth. Suddenly something ran through the undergrowth near them. They all gasped and the ferns and grasses at the edge of the forest dipped and then sprang back. They tried to hurry and, turning uphill again, rounded the corner by the sledge run. There the sudden plunging rush of water pouring into a culvert startled them badly. They could not tell how near to the edge they were. Looking back, Selda saw the lights of the town flickering in the distance and when the church clock chimed a half hour, the forest rustled and moved and consumed the sound so that they were only left with its echo.

'When we first came here my mother wondered if there were wolves and bears up here,' said Selda and, though they laughed at the idea, they all understood what Sevgi Hanım had meant.

'That's it!' cried Giselle at last and ahead of them Selda could make out a clearing. Her heart beat so fiercely that she could barely speak.

'Is, is that it? The bird-watcher's hut?' she whispered.

'Yes.' Giselle nodded. 'Well, go on. Make that call, like your brother said. Go on.'

But she couldn't. She couldn't make a sound in all that darkness.

Anton shook her arm impatiently, then raised his head and called clearly: Brownie! Brownie! Brow-nie? Where are you? Where *are* you?' His voice was sharp and, when Giselle

239

joined in too, Selda almost expected some adult to appear and order them to be quiet. Anton had begun to crumble the bread on the ground and was looking about him as though he expected the rabbit to hop up straight away. Selda tried to force her eyes to see into the blackness but she could make out nothing beyond the outlines of the trees and bushes. 'Say it' hissed Giselle and, somehow, she managed to call faintly into the waiting shadows: '*Das ist es*,' and the three of them froze, like figures of stone.

And something did move. Up there, where an undergrowth of hazel and bramble had piled up thickly along an old water course, something moved.

Selda started forward.

'I'm coming too!' cried Anton, springing to her side, trying to find her hand. 'Don't leave me alone in the dark!'

'I'm not. Giselle's there,' whispered Selda, trying to push him away gently. 'Look, you have to stay there in case Brownie comes. He won't be up here in these brambles. Please Anton. I have to . . . look at something.'

'Look at what? Let me come,' he whined and, catching hold of her jumper, clung on, dragging her back.

'No Anton, let me go!' She tried to prise away his fingers but he held on. She gave him a push and he screamed. He screamed and screamed as he had done that day in the playground. His voice rose higher and higher and somewhere near, a dog howled. They heard twigs snapping and cracking and the sounds of things brushed aside. The dog howled again, more loudly, and Anton's noise stopped and he ran back to Giselle in terror. Selda, siezing the opportunity, scrambled up the slope through the brambles. She held one arm in front of her face to keep off the springing branches and with her other hand she tried to tear off the brambles. Once she tripped and fell so that her hands were pressed through the dry surface into the cool dampness of the forest floor.

'Selda?'

So, He was there.

'Ferhat?' It was like magic should be, with all her dreams and hopes suddenly fulfilled and roses blooming instantly around the door and black winter quite gone. She could tell him now. She could tell him how worried she had been for his safety, how sad she had been that they had not said goodbye. She could tell him how much she valued his friendship and his trust in her. And she could reassure him that she had not betrayed that trust: she had not told his secret and she never would. But she didn't. Pulling at the thorns and brushing the leaves from her hair, she hardly looked at him. Instead she chattered on, unable to be quiet.

'Ahmet Abi couldn't come and so I did. We did. I said we would, Giselle and I. We came together but we had to bring her little brother Anton. That's him down there. He was making all that noise. I really couldn't stop him, I know that somebody will hear, but I couldn't stop him, though I tried. He's afraid of the dark. And that dog frightened him, barking like that. I'm sorry about all the noise –'

'It's all right,' he said. 'I'm glad that you didn't come up here on your own.'

'Are you alone?

'No, no. My father's waiting over there. He didn't think it could be you. He said that it was just youngsters out in the night, but I knew it was you.'

'Did you?'

He must have nodded then, in the dark, for he didn't say anything more but just kicked at the leaves. She too fell silent and searched in her pocket for the address.

'Ahmet Abi gave this to me. It's for you. It's the new address.' She held it out and they both looked at the pale square of paper and he took it from her.

'Ahmet says that you must ask for a Herr Stamm.'

'Stamm? I think I've heard of him.'

241

'Good. Ahmet says that he's expecting you. He runs a decorating business, I think. But that's all I know.'

'That's more than enough. It's fine, Selda. It's better not to know any more. If we don't know anything, then we can't tell anything, if the police do pick us up. It's safer that way.'

'But they won't pick you up, will they?'

'No. Not now.'

'Are you sure?'

'Sure.' He was folding the paper up very small and still kicking at the leaves.

'But what will you do?'

'Go to this address.'

'But – '

'Look. We'll walk through the woods to the next station. Nobody will be looking for us there. We'll catch a train back to Zurich and then another on to this address. We'll be there tonight.'

'Have you got enough money?'

'Yes. You mustn't worry so. We'll be all right. Really.' He put the paper away inside his jacket and continued to kick away the leaves and pine needles until his shoe was kicking up the bare earth of the forest floor.

'Did you find the other money then?' he asked at last.

'Yes.'

'And the letter?'

'Yes.'

'Did you read it?'

'Yes.'

'And?'

And what could she say? She watched him and dug her hands into her pockets and shivered in the night air. Her fingers touched the two small rolls of paper which she had almost forgotten. There they were, the black and the white, like the two halves of her life, her past and her future.

'Here,' she said, drawing them out. 'You can have these, if

you like. That's my grandmother's address. It's the old house in Izmir where I grew up. My grandmother lives there now. You remember, the one I told you about, who likes dancing bears, the one who has learnt to write. If you wanted to write . . .'

'And see you?'

'See me?'

'Yes. Why not?'

'But –'

'Selda, don't say "but". Not now. Not after all you've done. Not you. Some day things are going to be different. I shan't go on living like this for ever. I can't and I won't. People shouldn't have to live like this. That's what you always said. Nobody should be hunted from place to place, like some dumb animal. It's wrong Selda and I won't let them do it to me. One day –'

'Ferhat!' It was his father who had called. Selda could see his outline now amongst the trees.

She found her friend's hand in the darkness and put the two rolls of paper into it and she felt him close his fingers carefully around them.

'What's this other one?'

'That's my fortune. You know, the one the old blind fortune teller gave me in Istanbul. It isn't anything, really, but you can have it, if you like.'

'Thank you.'

'So.' She stepped away from him. 'Good luck, then, to both of you.'

'Thank you. And thank Giselle for me. If she hadn't warned us we'd never have got this far. I'm glad she's your friend.'

'Me too. I'll thank her.'

'Ferhat!' His father called again.

'You must go.'

'Yes.'

'Goodbye then. Go safely.'

'And you, Selda. Go safely.'

Then he was gone. She stood there and listened to them moving away through the trees and then she turned back and made her way very slowly down, quite blinded.

'Did you hear that wolf?' asked Anton as soon as she joined them. 'I was really frightened. Well, not really. Just for a moment. But I bet that rabbit was. Giselle saw him. Honestly. You did, didn't you, Giselle? So he's all right. I nearly saw him.'

He had his arms very tightly around his sister and as she hugged him to her, Giselle asked, 'That was him, wasn't it?'

'Yes.'

'Was he all right?'

'Yes.'

'Then why –?' began Giselle and then stopped and all three of them began to run back down the hill and Selda was glad that there was no moon to light up the tears that ran down her cheeks.

When they got back to Giselle's house they were relieved to find that Herr Hebel was still away. They managed to get Anton to bed and had returned to the white kitchen before Herr Hebel came in. For a moment he looked startled to see a stranger sitting there, in his house, but he said nothing. Selda realized that although he was older than her own father and white haired, he was as smart and sleek as any young man. His shoes shone, his clothes were uncreased and the nails on his hand holding his glass had been manicured, she was sure. He wore a pale green shirt and a tie of the most violent purple and green. As he poured himself a drink from a large cut-glass decanter the ice in it tumbled and chinked.

'Your mother seemed quite well when I left her,' he said, glancing at his daughter and ignoring Selda. Giselle did not look at him but shrugged.

'I mean, it's not as though she's a stranger there, is it?' He sipped his drink. 'She knows them quite well now.' He actually sounded quite pleased about it. Giselle said nothing but picked at a splash of mud on her jeans. In the quiet kitchen the only sounds were the scrape of her nail on the cloth and the chink of ice.

'I expect we'll have her back in a few days,' he continued and tipped up the glass. 'She'll be as good as new then.' It was supposed to be a joke but Giselle didn't smile and Herr Hebel straightened his perfect tie.

'They say it's the best place in Zurich. It's certainly the most expensive. You should have seen the flowers there today.'

'Will she be home for Easter? Giselle asked suddenly, bending even lower over her jeans.

'That depends on her doctors,' replied Herr Hebel absently. 'It needn't worry you. We can still have our holiday. I can do with some fresh mountain air.'

'What about Mother?' Giselle finally looked up at him.

'What about her? You know that she doesn't like the mountains. She always complains that they are boring. Anyway,' he poured another drink, 'I need a holiday.'

'I won't come,' said Giselle, 'not without Mother.'

Herr Hebel's face changed. Selda saw the colour drain from it. He lifted one eyebrow in a very artificial way and stared hard at his daughter. She bit her lower lip and stared back as he drained his glass in one go, sucking the last drops from between the cubes of ice.

'Well girls,' he said, suddenly brisk and cheerful again, 'I've got a busy day tomorrow.' He turned to leave the kitchen.

'And what about Selda?'

'Selda?' He looked bewildered.

'Yes, Selda. I promised her father that we'd take her home by car.'

245

'Giselle, how thoughtless can you be? And stupid. I've sent the chauffeur home. Do you expect me to drive?' His anger was cold and suppressed.

'I promised,' Giselle muttered stubbornly.

Herr Hebel looked around him and seemed to see Selda clearly for the first time.

'Which of your friends did you say this was?' he asked.

'Selda.'

'Selda? Selda who?'

'I'm Selda Abbas. I'm in Giselle's class at school' Selda was glad to have a chance to speak at last. 'And it's all right, Herr Hebel. I don't want to be driven home. It's not far. I can easily walk.'

'Of course you can't walk at this time of night. You never know who will be out on the streets nowadays. Of course I have to drive you, Sel-Selda? Did you say that was your name?'

'I'm sorry to have caused this trouble,' she said firmly, for she had heard the suspicion in his voice. He looked from her face to his daughter's and then back to her's again and Selda knew that he was comparing them.

'Well, Giselle, he said, 'you'd better come along too. She's your school colleague, after all.'

'She's my friend, Father. My best friend.'

'Really?' He raised the one eyebrow again and jangled the car keys.

'Yes. She . . .' Giselle stopped and began scratching again.

'Giselle, don't be so infuriating. It's very bad manners to begin something and not to finish it. Now do hurry up.'

'She wants to come to St Moritz with us. At Easter. If we go.'

'What?' He was startled and showed it.

'That's right,' said Giselle. 'And you promised me. You said that this year I could take anyone I liked.'

'Yes. Yes I did. And I'm a man of my word. But I meant,

246

dear, well, I meant any girl of our . . .'

'You meant, "any Swiss girl".'

'I never said that, Giselle.'

'Well, Selda's my friend and I've asked her to come. I won't go if she doesn't – especially if Mother's not there.'

She tossed back her fair hair, defying him as Selda had seen her defying the teasing crowds in the playground at school. They scowled at each other, father and daughter, and they did not understand one another at all. Selda watched quietly and knew how each felt.

'I'd have to ask my parents first, Herr Hebel,' she interrupted, 'but I don't think they'd let me go with you. It was very kind of Giselle, and you.'

'Not let you go with us?' His voice had changed again. His neat hand again straightened his neat tie. 'Oh, I'm sure they would. What I mean is, I'm sure they would once they know who I am – who Giselle is.' He smoothed down his hair.

'They do know,' said Giselle.

'Ach so.' Then he led the way out to the car, without looking further at either of them.

The large car glided slowly down the hill and swung a wide even circle in front of the flats before drawing to a halt beside the rubbish bins. They exchanged polite goodbyes, but at the last moment Giselle wound down her window and called out to Selda who was staring up the steps: 'Don't worry. It'll be all right?'

'Of course it will,' repeated Herr Hebel, slowing the car again. 'Of course it will be all right. We'd love to take you with us. I don't think your father will say no to me.' The car accelerated swiftly back up the hill.

Selda began to climb the steps very slowly. She dared to think of him now. She only had this space, this time, marked out, step by step, to be alone. She thought of Ferhat and willed him to be all right. When she entered the flat she knew that they would overwhelm her with their concern and their questions. There she must not think about him. She must bury her knowledge of him deeply away, so that she could keep him safe. So she climbed up the steps one by one and distantly she heard the sound of a train making its night way into Zurich.

Fourteen

At her first knock the door was flung open and Selda's family surrounded her and drew her into the warm little room, bombarding her with their anxious questions. She did her best to answer them. She described the house and the car and Herr Hebel and the rooms and Anton. She was even able to reassure her mother that no, she had definitely not eaten pork for supper. Only Pembe, who wanted a detailed description of Giselle's clothes, was disappointed. They hardly asked her about herself. They were not interested in what she had done so she did not have to mention the trip up to the forest at all. She was glad she did not have to lie.

Turgut Bey who had been unusually quiet, went off to bed early as though glad to get away from the rest of them. Selda too was very tired after the day's excitement, but she was determined to stay awake. She had to see Ahmet when he came in from the restaurant. She chatted quietly with her sisters as they got ready for bed, but when they had fallen asleep beneath the pink bed spreads, she kept awake by thinking of her grandmother, back in Izmir. She could see the stiff, heavy figure in the home-made print dress sitting at the kitchen table. It would be almost summer there. Her grandmother would be sitting square to the table, bending over it with a letter spread out on the old flowered oil-cloth. The back door would be open on to the garden to let in some light. There, in that warm sun, this year's crop of hopeful kittens would be sitting with their mother, just beyond the step. They would be watching her grandmother with gentle and expectant eyes as she moved a stained forefinger slowly along the lines of a letter. It would be one of Selda's letters. In this letter she would have told her grandmother all about Ferhat. Now the old woman moved her finger more slowly, going back sometimes, and Selda thought that she heard the touch of the roughened skin on the rustling paper. The old woman mouthed the words and shook her head in dissapproval, but read on. She read on to the end of the letter and understood it all.

Then she slowly got up from her chair, pushing it back so that the wooden legs squeaked on the tiled floor. She walked to the door, softly, so as not to frighten the kittens and she watched them in silence. Then she folded the letter up and put it back into its envelope and went into the bedroom. She opened up her trunk and put the letter safely away amongst the old linen and lace-edged sheets, where no one else would ever find it. As she shut the lid of the trunk with a click Selda was startled into wakefulness.

'Selda?' She was already scrambling out of bed when Ahmet put his head cautiously round the door.

'I'm coming, wait a moment.' She felt around for a jumper to put on over her pyjamas, and was awkward in the dark, as though her mind still dreamed. Yet when she crept down the hall to the kitchen, she felt almost light-hearted.

'Plant roses in your garden,
Plant sweet herbs by your door,
But bury secrets in your heart
To keep them safe for evermore.'

She knew now that she could write to her grandmother. She'd tell her all about Ferhat and she knew that though her grandmother might not agree with what she had done, she would still keep the secret quite safe, because she would understand.

Selda paused in the doorway, looking at her brother, this favourite brother, and she wondered unhappily if she had

250

been right to trust him. After all, why should he help them? For him, weren't they . . . just money? Could he have become greedy for more?

'Well, did you find them?' Ahmet asked as soon as he saw her.

'Yes.'

'And no problems?'

'None at all.' She described briefly what had happened.

'Selda,' he said, pouring himself a glass of orange juice from the fridge, 'why should you bother about one illegal immigrant and his father? You are an odd one.'

'Me? Odd?'

'Yes. And if you think you're going to change the world, I can tell you, you're wrong. We have to look after ourselves. So, Selda, I'm warning you, little sister, don't ever do anything like this again. Promise?'

'No, never! I'm not the one who's odd. You are! You're the one who's changed, but I'm the same me. I'm Selda. You may criticize Father, and you're right. The problem is, you're getting just like him! Look at yourself, Ahmet! You're so keen to save up your money that you don't care how you earn it. How could you take it from people like Ferhat and his father? You've helped to make them into slaves. People should be free and it's wrong to enslave them.'

He fiddled with his glass, rolling the last drops around the bottom. She was right, of course, this little girl, whom he had thrown up into the air and twirled around in those distant village days when he had still felt like a hero.

'I'm glad that they got away safely,' he said, at last, trying to make his peace with her. 'Don't worry, Selda, they'll be all right. That Herr Stamm is a decent man. We've sent people to him before. He employs all sorts, Turks, Romanians, Poles, anybody who can't get a work permit. They'll be all right there.'

'For how long?'

'Selda, you can't do anything more for them. I know you'd like to. I'd like to, honestly, Selda. I don't wish them harm.'

'Somebody does,' said Selda, bluntly.

'I know.'

'But who, Ahmet, who? Who would report them to the police and why?' She had thought of everyone she knew. She had even guiltily wondered if kind Fräulein Altmann had reported them. After all, the teacher had once said that one shouldn't 'break the rules' ... Then she remembered Paul Bauer.

'The old farmer told me that people in the town were always making trouble for him,' she added. 'He said that they wanted to get his land.'

'I can believe that,' said Ahmet, 'but lots of people must have known that Ferhat and his father were on that farm. However careful you try to be, you can't be invisible. They were taking a risk. I suppose somebody, somewhere, was watching and waiting and biding his time. Then, when it was safe, he made his move.'

That description reminded Selda of Adnan Hoca. He was a man who watched and waited and then, when it suited him, made his move, or got somebody else to make it. She remembered how he had sent his wife to make that trouble for Pembe. Could Adnan Hoca have gone to the police, or, more likely, sent someone else to them? And if so, why? She shivered.

'You're cold,' said Ahmet.

'I'm not. I'm just . . . scared . . . '

'What of? You shouldn't be; it's over now. They've gone. You'll never have to see them again, so you can forget them. Hey, you really are shivering, aren't you? You must have caught a cold, up in the forest. Get back into bed now, go on, snuggle in and you'll soon be asleep.' He patted her shoulder and took her back to the bedroom door.

She did as he said and pulled the quilt up over her ears, but she could neither get warm, nor fall asleep. She remembered the coldness in Adnan Hoca's eyes as he watched her across the *Fasnacht* procession . . .

The last two weeks of the school year were very busy, and though Selda thought often of Ferhat, she had many other things to do. Fräulein Altmann kept them occupied finishing their work and cleaning out the classroom. She was taking down pictures, dismantling exhibitions and getting everything ready for the move to the fifth class after the holiday. Selda and Giselle stayed regularly after school to help with the extra work. On the afternoon before the school trip, Giselle was buried in a cupboard picking out bits of coloured chalk and Selda was stacking piles of half-used exercise books into the rubbish bag. Fräulein Altmann regretfully tossed in two or three old atlases, then took one out again.

'I don't suppose any of this would be of use to that friend of yours?' she asked Selda.

'Not now.' Selda shook her head and only then realized what the question meant: it meant that Fräulein Altmann had *not* known that Ferhat had left the town. It meant, therefore, that she was not the person who had reported him to the police.

'Has he given up studying German?' asked the teacher.

'Oh no. I'm sure that he's still studying it,' Selda replied guardedly.

'I see. Is everything all right, Selda?'

'Yes. Yes, Fräulein Altmann. At least, I hope so.'

'Then I hope so too.' Fräulein Altmann tied up the neck of the bag. 'And things are looking better for you too, I hear.'

'Me?'

'Why yes. I met Herr Hebel in town yesterday. He told me that in the holidays you're going to St Moritz with the Hebel family.'

'Did he?' A startled Giselle drew her head out of the cupboard so swiftly that she banged it on a shelf.

'But . . .' began Selda who was startled too. Then she stopped and said instead: 'Yes, I'm looking forward to it.' These days she was much more tactful.

'I told him,' Fräulein Altmann said, smiling at the girls, 'that he'd better take good care of you because he'd have two of my best pupils with him!'

'Did you?' Giselle looked very pleased.

'Yes. Anything wrong? I was telling the truth, wasn't I?'

They looked at each and shrugged and finished up the work quickly. They both wanted to get to their homes to find out more.

Sevgi Hanım met Selda's questions with puzzled indifference. She said that she had heard nothing about a proposed holiday in St Mortiz.

'Why should I?' she said bitterly. 'Nobody tells me anything. You'd better ask your father.'

'Now, don't try and rush me,' said Turgut Bey, when Selda asked him during supper. 'I was going to mention it, in my own time. Actually, I fixed it up for you a couple of days ago. I had a . . . a chat . . . with Herr Hebel. He's not such a bad chap, for a Swiss.' Turgut Bey looked very pleased with himself.

'Was *that* it?' interrupted Ali. 'I wondered why the foreman sent for you on Monday. I thought there had been complaints about that last batch of goods!'

'Herr Hebel didn't "send for me",' snapped Turgut Bey irritably, 'we had a . . . a discussion. The foreman just passed on the message, for Herr Hebel. We talked about things, he and I.'

'What did you talk about?' asked Selda.

'Well . . .' Turgut Bey looked around him in a satisfied manner. 'Well, while I had the opportunity, I did mention one or two of Adnan Hoca's plans . . . '

'But what about me?' gasped Selda.

'You?' he looked at her. 'Oh, I said you could go. Up to some mountains, isn't it?'

'Was that all?'

'My dear girl, I don't think you quite understand. When an important man like Herr Hebel talks, personally, to one of his long-standing employees, they don't waste time on holiday plans. We talked about important things.'

'But when can I go? Didn't you ask?'

'Well, not in so many words, like I said.' Turgut Bey was irritated.

'I don't suppose Father had time. He was only in the office for half a minute,' said Ali.

Her father blustered and shouted at them, but Selda realized that it did not really matter. The Hebels had invited her into their family and her father, for whatever reason, was allowing her to go. That was what mattered. It could not have been easy for him, whatever he pretended. She went over to him and sat down beside him on the sofa, which she had not done for a long time.

'Thank you,' she said and she took his hand and squeezed it and in his surprise he stroked her hand back and smiled at her with some of the distantly remembered warmth of her early childhood days.

Then, the next moment, he turned on the television loudly and she hurried away to the white bedroom so that the moment of pleasure remained unspoiled.

She slept well that night and so deeply that in the morning she could not wake up.

'Selda! Selda! Wake up! Giselle is already here, wake up!' That was Sevgi Hanım's voice, but Selda would have shut her eyes and even then returned to the dream that was already slipping away.

'Selda! It's your class trip!'

Of course. How could she have forgotten? Today was Thursday, the day of the fourth class strip. Now that she was fully awake she remembered that they should have been in school by seven. Now they had only ten minutes to get there.

'I'll go and get that food ready,' said Sevgi Hanım and yawned, but hurried cheerfully and busily towards the kitchen. Selda got dressed swiftly. When she went into the kitchen her mother was already filling a large polythene bag with things from the fridge. Giselle, immaculate in proper walking boots and a new rucksack, watched the hasty preparations in silence. In another minute they were both running down the road. Selda was awkwardly clutching the bag which was filled to the top with packets of food. At the corner she turned and looked back and saw her mother standing out on the balcony, watching them go. She nudged Giselle and they both waved and Sevgi Hanım waved back and called out, in Turkish 'enjoy yourselves'.

The bright yellow post bus was waiting in front of the school and its engine was already running when they scrambled up its steps.

'At last!' gasped Fräulein Altmann in relief. 'Another ninety seconds and we would have had to leave, or we'd have missed the train.' The rest of the class and a couple of parents who were accompanying the trip, looked at them reproachfully, for they had disrupted the programme. They flung themselves into a couple of empty seats, panting for breath and laughing.

Selda was excited. It was the first time that she had been on a journey since they arrived in Switzerland. Perhaps she was like her Kemal Amca with his love of travelling. It was odd to recall now that first journey of last summer: what a little, worried girl she had been, setting out from Izmir, clutching that other bag and scared of what people might think of her. She wasn't scared any longer, or not of foolish things like that. Now she was ready to see anything and this was to be the first of the journeys.

The post bus took them some distance outside the town to a railway station. There, they were to ascend the mountain by a special 'ratchet railway'. It was, the teacher told them, 'a wonderful example of Swiss engineering'. This was a mechanical train, and not one driven by steam or diesel.

'We're so lucky that it's a clear day,' said Fräulein Altmann as she ushered them into the train. 'Sometimes it's too misty to see anything. Now children, look up there.' She pointed and there, in the near distance, was the mountain peak. 'That's our destination,' she said.' Now, who can remember how many metres above sea-level it is?' In the scramble to get a window seat nobody bothered to reply.

Red-headed Christian, the policeman's son, leant over and tapped Selda on the shoulder: 'I don't suppose you've seen anything like this train before, eh Selda?' He grinned at his neighbours and put his dirty boots on to the seat beside Selda. 'I expect you usually go by donkey!'

She looked at him. For one second she thought about the Bosphorus Bridge, but she didn't mention it. She knew a better answer: 'Yes.' She smiled, glancing down at his muddy boots. 'We do have donkeys in Turkey. They are very useful for people who don't know how to behave in trains!'

It wasn't much of a joke, she knew, but it was enough. Several people pulled faces at Christian and he swung his feet down and began to look out of the window with great concentration.

The train began the slow crawl upwards. It passed through the lower slopes of deciduous trees where the spring leaves were as brilliant and tender as high summer flowers. They pulled down the train windows and breathed in the air and heard the noises of the woods. But when they entered the forest, all was quiet. When they leant out now the air from the battalions of red-barked pines smelt of dried resin and the hidden, dusty lairs of animals. Once they saw a herd of deer: the does, followed by their dapple-backed babies, rippled like sunlight between the tree trunks. The train moved steadily upwards. Bridges carried it over vanished streams that had cut deeply into the rocks. Selda could not see the water, but she could hear its roar and looking back, she saw its rainbow-flecked spray above the tree tops. She stared out on huge grey boulders embedded in the sides of mountains. Fräulein Altmann told them that these massive stones had been dragged here by glaciers millions of years ago. They had been carried by the ice and then, as times changed, they had been abandoned. Now they remained, as dead sentinels of another age and had imprinted on them moss and lichens and sudden, unexpected mountain flowers.

It was a different world up here. Selda watched it all in silence and thought of Ferhat and wondered if they would have to cross country like this.

The temperature had dropped and though Selda would not have admitted it, she felt frozen. This then must be the cold which Giselle had spoken of: the winter that clung on in the high mountains long after spring had come to the lowlands. She shivered and wished that she had dressed in warmer clothes. Then, at last, it was time to move. Fräulein Altmann called out that this was the end station and they must all get out. One of the parents came round checking that nobody had forgotten anything.

'What a shame,' she said, looking at Selda, 'you haven't even got a rucksack, you poor thing. One does need the proper equipment in the mountains. It's going to be very difficult for you, with that bag in your hand, dear.'

'Don't worry,' said Giselle quickly, 'we'll share my rucksack.' She opened it up and put in most of the things from Selda's bag.

'Oh Giselle!' The lady gushed effusively. 'What an *example* you and your family are to us dear.' Then she blushed deeply and hurried off, pushing her way through the quietly waiting line of children as though she had just remembered something desperately important at the other end of the carriage. Giselle shrugged and Christian muttered 'hypocrite', and then he tapped the girls on the shoulder again and said, in a careless voice, that he wouldn't mind carrying anything extra for them.

'It's all right,' said Giselle, 'but thanks all the same.'

Selda, who had seen that Giselle's new rucksack was empty of all but a single, fluttering twenty-franc note and a packet of plasters, said nothing. Then the three of them climbed down from the train and began to walk together up the mountain path behind the rest of the class.

It seemed to Selda that they had suddenly come very near to the clouds. While the forest lay thickly below them, this summit was bare and not what Selda had expected. It wasn't exactly ice covered, though there were deep crevasses of ice and snow which they were warned to stay away from. She would hardly have known that it was a summit at all, if there had not been a notice to say so. But this was it, and she had reached it with barely a climb. Even so, she was cold and tired and glad that they were to stop for lunch.

Fräulein Altmann pointed out the picnic area and showed them where they could light a fire and the children set to work. Soon they were impatiently blackening sausages over wood that was not properly alight. Selda and Giselle had nothing to grill and so they sat apart from the others and began to unpack what Sevgi Hanım had put ready. It was a small feast of Turkish food. There were several kinds of olives and two kinds of Turkish cheese. There were rolled vine leaves and slices of spinach pie and little diamonds of lentil paste and cabbage leaves filled with rice and nuts. There was even a sweet, soaked in lemon-flavoured syrup. And it was not a feast for one. It was only as they unwrapped it and spread it all out on the flowered cloth that Sevgi Hanım had carefully put in, that they realized it was a feast for two. There were two of everything, even two forks, wrapped up in real cloth napkins. Selda understood that this was no picnic hastily thrown together from the leftovers in the fridge. Sevgi Hanım must have been secretly planning it

259

for days and she must have got up, very early that morning to prepare it all.

They began to eat in silence. Giselle picked up a couple of meat rolls and walked off by herself, to look at the view. She scrambled up on a rock and sat there eating and swinging her legs. Selda guessed that she might be thinking of her own empty house where there was no one to get up early and prepare a surprise like this. She stood up and would have gone over to her but at that moment some of the other children crowded round and stared at all the 'odd' foreign food. Then Fräulein Altmann joined them and begged just a taste of this and that, and then everybody began to do the same and the rest of the sausages were abandoned to their fate over the fire. It was like a party with people tasting and exclaiming and praising.

Selda left them to it and climbed up on to the boulders beside Giselle.

'Even if my mother *had* been at home, she wouldn't have bothered to get anything ready for me,' said Giselle miserably, scuffing the leather of her new boots against the rocks.

'But she's ill,' comforted Selda.

'All the same!'

'But you could have got something ready,' suggested Selda, not looking at her.

'Me? How? I can't cook! I don't know how.'

'You could learn, couldn't you? I mean, I know quite a bit. I used to help my grandmother in Izmir. She was impossible, but she taught me. She criticized everything that I did, but it was just her way. When you weren't there, she praised you. I've heard her. I baked some biscuits once and she made such a fuss, said that they were burnt, that I'd wasted good ingredients. She grumbled that she almost broke a tooth on them, but then, do you know, the next day I overheard her telling a neighbour what a good cook I was. It just seems funny now and not all that important.'

'Can you really cook?' asked Giselle.

'Yes. Enough to feed myself, anyway. I could show you, if you liked . . . '

'When we're in St Moritz?'

'Yes.'

'Perhaps my mother would be interested,' said Giselle very quietly. 'It might seem different,' – she looked away – 'mightn't it, eating foreign food?' The thought seemed to cheer her. 'Come on, let's get back to the others.'

The fire had died down and the class stood in a close circle around the embers enjoying their last warmth before stamping them out. As Selda and Giselle came up, Christian told the others to make room, and they did, shuffling around so that there was a place for them.

'That spinach thing was terrific,' said somebody, and Selda smiled with pleasure and wished that her mother could have heard the praise.

The walk down was to be by a different route. At the bottom they were to catch another train into Zurich before returning home. This face of the mountain was windy and more exposed and the snow had been blown into deep piles between the rocks. They had to walk down the path in single file and carefully. Selda was following Giselle and trying not to look at the steep drop on their right, when something made her look up. Something up there had sparkled or shone, suddenly, there below the sky. They were crossing a rough stone bridge beneath which another mountain stream ran thinly and noisily. Some of the water had splashed out on to the rocks and frozen there, and now it glittered in the sunlight. Above, something flashed again. As she looked higher up she could see icicles and great spears and chains of frozen water, hanging from the black ledges like tossed, torn lace.

There, at the top, catching the sun, where the water first fell over the edge, was the frozen waterfall. It was as though the stream had stopped and hung there in the air, like the swelling crest of a winter wave in a wind-whipped Izmir bay. But this wave had not rolled on. It had not broken and foamed against the rocks and it was not white as it hung there, just under the sky.

Selda stopped dead and stared up at it. The children behind her bumped into one another and grumbled and made to push past and somebody called out that it was dangerous to stop like that, on a mountain path. She stayed where she was, staring up at it. Somewhere, in all the frozen intricacy of its crystals, there was the blue of the sky and the green of the leaves and all the wonderful and changing spectrum of colours. She was sure that she could have seen them all, if only she could have stopped and watched for long enough.

'Look at our Selda,' joked Christian, giving her a gentle shove, 'she's never seen ice before!'

'No,' she said. 'Poor little me.' She snatched up a handful of the coarse snow beside the path and she managed to drop a little down the neck of his shirt, and then she laughed and walked on.

But she had seen it all the same. She had seen the frozen waterfall. She had seen that rushing vein of water stopped and held in the air like the white, clawed hand of some undreamt-of creature from long ago, from the time when all this landscape had been covered by ice.

'Did you see it?' she asked Giselle, excitedly.

'Yes, but that was nothing special. You should see the ones near our house in the mountains. They're much bigger, ten times as big.' She kicked a stone off the path and they heard it fall and fall, going down from rock to rock.

'You will come to the mountains, won't you?' asked Giselle.

Selda nodded. Nothing would stop her now.

They were leaving the higher slopes which were almost bare of trees, save for some which where wizened and colourless and crouched closely to their rocky crevices. Now they re-entered the band of forest that ran along the valley like a constant shadow. The forest floor was deep with pine needles and, here and there, unexpected and fragile, sprung clumps of white spring flowers. Someone called out that they had seen a black squirrel and they all paused, looking up to where something had moved and had made the uppermost branches spring and tremble.

It must have taken them about three hours to walk down to the station. In that time they had passed from the bare summit through the forest and out on to the green, green pastures around the lake. The best of the afternoon had gone and it was cooler even there. In a nearby field the cows were being brought in for milking and the strange, repeated notes of their bells tolled tuneless but clear in the lengthening shadows. Overhead the gulls called and circled and called again before returning to the waters of the lake. Here at the edge of the path there were buttercups and clover and an early butterfly fluttered amongst the waving flower heads, whereas up there, on the summit, Selda knew that the sun would set on the hardening edges of the ice.

She walked more slowly. She was tired. They all were. They walked in small groups, chatting of this and that at the quiet end of a happily shared day. And it was not finished yet. They were to change trains at the main station in Zurich and Fräulein Altmann had said that since there was half an hour to wait, they could buy themselves something to eat and drink if they wanted to.

It was the evening rush hour when they arrived. The station was brightly lit and alive with hurrying crowds. The notice boards for arrivals and departures clicked over busily. Business men with smart briefcases checked their watches and quickened their stride towards the correct platforms. Every now and then, small, quiet trucks, pulling rows of mail bags, picked their careful way through the crowds like cats finding a path in a busy bazaar. Yet it was all so different from the busy places of Turkey. Here all was bright and sharp and clean. Most of the children had begun to make for the snack bar and the vending machines. Selda, who had no money to spend, was happy to stand and wait while Giselle got something for both of them. She read down the list of destinations: Munich, Vienna, Naples and Bucharest. How Kemal Amca would have enjoyed himself here. The train that was standing near by was going right through to Romania. There was a carriage of sleeping cars and other wagons with seats. Outside one of these wagons a group of people struggled with their luggage. Selda guessed that they were Romanian workers about to return home. They were shouting and trying to push a large television in through the train window. The railway guard walked to and fro a couple of times and glanced at their luggage and raised his eyes in despair. Selda wondered what it felt like to be going home, finally. Two or three Romanian children stood to one side, eating hamburgers and watching the adults anxiously. She understood just how they felt. Fräulein Altmann was watching them too and she and Selda exchanged a sympathetic look. Selda glanced once more at the destination board, and then she saw him.

She saw Ferhat threading his way through the crowds. She recognized him instantly. She knew his red-checked shirt, knew him from the way he moved, restless as always, pushing through the crowd with that bag slung over his shoulder. And there was his father, left some paces behind. She had never thought that the address Ahmet gave them would be in the area of Zurich and he had not told her.

She so wanted him to turn round and see her. She imagined it: he would turn round and smile with joy at seeing her and hurry over, and people would step aside for him, understanding that he must reach her through the crowd. Then he would run towards her with his arms outstretched and she would greet him and turn to Fräulein Altmann, who would be watching them, and she would say: 'Fräulein Altmann, this is the friend I told you about . . . '

Then she saw Giselle returning with two cans of drink and a packet of something clenched between her teeth.

'Selda? Is something wrong, you've gone as white as chalk,' said Fräulein Altmann kindly.

'No. Nothing is wrong. I think I'm tired.'

'Yes, I'm sure you are. It was a long walk, and do you know, I sometimes think that climbing down is much more difficult than climbing up.'

Now the Romanians had hoisted up a battered suitcase. It was tied around with string and even Selda could hear the things slipping and clinking inside it and one of the women was shouting, perhaps telling them to take more care. The railway guard came back and stood and watched and checked his timetable. They heaved the case up again, balancing it on the edge of the window.

'I hope our children won't be late,' said Fräulein Altmann, looking at her watch. Giselle and some of the others were almost back.

Ferhat was walking along the platforms reading the names, looking for the right one. He was dressed in overalls, the sort that houses painters wore, thick, white overalls with paint splashes on them. He was so near to her now. The sleeves of his check shirt were rolled up and she could see a fine spray of grey paint over his hands and wrists. He was so near. He must see her now.

He did. He looked and saw her.

The guard shouted at the Romanians and pointed to his watch and to the train. He shouted again and they shouted back and one of the children began to cry fearfully.

Ferhat stood still, holding the bag over his shoulder, watching her.

The guard put a hand on the shoulder of one of the Romanians who threw him off and shouted in rough German

265

that even God would have allowed him twenty seconds more to load his luggage. Ferhat's father had caught up with him. Then he too saw Selda, but he turned aside immediately. He plucked at Ferhat's shirt, then pulled his arm, but Ferhat stepped towards her, his eyes darting around like an animal coming out from its lair.

The child behind them screamed as its mother jerked its arm: the train was about to leave.

Giselle walked very slowly, trying to open the packet with her teeth. She had her head bent down and so did not see Ferhat. The guard blew his whistle sharply. The Romanians began to panic and shout. Everybody turned to watch them. The child froze where it was, shrieking, refusing to climb up the step into the train. Ferhat's father began to walk away, leaving his son still standing, staring. Selda's class, now almost all assembled, moved closer together and watched the scene with mounting horror: surely the train couldn't move off with some of the passengers left behind. But it moved. The guard blew his whistle again and two policemen appeared and strolled over to find out what was up. They were between Ferhat and his father. They called out to the guard who called back and pointed to the Romanians. The mother had almost got the child up the step and the man, the father perhaps, turned on the police to keep them away. One of them flung out his arm, as if to prevent the Romanian from doing any-thing, and struck Ferhat's father on the back. And Ferhat's father ran. He darted back into the crowd. The policeman turned in surprise and called out. Ferhat's father spun round, hemmed in and trapped. Selda saw him look back at the mass of people and away to the empty platform beyond the train. She saw the black iron wheels move and saw the blind terror in his eyes and she cried out: 'Stop!'

But he didn't. He just ran. He ran away from the crowd. The two policemen began to move towards him. They went carefully and steadily and one began to speak into his radio.

'Stop!' cried Selda. 'Stop, stop!' But he was beyond hearing. He ran down the emptied platform, past the quietened child, and past the waiting passengers. He ran to the end and when the police closed in behind him, he did not stop. He ran on to the track and perhaps did not see the train that was drawing in to the other platform, and the iron wheels screamed and screamed above all the other terrible sounds of the station.

'Don't look,' cried Fräulein Altmann. 'Don't look, children!' She held out her arms and tried to draw them all to her, shielding them as best she could.

'Don't look,' she said again. 'It's too late now.'

Selda looked. She stepped beyond the reach of Fräulein Altmann's arms and stood apart so that she could see, and then she looked for Ferhat. She saw all the busy evening home-goers stop, open-mouthed and horrified. She saw them put their hands up to their faces and then hurry on their way. Even when their train finally pulled away from the station, she could not sit down but stayed at the window, searching for him, but she never saw him.

The children were restless and couldn't keep quiet, but must get up and down and ask each other, 'Did you see it?'

'It was just like . . .' began Christian loudly.

'Don't!' screamed Selda, above them all. 'Don't!'

'Honestly, Selda,' he protested, 'I only meant . . .'

'I told you,' she said. 'Don't.' He didn't, and sat back, slumped in a corner. They all looked at her and then left her alone. Only Fräulein Altmann returned again and again, and just before they came in to their station, she came over and asked quietly: 'Did you . . . did you recognize anyone, Selda?'

'No. No, I didn't.' She buried it all deeply and safely, for it must be what he would want.

A large crowd of anxious parents was already gathered at the station. The awful news of a tragic accident to 'an unidentifiable man, possibly a foreign national', at Zurich Station, had been on the television. They all pushed forward as the train carrying the much-delayed class drew in. There was the red-haired policeman, Christian's father, and there were two other teachers from the school and Herr Hebel and Anton, at the centre of a group, and there too, on her own, was Sevgi Hanım. She stood tensely at the very back of the crowd in her best coat and shoes as though this were a special occasion. And it was, in a way: this was the very first time that her mother had left the house and gone anywhere on her own in Switzerland. Selda made her way towards her mother and they put their arms around each other.

'Fatma told me,' said Sevgi Hanım. 'She and Ramona saw it on the news and I thought of you. That afternoon at school your teacher told us that you'd come back through Zurich Station. I remembered. Did you . . . did you see?'

'Yes.'

They began to walk arm in arm, but she knew that she must not tell, not yet, not until she knew what he wanted to do. It was hard though, when Sevgi Hanım had done this for her.

'And thank you for the picnic,' she said, willing her mother to understand.

'Oh! That!' Sevgi Hanım laughed shyly.

'But it was wonderful. Everybody said so and they all tasted it; they liked it too, they really did.'

'Did they?' she asked proudly.

Then the Hebels' car drew to a quiet halt beside them. Giselle and Anton peered out of the back and Herr Hebel lent over and opened the front door for Sevgi Hanım and invited them to have a lift home.

'Oh, no! I couldn't,' gasped Sevgi Hanım in Turkish. 'Tell him, Selda, tell him that we couldn't.'

'Why not?'

'Well, well . . . '

They waited. Selda and the Hebel children and their father watched her and waited and then Anton leant over and patted the front seat like you would to encourage a child and he said very clearly: 'Come, come,' and she climbed in. Awkwardly she got into the front seat and pulled her best coat straight and said, '*Danke sehr*,' and they were perhaps the first German words she had spoken.

In a couple of minutes they were outside the flats. Herr Hebel said good evening very politely and then the great car glided away up the hill with Giselle and Anton waving from the back. Selda and her mother climbed the stairs very, very slowly, both wondering what would happen now. Turgut Bey did not get up to greet them. He called out sourly: 'And where do you think you've been until this time?'

Sevgi Hanım unbuttoned her coat carefully and hung it up and stepped out of her best street shoes and then she went into the sitting room nervously touching her hair.

'Turgut Bey,' she said, hesitantly. 'Selda needed me. So I went down to fetch her.'

He looked up at her, astonished. 'But it was supper-time.'

'Supper will be late this evening,' she said, picking up an empty glass, 'so you'll all have to wait.' They stared at her as she went into the kitchen to begin her work and they listened in silence as she began to run water into the sink. Selda, too tired to answer any more questions, went into the white bedroom and climbed into bed fully dressed and fell instantly asleep.

Fifteen

Fräulein Altmann and her class were much affected by the accident. At first there were awful jokes about it. Then a game called 'going under a train', appeared briefly in the playground. Finally, everyone was quieter and more thoughtful. Walking round the concrete playground they hardly ever mentioned what had happened, but now Selda found that she was no longer left on her own. The local newspapers had written sympathetically about the desperate lives of these foreigners who lived on unknown and isolated in a country that did not wish to know them. There was even a short film on the television. Selda listened and read and watched it all but she never ever said anything. She was sure that Fräulein Altmann suspected something, but she never asked directly and Selda never told her. It was reported that the police knew that the unidentified Turk had not been alone and Ali said that they had come to the factory asking questions, but no one seemed to know anything about the man. At home Selda and Ahmet avoided talking about it.

Adnan Hoca was the only person who mentioned the accident repeatedly. He brought his family round one evening and sat dipping chocolate biscuits into his tea and then eating them with a disgusting sucking sound. Then he stirred the thickened tea and said: 'Well, with people like that, there's no real loss, is there?'

The little room was quiet. His wife nodded bravely in agreement and his daughter spat daintily on the diamond in her engagement ring and polished it on the arm of the chair. Turgut Bey coughed nervously and opened his mouth but lost his courage and asked for more tea instead. Sevgi Hanım got up to take his glass and then paused by their visitors' chair and said unexpectedly: 'I think, Adnan Hoca, that a life is a life. Now, will you have some more tea too?' She held out her hand for the soiled glass and he handed it to her without a word. Instead he smiled to himself in a satisfied sort of way as though reminding himself that he knew things that simple people like them didn't know.

Selda, who was watching him closely, remembered that this was exactly how he had looked at the *Fasnacht* procession. Surely the smile which curled the corners of his cold, cruel mouth was that of a traitor. She could have snatched the tea from her mother's hand and dashed it all into his hateful face, but she didn't. It wouldn't have helped Ferhat now. She got up and opened the balcony door and stepped out into the evening breeze and looked out over the black lake and then she glanced along the road he had walked up, carrying that bag of bread, after the day's work was done. It was pointless, but she still watched for him.

The first days of the school holiday passed slowly. Frau Hebel had come out of the clinic and so Giselle was busy at home. In a few days' time they were to leave for the mountains and Selda was to go with them. It had all been arranged. She had been up to the house once to try on some of Giselle's old ski clothes and had returned with a large bagful, much to Turgut Bey's annoyance. He grumbled bitterly that he didn't want charity from anyone and then comforted his wounded pride by saying that she would probably break a leg at least, up there in the mountains, and that he was only letting her go as a favour to Herr Hebel, his friend.

Selda herself longed to go. She longed to escape the cramped flat and the fetters of concern that had begun to chafe and hold her back. She looked down on the still lake with its pall of grey mists and she dreamed of the sunlit summits where flowers would bloom out of the rocks and where the waterfalls would hang frozen beneath clear skies. It would all have been so perfect if she could just have known that he was all right. Nothing more.

The day before she was due to leave her mother called her aside and pressed into her hands a small sum of money that she had been saving from the housekeeping.

'It's for you, dear. To spend while you're with them. You know, like Swiss do, just to waste, if you like, dear. Now put it away quickly and we won't mention it again.' She understood what her mother meant: poor Fatma had been suffering agonies of envy. It did seem so unfair that Selda should be the one to go off to the mountains and have the chance to ski!

That afternoon, after she had packed, she went down to the library and did not return by the short cut up the steps. Instead she went the long way round by the road. That was the way she and Giselle had always cycled. It had rained heavily that morning and the clean pavements were wet and black and the underground water still roared down towards the lake. A gust of wind blew a shower of raindrops off an overhanging branch and into her face and in the wind she smelt the sharp reek of the pigs. She paused where the path to the farm branched off between the fields. She could hear the shrill cries of the young piglets. She hadn't been to the farm since that day. There had seemed no point. Now, glancing to her right, she saw that the old apple tree was in bloom and the fields beyond had been sown. The rains had drawn up a covering of fine, bright green. So someone else was working there. She went over and looked down at the pigs who were cheerfully rooting about in the mud. Then up near the farmhouse, something moved. A man appeared to be standing behind the hedge in the vegetable garden. He had his back to her and was now standing very still, watching something, perhaps. The yellow scarf around his neck must have worked loose, for it was flapping in the wind.

She wondered if she was imagining it. She wasn't scared

but she had to know, so she began to walk slowly towards the farm. A gust of wind ruffled her hair and blew a shower of blossoms down on to the muddy backs of the piglets and the scarf flapped again and a flock of sparrows was startled up into the hedge.

'Hey! You!' Someone called and Selda jumped but the man had not moved.

'Hey!' The old face appeared at the window and the old stick beat noisily on the glass.

Then a stronger gust of wind freed the yellow scarf and the figure swung slowly round and Selda saw that the forgotten jacket and scarf had been set up upon a stick and filled with straw and left out to scare away the birds.

'Come here!' Paul Bauer was beckoning to her and Selda began to run. She ran down the bank, past the rows of cages by the barn door and past a fair-haired man who was forking in fresh straw.

He called out to her but it was not in a language that she understood. She pushed open the kitchen door but hesitated to step in. Someone was coming down the stairs, very slowly, one step at a time. The dog pushed past and reached her first and pushed his whitened muzzle into her hand. She bent down and scratched his head and watched as Paul Bauer painfully eased himself off the last step.

'At last!' he said, banging his stick in front of him, 'I thought you'd forgotten us!'

She did not know what to say but just stood there letting the wind bluster in and rattle the windows.

'Do you want me to freeze too?' he asked irritably and tapped his way through the kitchen to a dark, old-fashioned sitting room with panelled walls and curtains made of thick, yellowed lace. She followed him and there, waiting for her, coming over to her, was Ferhat.

The old man settled himself in a high-backed chair and the dog lay down across his feet. It was even colder in this room.

There were old photos in tarnished frames on the mantel-piece above the unlit stove and one wall was covered in black-framed certificates.

'Why didn't you come before?' repeated the old man.

'I didn't know.'

'Well, you should have. I told you he was a good lad. You should have listened to me. Where else should the boy go, and in such trouble. He should never have had to leave in the first place. Why couldn't they have left us in peace? But I'll tell you this, they'll never get my land. Never!' He reached stiffly down to stroke his dog. 'Well, Miss, lost your tongue?'

She nodded.

'I suppose you'll both be wanting to speak that awful language of yours now. I can't think why. Not when there's a decent language like German to speak. Still, there's no pleasing some people.' He picked up a newspaper and began to turn the pages awkwardly with his deformed hands. Then he looked sharply over at Ferhat. 'But don't talk too long. Not after all the trouble you've caused me.'

'Have you been here all the time? I mean, since.'

'Almost. I walked back here that same night. When I saw it happen and knew that it was all too late, I just turned round and walked out of the station, out of that crowd. I still don't know how I could have done it. Left him. But I did, I knew it was too late. Perhaps it always had been, for him. He was never going to learn to live here. He couldn't. So I walked away. I followed the signposts and followed the road along by the lake until I saw Bauer's farm and then I came up here and hid in the barn that night. The dog found me in the morning. And old Bauer took me in and hid me. The police came once and looked around, but I don't think they wanted to find anything. They seemed really sorry about what had happened. I wanted to get in touch with you, but he said I shouldn't. He said that it wasn't fair and that you'd find me, if you wanted to. He said that it could make real trouble for you and your family but that it didn't matter for him. He has no one to think of.'

'But he's been so good to you.'

'Yes. It's odd, isn't it? Sometimes it's the people you least suspect in all the world. They're the ones who really care enough to help.'

'That's like my grandmother. She can be so horrid sometimes, but she cared enough to learn to write so that she could write to me. Whatever she says, she'd always help me. I'm sure of it now.'

'I've still got her address safe.' He reached into his jacket and brought out the two little rolls of paper and smiled at her. 'So, how's that other friend, that Giselle?'

'She's fine. Better, actually. I'm going to stay with her family tomorrow, in the mountains. Do you remember how she used to talk about it?'

'Yes. I'm glad for you, Selda.'

'And you? What are you going to do Ferhat?'

'I'm going away too. Herr Bauer has arranged it for me. It is strange. He was so mean when my father and I worked here, and he still is. He's got that poor Romanian working for him for even less money, but do you know that he's done for me, while I've been in hiding? He's arranged for me to go and work for a friend of his, in the south. It'll be a proper job with a proper wage and this man is going to apply for residence papers for me, after I've been there a bit.'

'Do you trust him?'

'Yes. I have to.

'But why has Herr Bauer done this?'

'I don't really know. But do you remember, he used to talk to me, while I was ill. Well, I didn't understand it at all then, but I now think it's because I remind him of his son.'

'I didn't realize he had any family.'

'I think this son was killed years ago. Look.' He pointed

towards one of the faded photographs on the mantelpiece. It showed a young man dressed in old-fashioned climbing things, smiling out against a background of white mountains. 'I think he was killed in that European war. I still don't understand everything he says, but it was something to do with helping people to escape over the mountain passes from Germany into Switzerland. It makes sense, doesn't it?'

It did make sense and, looking at the photograph in her hands, Selda could see that there was a likeness.

'So you're really going?'

'Yes.'

'And if it doesn't work out?'

'Then I'll move on. I'll do something else. I have to try this. It's like you said, we have to try.'

'When will you go?'

'In about an hour. The man is coming back for me. We'll drive down there tonight. And, if it goes well, I can get that permit, Selda.'

'And then you can stay?'

'Yes. But even better, I can go too. When I have saved up the fare I can travel back to Turkey and see my family and come back again. It means that I can be free.'

'It's wonderful! If only –'

'Don't say it. He would have been pleased. It's what he wanted. It's what we planned at the beginning. It was just that he was too frightened. He lost all hope as time went by. I think he feared that there was no escape, ever. He would have been pleased for me. I know it.'

'I'm sure he would. And I'm so happy for you, now.' She was, too. She hadn't expected to feel like this. It was like some great burden taken from her, some iron door opened and fresh air let in.

She suddenly wanted to go. She wanted to say goodbye.

'Do you think I should wake him?' She nodded towards the old man but when she reached to put the photo back she saw that he had not been asleep but was looking at her with tired sad eyes.

'He liked animals too,' he said gruffly. 'You can always tell a person by a thing like that.' He refolded the paper noisily.

'I have to go,' she said softly, 'but don't get up.' She took his old, bent hand in hers and kissed it and touched it to her forehead and then walked away. Ferhat came with her past the cages and past the barn and up to the lane which ran between the fields.

'Goodbye then, and go safely.'

'You too, Selda, go safely.'

She hurried away down the path. This time when she looked back he was still standing there waving.